JURASSIC DEAD

Rick Chesler and David Sakmyster

The authors would like to thank our first readers, Phillip Tomasso, Jonathan Maberry and Daz Pulsford for their encouragement and support. Thanks of course to Gary Lucas and Severed Press for breathing life into our creation, thanks to Finn for providing inspiration with his dinosaurs on the floor, and thanks to you, the readers... we hope you'll stick along for the ride.

1.

Antarctic Circle–Russian Drill Site Theta-1, five miles south of Vostok

Alex Ramirez wished he had stayed at the surface. Halfway down the freshly-drilled pit, the temperature had actually warmed to a balmy minus twenty degrees Fahrenheit, and at least they were out of the brutal whipping winds, but the cold was preferable to this. In fact, he began to wish he had stayed back in San Diego altogether.

How did he let Tony talk him into this madness? This insanely death-defying stunt to strike at the heart of two heartless nations trying to profit at the expense of the natural world?

Oh right, Alex thought, *because my father is one of those heartless bastards.*

In a modern-day spin on the Cold War, Russia and America each had set up shop on opposite sides of a massive underground lake, above a discovery that had the whole scientific world abuzz. All that pressure from two thick miles of ice, over millions of years, had created a pocket that had expanded, heated, and melted the glacial ice, eventually forming an enormous underground lake. From initial surveys, it appeared to be teeming with microscopic biological organisms. Some possibly hundreds of millions of years old.

Following the notion that competition spurns innovation and success, the U.N. sanctioned a race to see which nation could get there first. Much more than pride was riding on the outcome, for the research spoils as well as the biological and mineral output down there could be considerable—and worse, from Alex and Tony's points of view—could lead even to more exploitation of the last pristine continent left on Earth. Antarctica was the only place left on the planet still untouched by corporate greed. If no one else was going to step in and protect those tiny life forms— which certainly could not stand up to modern-day contamination, let alone further drilling, mining, erosion, and utter destruction of their natural habitat—then he would take it upon himself to do just that.

Alex adjusted the camera mounted around his neck. It was set up for dual-action filming, both away and toward his face as he rappelled. "How much farther?" he shouted into the mouthpiece under his hood.

He could barely hear Tony's answer through all those layers. Through the perpetual gloom above, and all this darkness here, his night-vision visor barely registered the glowing form twenty yards below.

"What?" *Come on, man, don't leave me hanging—literally.*

The ice sheet tapered at this point, moving to a steep incline as the Russian drill had angled, veering for a sloping entrance to the lake. It was about a half a mile ahead, according to his GPS. Unlike the American site, this one offered more varied approach advantages, including this sloping angle, but perhaps it required more finesse to avoid bedrock and other impediments than a straight linear descent.

He checked the screen mounted to the camera and confirmed their distance, seeing his and Tony's icons slightly apart.

"…setting the charges," came Tony's voice crackling in his earpiece. "Almost there."

"Stop smelling the roses! Remind me again why you need me down here? I could have stayed up top, securing the climbing gear, and made sure your ass didn't fall and wind up in the lake."

"Redundancy!" Tony yelled back. "This mission is too important to fail. We only get one shot at it. So yeah, redundancy…and heat signatures."

"What?"

"The Russian base was right there, man. Come on, even though it's nearly pitch black up there and surrounded by winds, you can bet your ass they have infrared cameras and sensors. We got lucky we weren't spotted."

"That's not luck," Alex said, grunting after his boots struck awkwardly and he broke into a half-run, half-leaping descent, finally tugging on the clamps to slow his approach. He was almost at Tony's location, but still could barely see anything.

"We trained for this," he added after digging in his boots. "Used up all our considerable Kickstarter funding with these fancy gadgets and schematics, diagrams of the bases and the security movements and... not to mention chartering a plane from Chile."

"Should have paid for you to take a few extra flying lessons."

"I have my license!"

"Yeah, but clearly not enough logged hours."

"You know what they say, any landing you can walk away from..."

"We walked away, but barely, and that plane's toast. Hope you didn't leave a hefty deposit."

"Insurance rules, and hell, we're probably not coming back, at least not of our own volition or without chains. That was the plan."

"Prison barge, only way to go." Tony fastened some more wires, packed ice around the C-4 and rubbed his hands together. "Anyway, we had nothing to worry about. Security was a joke up there." Tony raised his hand as Alex approached. He moved to the side and Alex winced with the sudden light from Tony's flashlight—highlighting the pack of C-4 wedged into a crevasse he had created with a small pickaxe in his left hand. "It was like they were all out on a vodka break. Let's hope the American side is more of a challenge."

Alex shrugged. "How about we count our blessings?" Still, the ease with which they got this far bothered him. He had never expected it. In fact, he had fully anticipated that he and Tony would be in Russian custody at this point, and if they allowed him one phone call, it would be to his father across the ice, to break the news that once again, his useless prodigy had found a way to be a major pain in the ass.

At least, then good old Dad would have to pay him some attention. His father had run all over the world, gone throughout Alex's childhood, hunting down old fossils and ancient teeth, caring more about the long dead than the still living. That included his sick wife, Alex's mother. At this point, Alex wanted nothing more than for his old man to suffer, in whatever form it took. Even if it was having the embarrassment of a lunatic liberal son doing ridiculously dangerous things to save the environment and protect the smallest of Earth's defenseless creatures.

"Set the charges," Alex said grimly, "and then let's pay a visit to the other team and leave them an equally generous gift."

"Double kaboom," Tony said with flair, and Alex could just about imagine the grin stretching under that visor. "All set here, let's get down there, steal the sub—which better still be docked there—and haul over to the Americans to set those charges. Then we kick back and—wait, what's that?"

Alex followed the direction of the flashlight beam…Down.

The glare affected his vision through the visor, adding to the ice and fog. He wiped at it and squinted.

"Oh shit. The Russians."

They were coming, rising up from the pit, from the shadows. At least a dozen men.

"Where are their ropes?" Tony asked, incredulous.

Alex focused harder. The air temperature dropped, and those dark forms, loping, leaping, darting faster than anything should have been able to climb, moving as if in silent communication, and with a purpose. "Don't see any, they're just… climbing."

Fast.

A wave of sudden, absolute and animalistic terror washed over Alex in advance of the approaching figures, and he had the sudden certainty that whatever those things were, moving with impossible speed and dizzying, jerking motions, they weren't Russians. Not anymore.

"We have to get the hell out of here."

They turned, attempting to climb, knowing it would be futile—and saw that up was no escape either.

Another wave of figures perched at the top, waiting silently, patiently.

Hungrily.

2.

"One chance," Tony said. "Follow my lead!" Ever the daredevil, Alex was sure this wasn't going to be good, but they had no choice. The Russian figures were a green-black blur in his night-vision, and a wave of icy terror shot ahead of them, rooting Alex to the spot. He felt the tug of gravity, the pull of the blackness down there, and thought he heard whispers in his head beckoning him to come on down and explore…

Maybe Tony heard the same thing, because a moment later, just as the sound of a multitude of scrabbling boots mixed with some sort of inhuman, almost reptilian hissing echoed off the smooth icy walls of the pit, Tony literally cut the cord.

"Wait—" Alex started as he felt the vibration in his harness and the tug, and then—Tony was gone. A snap and he shot away and down, tucking like a circus performer shot out of a cannon. He was a rolling blur, blasting right between a gap in the approaching soldiers who turned and swiped at him, but missed.

"Tony!" Alex struggled, hanging and flailing his arms, adjusting to the lack of weight now that his partner had disconnected. He reached to his belt, fumbling around. *Where—*

Got it! The knife…but the latch was frozen. He tugged and pulled. *Oh God, I have no time—*

They were almost upon him, and in a glance that he immediately regretted taking, he saw their eyes—glowing and alien-like, ferocious and more than hungry—*starving*. It was the look of carnivores left in cages for weeks and then tossed a bloody chunk of meat.

However, it was all Alex needed to galvanize his muscles. That and hearing Tony's grunting screams, as if he was rolling and crashing into things down there.

He couldn't think about Tony's fate. There was no choice but to take the same route. Another moment and they would be upon him. He released the knife, turned backwards and slashed down hard on the cord—and it didn't break. Only halfway.

"Shit!" He screamed and bent his legs, slashed down again as he launched upward. Just in time, he barreled backwards, crunching through a flurry of bodies. Hands and arms reached for him but had no grasp on his Gore-Tex coat. He soared out into the air and sideways for he didn't know how long, before reconnecting with the incline, jarring hard on the glacial wall, slamming his shoulder, and then rolling and launching into the air again. The camera shattered, but remained attached, twisted around the side of his neck. His visor cracked, and all he could see was a spinning, jarring, green-flecked darkness punctuated by flashes of lighter walls, and in the direction he thought he had come—a multitude of forms, like tiny bats, fluttered after him.

Shit, he thought. They leapt down toward him in pursuit. *What the hell are they?*

He didn't have much time to think, as in the next second, his body flattened out and he slid feet first like an Olympic luger. Looking down past his boots, he couldn't make out anything at first, and then he saw the tiny flickering glows of what could only be small flares. Nearing the lake shore, he felt the incline leveling slightly, as his body bumped and jarred with the terrain. He dug in his heels as much as he dared without flipping himself over, and reached out—with the knife still in his right hand. Surprisingly, he hadn't stabbed himself, but now he slammed the blade into the ice, then spun around and grabbed the hilt with his left hand as well.

It almost wrenched from his hands, but he held on, forcing a huge gash through the packed snow and ice as his descent began to slow.

He looked back and saw the flares glowing and bathing the area in a dull but painful glare. He took in a wall of crates and machinery, smaller cranes and a generator, and by the shore—something that may have been a two-person submersible.

Then he dared a look back up, and amidst the ice shards kicking up in his wake, he saw the thing he most feared.

The pursuers were not slowing.

They were gaining, and fast.

As soon as he could, Alex let go of the knife and pushed up with his frayed gloves. Launched to his feet, backpedalling and then leveling out. He had a moment of fright that he would trip on something and crash backward into the lake, but just before tumbling, a dripping wet hand caught his shoulder.

"*Run,*" Tony said—and his voice sounded like he spoke through lungs filled with ice water. He shoved Alex with surprising strength. Shoved him far and hard to the left, toward the submarine and one of the flares.

Alex tumbled and rolled, then slid on a sheet of ice. He yanked off his visor and wiped a sheen of sweat off his face. It was so much warmer down here, almost tropical. He was suffocating in his coat, but he looked back.

Tony was framed in a red glow from a dying flare by the shore of the formless expanse of the lake. He spread his arms wide as he faced the tunnel to the surface.

The Russians burst from the shadows.

Alex's vision adjusted to the illumination and he noted the device in Tony's right hand. His friend turned, and in the flickering light, his face looked almost *scaled.* The flesh around his cheeks was yellow and brittle, his eyes slanted and almost reptilian, and there was only the barest hint of humanity in those pupils—a hint that flashed and winked at him an instant before the horde of Russians swarmed upon him, an instant before—

—he pressed the detonator.

3.

Transfixed, Alex barely heard the muffled explosion over the screams and sounds of rending, biting and ripping. It was like a pack of rabid dogs were attacking one of their own. Alex shuddered and hesitated, then was about to turn to the sub when the mob just... stopped. One of the figures stepped back, holding what looked like a shredded limb, looked at it, sniffed it, and then just dropped it. The others backed away in a semi-circle from the figure on the bloody ice. Tony was barely recognizable, his coat shredded along with his flesh, his ribs protruding from huge bite marks, but a viscous darker mass oozed from lacerations on his face and neck.

All this Alex could only register in an instant, before mind-numbing fear took hold, as the entire horde of Russians turned toward him, tensing, about to rush him when—a wall of ice and snow roared over them. A massive avalanche collapsed the tunnel with hundreds of tons of glacial ice, silt and earth, and a rolling wave of demolition swept over the soldiers, annihilating everything and sweeping them into the lake.

It was just the impetus Alex needed to turn and run. The tunnel was gone, the flares winking out, all but one... Sounds of scraping and growling in the darkness behind him. Splashing feet...

Alex got to the lake edge and hauled open the sub's hatch. A two-seater...perfect. He angled the nose toward what he hoped was the American side, pushed it free of the shore, and jumped in. He locked the hatch back down and powered on the control systems. Refusing to waste time trying to interpret the Russian symbols, he piloted by instinct, knowing it couldn't be too different from flying a Cessna or a Beechcraft, and he had studied the schematics for one of these for weeks back home.

He could do this.

Now...find the exterior lights.

He flicked them on, swelling with satisfaction as the twin halogen beams stabbed out into the gloom. The depth gauge immediately caught his attention. The sub was drifting down, fast, so he found the thrusters, angled the control joystick and veered back up. *Compass...? There. Guide it, come on. Accelerate.*

Imagining a small army of swimming figures pursuing relentlessly underwater, Alex resisted every urge to look back.

Sorry Tony.

Staying on course, keeping the shoreline (or what he hoped was the shoreline) on his left, he maintained a depth of twenty meters and kept moving straight. Fifty meters. One hundred. He shrugged off the coat and threw it in the empty co-pilot seat, breathing a sigh of relief. Then he took a moment to study the environment outside.

The water—and the creatures in it. Floating particles, some of them exhibiting non-random movements. Alex could only imagine what he couldn't see: the microscopic bacterial organisms—those plentiful, ancient life forms he and Tony had set out to preserve and protect.

He swallowed hard. Thinking... thinking again about the lake. About Tony, and the Russians. He had fallen in, and certainly had been cut up. Did bacteria infect him, get in his bloodstream? Had the same thing happened to the Russians earlier?

Did what we had come to protect, instead see us as hosts, and attack?

What had happened to the Russians, and what was happening to Tony?

Alex studied the inner structure of the sub, breathing hard. His lips were dry and he cut his speed, worried suddenly about striking a rock or a wall, breaking the Plexiglas and letting in those...things.

He cut the thrusters just as the sub entered an area that had its own illumination. Brighter lights bobbed in the water, and beams were projected from above.

Welcome to America, he thought, slowing and preparing to descend again, hopefully out of sight before anyone noticed. He would make his way carefully to the far wall and rise to where—according to the American schematics—there should be a dock and an exit ladder.

First... he turned the sub gently—but stopped before he began to accelerate. Something huge was in the way.

Apparently lodged in the muck and rising some…fifty feet at least, according to his gauge, Alex had no idea what it could be.

A rock formation, or a huge glacial deposit?

Alex steered, trying to go around it to the right. Moving in closer, the bright beams focused and reflected off patchy green flecks, like aquatic lichen or bioluminescent sponges. Here and there were deep gouges taken out of the surface of whatever this thing was, segments plucked out in ways that Alex figured were far from natural. He was no geologist, but the manner of erosion—or whatever this was—seemed…violent and…

The sub, carried by an imperceptible drift, jarred to a halt as he suddenly pulled back on the joystick and reversed thrust.

Impossible…

Angling the nose of the craft, he aimed the lights dead-on toward the apex of the formation—where he figured the object was angling and narrowing, providing evidence it had grown like a crystal structure. Except…this formation had something it shouldn't have. Nearly frozen, perfectly preserved down here in the ice until the pressure and weight created a lake of sludge that somehow preserved it…

This… He couldn't believe what his eyes were seeing. Perched above more gashes, torn scales and what he now realized was *flesh*, rested *a single huge eye.*

Not daring to breathe, Alex could only gape as the sub reversed slowly, his hand on the controls…until suddenly, the eye *blinked.*

It seemed to attempt to focus, and then the pupil narrowed and turned almost yellow-white. An enormous set of teeth flashed into the brilliance, as the jaws opened, spreading moss and weed-like debris everywhere.

Losing control in a flurry of ice and bubbles, the craft spun in a one-eighty and slammed into the side of the creature. The viewing dome cracked. Water sprayed inside the submersible, Alex's head slammed against the hatch—and everything went black.

4.

Antarctica: American Drill Site Montgomery-Alpha

"Imagine my surprise," Marcus Ramirez said when the soldiers brought Alex into his office, two miles above the lake site. "Here I thought we had captured a Russian agent in violation of our exploration treaties, and I would have to initiate numerous international protocols and cause a huge scene involving multiple government agencies, and instead, I find that the criminal trespassing onto my secure research site is…my own goddamned son!"

He leveled a glare at Alex as icy as the frost on the windows obscuring his view of the perpetual gloom outside Montgomery station. Somewhere out there were two huge cranes poised like giant frost guardians over the pit—except these instruments would be used not for defense, but for extraction.

Marcus sat at his desk, a mahogany behemoth that would have been better suited to a banker's office than a paleontologist's field station, but that was par for the course for his benefactor. William DeKirk spared no expense, and wanted his people drowning in opulence, as if wealth and the mere presence of overpriced equipment could produce the discoveries he expected.

Maybe in this case, it had, or perhaps it was just dumb luck—or, Marcus liked to think, his own persistence, research, painstaking work and informed hunches, that had convinced him to outbid the Russians in this dual-nation race-for-the-lake mission. He had lobbied for the more difficult western approach. The underground lake was deeper at this section, less accessible, without any gradient allowing for a motorized approach along an incline. Marcus still recalled the months of persuasion and insistence on his part. If DeKirk was really after something more sizable—more media friendly—than microscopic organisms, his best bet was the deeper sediments on the western edge, where all the sonar and initial probes indicated an earlier basin more in line with the natural habitats and feeding areas of the larger dinosaurs.

Alex cleared his throat and raised his wrists—still bound with flex-cuffs. "If I'm damned, we may as well both be." He looked wet and miserable, shivering in a blanket between the two hulking soldiers. His long, partially dread-locked hair was tied back in a ponytail with a length of rawhide. He wore a crude necklace featuring a single, dull stone.

One of the soldiers moved forward and carefully held up Alex's pack, which he had hidden in his coat—a tightly-packed collection of clay-like bricks, along with wires and plugs.

"C-4?" Marcus said. "Oh God, Alex, what were you thinking?"

His son lowered his head. "Dad, I know it's been two years, and I know what you think of me, but—"

"I don't believe this. Now, of all times, you show up again in my life?"

Alex fumed at him. "I'll disregard the hypocrisy in that question, and ask you another one. Do you know that thing down there is alive?"

"So you saw it," Marcus said, lowering his voice, "what we have down there?"

Alex shook his head hard. "Yeah that... it's freakin' unbelievable, and congratulations on the discovery of a lifetime, but I swear, it's alive."

Marcus shook his head. "It's not. Average water temperature down there has been around twenty-seven degrees, most likely for millions and millions of years, and before that, this thing would have been frozen solid in a glacial layer. A veritable ice cube. No metabolic activities can function in those conditions, not to mention the fact that it couldn't breathe or eat or anything, even if you thought it was an evolutionary marvel like the Loch Ness Monster or something, it still would have had to eat."

"Dad, it opened its eye, and its freakin' mouth."

"Gas bubbles maybe, escaping from its gut as your sub's thrusters stirred up the water, changing the pressure."

"Bullshit."

"Really? Then what's the alternative? That a sixty-five million year old dinosaur has been taking a little cryogenic nap all this time?"

Marcus could tell his son was thinking, trying to reason out alternatives. He had to settle this and move on to more pressing matters. "Listen, you hit your head pretty bad, and you've been out in the extreme cold for I don't know how long. All these elements, and if I know you, no sleep… It's not surprising—"

"We found this too," one of the soldiers said, holding up a camera with a cracked faceplate. "We'll have to run the images."

"Yes!" Alex insisted, a spark returning to his eyes. "Run it, and then you'll see."

Marcus frowned, looking from the camera to his son, seeing the boy's crazed eyes, a look touched with a fear beyond anything these soldiers could have instilled in him. "See what?"

"That you've got bigger problems than whether or not I'm hallucinating. Bigger problems than finding some prehistoric monster that shouldn't be here."

#

Marcus wasn't aware that Alex had been following his career, much less that he would have known about the distribution of Jurassic-era dinosaurs and their geographic prevalence. Although it might stand to reason that few laymen would have expected much in the way of fossils down at this pole, but Alex was right. The few previous discoveries in Antarctica had pointed only to the presence of certain avian-variety dinosaurs and some herbivore species, as well as a new carnivorous species—dubbed a *Cryolophosaurus*, of which only a sub-adult had been found so far, so descriptions about the adult's size and attributes were just guesses. Marcus had theorized that the landmass that had once connected Antarctica and Australia would have been more than capable of allowing for a greater variety of dinosaurs during a time when Antarctica was lush and subtropical. It was exactly this theory that brought Marcus to the attention of billionaire DeKirk. Whatever DeKirk's motives (and he certainly hadn't shared them with Marcus), he was sure that they involved Marcus's theories. Today, this discovery apparently had DeKirk wild with excitement.

Alex's presence, a veritable thorn in his side, couldn't have come at a worse time.

"The Russians," Alex insisted. "The other side. We started there and…"

"Sir!" Another soldier just ran in, skidding to a halt beside his colleagues. "Just received word. A seismic event was recorded two miles east. Theta-1, it has to be…"

Marcus shot a glare at his son, then to his backpack full of C-4. "What did you do?"

Alex struggled with the handcuffs and against the restraining grip on his arm. Finally, Marcus nodded and made a wave with his hand and the soldier produced a key to release the cuffs.

"Thanks. Listen, so there *may* have been an explosion over there, but Tony and I—"

"Oh no," Marcus said in a low voice. "Not Tony Harrison?

"Dad, just listen."

"Where is he?" Marcus looked to the soldiers, then back to Alex. "What did you two do? Gary, contact Theta-1 and—"

"Tried sir, no response."

"Dad—"

"Try again."

"*Dad!*"

Marcus turned back to him. "What?"

"Tony's…dead."

"Oh, Alex."

"It was…an accident. At least at first. We fell down the pit. He was all cut up and landed in the lake—"

Marcus blinked at him, imagining it, but something in his son's voice held back his own questions.

"The Russians, they were there…they…were not right. Attacked us, and I'm telling you—"

"Wait, they attacked you? Oh Christ, now we *do* have an international incident." He could see it now. American intruders, they would be branded as CIA operatives or something, and the Russians would be in the clear for defending themselves. An American activist dead, another wanted for criminal actions. Marcus held his head in his hands. It was all falling apart fast.

"Dad, the water! I'm telling you, there's something about those microbes. You have to get your men out of there, pull them all up and—"

"Impossible," Marcus said. "We're beginning extraction of the *T. rex* today, and the other two…"

"What?" Alex frowned, and then looked to the desk, where Marcus had three monitors, two showing split screens of various artificially lit views of the infrastructure down at the base of the pit, the catwalks, wires and mesh netting, the six submersibles and five inflatable boats. "Jesus, so that was a *T. rex*? Did you say, *other* two?"

"Alex, we've got a team of fifty trained technicians down there with state-of-the-art equipment. We're talking military-grade harnesses and hydraulic load-bearing gear with computer-assisted winches and other stuff that isn't even on the commercial market yet. All set to raise one of the greatest finds in paleontological history. A perfectly-preserved *Tyrannosaurus rex*! Yes, last week we located in the sediment two more *Cryolophosaurs*. Sub-adults both, but also perfectly preserved. At only twenty feet long, their extraction is a far simpler matter."

He pressed a few keys and the screen flashed, showing from a distance what looked like two wet, frozen dogs, and Marcus could just make out the telltale crown-like appendages on their heads, the ridges on their skulls, and the rows of nasty-looking teeth in their jaws.

Marcus beamed, but just then the third monitor flickered and a Skype call came in. A grizzled face, heavy with scars like an ancient roadmap across his leathery skin, William DeKirk's wild eyes, slightly off-jade, loomed in the screen. His hair, silvery and thin, fell over his face but couldn't block his enthusiasm.

"I want minute-by-minute updates, Marcus. Patch me in to the operation."

Marcus immediately pulled the screen to an angle where, hopefully, DeKirk couldn't see his son, or the soldiers. *Please...*

"Yes, Mr. DeKirk, but... there's been an incident. We may have to wait."

"What incident?" His voice snapped like a cobra, and he hissed back. "What, the Russian explosion? Heard about that, it's of no consequence."

"You heard...?"

"I have my sources, and no, I don't care. I've alerted the American embassy in Moscow and they can handle it with the usual denials and claims of ignorance. Which is correct isn't it?"

His eyes peeked through the silver hair and blinked at Marcus, then tried to look beyond the camera's limited field of view from his end. "You *didn't* have anything to do with it, right? Even though there's the disturbing family connection…"

Oh God. Marcus flashed a look to his son, who just raised his hands.

"Sorry," Alex whispered. "My camera…it was a thirty-minute-delay live feed to our blogsite… at least until it all went nuts."

Marcus rubbed his temples. He closed his eyes, took a deep breath, and then looked at the screen again. "Sir, I had no idea."

"I'm sure." DeKirk pulled back, grinning devilishly.

"Really. I have Alex here. He's in custody, and I'll deal with him. Harshly or…" He looked at Alex. "Turn him over to the authorities if that's what's required."

"We can decide that later," DeKirk said, "depending on the situation and the level of response from the Russian side. I heard there were…casualties?"

"Regrettably," Marcus said, "Alex's…colleague, as it were, and—?" He raised his eyes to Alex. "The Russian scientists?"

"I'm not sure they were scientists," Alex said, walking around, now in view, so that he could see DeKirk—and vice versa. "I'm not sure they were…right. They just weren't *right*. Something happened down there, sir…"

"Alex, not now."

"What happened?" DeKirk asked, perking up again.

"I don't know exactly, but I was telling my father. The lake down there, the bacteria or the microscopic organisms, you can't just expose something millions of years old to present conditions without some consequences. Tony and I—we came here to protect an indigenous species, but after what I saw down there, after what I think it did to Tony, infecting his wounds…I don't know. It acted fast, and something—"

DeKirk nodded in an off-screen direction and just raised his hand. "That's fine, son. Your concerns are noted, but we've been studying the lake's…microscopic denizens… for several months now. We know what we're dealing with, and it's nothing to be worried about."

Marcus frowned. *We have?* It was news to him, and as far as he knew, he was the only true scientist at this base. The others—they were either technicians who operated specialized equipment, or else, they were all muscle. Mercenaries. A crew of ex-military contractors hired through DeKirk, but officially working on a U.S. initiated contract of exploration and polar research. If anyone was studying the water, it wasn't Marcus. So, was DeKirk lying, or was he just leaving Marcus in the dark?

"But, sir—"

"Alex, stop." Marcus turned to the screen again. "Look, the men are ready and we're close, but maybe we should listen to him. Give it another day or two. Make sure we're not in the middle of an international incident and that—I don't know—we're not bringing up something we can't deal with."

"We can deal with anything." Never had Marcus heard anything spoken with such confidence.

He sighed. "I'm not even talking about the microbes, but this is the first...the first preserved specimen from more than sixty-five million years ago. Who knows what viruses it might be carrying, or other bacteria? We can't expose it yet, I don't think."

"Not paying you to think," DeKirk shot back. "At least, not about this. You did your thinking and got us this far, for which you'll be handsomely rewarded. Money and fame is just the start. I take full responsibility for everything else, and we *will* contain it. Biologically, we have everything we need to keep it secure. My tanker is already en route to the port. We'll be there before you're done raising the specimen. I've had the hold outfitted to maintain it in optimal, biosecure conditions to prevent not only decay, but also the spread of any contaminants."

DeKirk grinned as his face took over the whole screen. "Dr. Ramirez, this is the find of a lifetime, a feat that puts you on par with Columbus and Neil Armstrong. You'll go down in history as a pioneer of new worlds!"

Alex shuffled closer. "But the *T. rex*... I saw it had wounds. Big chunks of flesh torn out of its hide. It could be that it's now infected with whatever infected my friend, and the Russians..."

"Why the hell is this person still making noises?" DeKirk asked. "I'm rethinking possible deliverance of this pest to the Russians. Control your son, Marcus."

"Yes sir, but I really feel that we need a little patience here. Bring in the CDC and other experts?"

DeKirk laughed. "I'm signing off right now to watch the extraction. Looking forward to viewing our prizes firsthand." He shook his head in wonder. "A *T. rex* and two Cryos! Fantastic work. See you in Adranos, Mr. Ramirez."

As the screen went blank, Alex asked, *"Adranos?"*

Marcus sighed. "DeKirk's private island and research facility in the South Pacific, named after some Sicilian fire god or something. I guess that's where I'm headed next."

"Fire god?"

Marcus shrugged. "It's got an active volcano."

"Wonderful. So…that's where they're bringing that thing?"

"Not until I raise it," Marcus said, "and after what you told me, I'm thinking we're *not* going to raise it. The hell with what DeKirk said."

"I don't think it's your call, Dad." Alex pointed to the window.

The cranes were lit up as they set into motion, turning, facing each other. On the screens, lights flashed, men on rafts waved glowing lights, water bubbled and steam arose in advance of a spiny cleft—a giant carapace breaking Kraken-like through the surface.

"We'll see about that." Marcus moved to the microphone and barked out orders to stop, but he knew it was futile. They were DeKirk's men, and this was no longer his operation—if it ever had been.

"Sixty-five million years," Alex said. "That thing is coming to us, and it's not coming alone."

5.

Retrofitted Oil Tanker Hammond-1, twenty miles off the northern coast of Antarctica.

The helicopter deposited its payload, refueled, and departed as quickly as it had landed, as if fearing to remain a minute more than necessary on the icy top deck of the giant tanker.

Xander Dyson pulled back his white arctic hood and lifted his goggles over his thick head of wavy blond hair. Despite having dressed in so many layers that he had lost count, he winced against the brutal cold and the biting wind as the three men approached. The flight from the port in Chile had been every bit of the white-knuckle hell ride that he imagined, and now to be here at the frozen toilet of the world, *ordered* here, no less, taken away from his research and the imminent accolades he was so close to achieving, was nearly unbearable.

"Captain," Xander said, addressing the bulky brute of a man in the middle whom he assumed was in charge. Although he couldn't really be sure, but usually, the control figures let their lackeys carry the guns.

"Mr. Dyson, welcome aboard."

"I need three things," Xander insisted. "One, immediate warmth. Two, a shot of your strongest alcohol, and three, an explanation as to what couldn't wait that I had to be rushed to this world of frozen misery."

The captain grinned beneath bushy white eyebrows crusted with flakes of ice. "The first two will pale in comparison to what we'll show you."

Xander frowned. "I doubt that. What have you got?"

"It's what Mr. DeKirk has found, and he insists he sees your reaction first hand. So come with us down below, where it's warm and the vodka is plentiful."

Xander bowed, and let them lead the way.

DeKirk. What did that old bastard have up his sleeve? There weren't many men who could order Xander halfway around the world and he'd go, but DeKirk was one of them. Certainly a man of Xander's genius, talents, connections and skills, didn't need

DeKirk, but he was one of several competing benefactors, stocking Xander's lab in Austria, bankrolling several lines of research and ensuring that his less-than-legal efforts failed to attract attention of the authorities. Xander's needs ran towards the very expensive, but his products were in high demand. He was near to closing several deals, pitting various agencies and governments against each other in a bidding war that would ensure his future—and his place in history, at only the ripe old age of thirty-eight.

They led him down a brittle metal staircase, and then across a lower deck teeming with crewmembers rushing about, preparing the great open area with winches and hydraulic cranes, de-icing the large cargo doors. Xander paused to stare as they opened the doors, expecting the hold to be filled with some sort of precious cargo.

Instead, as the doors completed their motion, they revealed an enormous empty space inside. Empty except for giant chains set to secure something immense.

"What the hell, did you find King Kong?"

Xander looked back to the captain for an answer, but found him disappearing into an open door, with the soldiers outside, flanking the entrance.

Following quickly, with just a backwards glance, as huge spotlights burst into light, aimed at the hold. The ship surged and Xander had to grip a railing or lose his balance. He didn't know what he hated more at this point: helicopters, boats, or just the brutal cold.

"What's your intended cargo, Captain?" he asked, as he entered and the door closed hard behind him.

A chuckle, and a shot glass was thrust in his face. The captain had tossed aside his coat and in a black wool turtleneck, he raised his own glass and drank with Xander.

"You won't believe me until you see it for yourself," he said. "You may need another shot, but here…" He approached a laptop on the desk in the cramped but warm room and turned to face Xander. "These will be your quarters, by the way, for the duration until we get to Adranos Island."

"What?" Xander swallowed the bitter vodka, licked his lips, and glanced around. Small bed, one desk and no windows. A bookshelf and of course the laptop and monitor. "I'm not going to any island."

Then the laptop screen sparked and resolved into the familiar visage of DeKirk's face. "Ah, Xander! Welcome to the party."

"Yeah," Xander replied, pulling up a chair and sitting level to DeKirk. "I don't recall having the option to RSVP."

"No need, my friend. Now, I hope you're ready?"

Xander shrugged, glanced at the captain, who was busy refilling both glasses, and now Xander wondered how many the man had already imbibed, *and what, exactly, made him need so many?*

"I'm sending you images from our American friends down at Erebus Station, Antarctica."

Great, Xander thought, *we're going somewhere even colder.*

"Hold onto your balls, and prepare to have your mind blown seven ways to Sunday."

Xander accepted the glass. "I'm intrigued. Bring it on already."

DeKirk pulled back and made some clicking noises, and the screen changed to a grainy bright view of an icy work site, an industrial place of cranes and platforms. Dozens of men in parkas bustling about, and then... a shift, and a view in a tunnel, something rising on a platform. Something huge, something...

Xander peered closer, squinting

His fingers flinched, opened, and the glass fell and shattered.

"Holy shit, is that...?"

"It is," came DeKirk's voice, barely containing his giddiness. "Perfectly preserved, and it's not alone. We've found at least two other dinosaurs, different species, but just as intact."

"This is it," Xander whispered, marveling. The cold, the flight, and the rough seas were all forgotten. "It's...everything."

6.

Monitoring the ship's bow from her darkened office with a small set of next-gen rangefinder binoculars outfitted with night-vision technology, Veronica Winters observed the helicopter's take-off. She waited with baited breath to see who could possibly be so important as to warrant a dangerous delivery to DeKirk's private and super-secret tanker.

She waited, hoping she'd get her first glimpse of his face, if the man dared remove his hood in the extreme winds and temperatures outside. She hoped that even from this distance that she'd be able to make an ID. If not, she'd have to break her cover as the *Hammond's* doctor, a cover her CIA superiors had worked hard and pulled several lucky favors to get in place. After spending the last two years in much more agreeable climates, such as Morocco and Monte Carlo, Veronica had no urge to consider heading out into less extreme conditions any time soon.

Come on, she thought. *Mystery man, show your damn face and save me the trouble.*

Already, she felt far too vulnerable on this mission: being the only woman, and a beautiful one at that, alone, with thirty female-starved crewmembers loaded with testosterone and bad manners, was not her idea of a good time. Every one of them would be feigning injuries at some point to book an appointment with the hot doctor, and for this mission, Veronica actually adopted a contrary disguise, toning down her looks, cropping her hair, and bundling herself in incredibly itchy and unattractive sweaters, but it did no good. Not with this crew of louts, or that ever-drunk captain always leering at her. It had been a long six days since cast-off from Chile.

Antarctica. She knew the destination from their Intel hacked from a rare less-than-secure email communication from one of DeKirk's contractors. A paleontologist, of all people, named Marcus Ramirez. What DeKirk wanted a fossil-hunter for was anybody's guess, but this had been a ten-year case of trying to nail DeKirk on anything, hopefully gaining evidence on a multitude of international crimes: money-laundering, sex-trafficking, drug running, artifact stealing, and corporate espionage were just a few of the possibilities. It should not have been this hard, but it was. He had deep pockets and incredible security. He was rarely seen in public, although he sat on at least twenty different boards, most with charitable leanings to provide himself some degree of legitimacy. He had no known romantic attachments, no indiscretions as far as Veronica could ascertain, and no weak links.

It was a nearly impossible assignment, and although she had come close on several occasions, she had come closer still to having her cover blown and the whole thing going up in smoke. Back in Morocco, she could have nailed him on a lesser charge of tax fraud, but held out when she had an indication that he was working toward something much, much bigger. Something with global implications. The highest secrecy, and something that involved a new direction for DeKirk: *genetics*. He now had teams of biologists and labs set up in several third world countries and islands in the Atlantic. That was the first priority, and Langley confirmed it, rushing to get her a new identity after intercepting the urgent communication from the American Antarctic base.

She shipped out to Chile, assumed the role of doctor on the tanker, and now... she was so close. She knew this mystery man wasn't DeKirk: far too fit and spry by his movements. He did have that the same arrogant, overconfident edge that DeKirk had, though, but he also had something else. Irritation. He was pissed off about being here, and that much was certain. So, he wasn't DeKirk himself or one of his lackeys. This was someone else, someone important and someone—

The captain approached with two thugs, and the new arrival pulled back his hood and lifted his goggles.

It was only a couple seconds before one of the soldiers obscured the view, but it was enough.

She could never forget that face. Those high, pronounced cheekbones, the comma-shaped scar on the left cheekbone, the angry blond hair. Those eyes: cruel and hard as nails.

His face was in every law enforcement's most wanted database. FBI and CIA had joint teams looking for him with Interpol assistance. He was a ghost, a phantom.

Worse, an assassin. He killed not with bullets or knives, but with rare toxins and biological agents. Viruses were his specialty, and if he was involved, Veronica's fears of a global initiative with DeKirk's funding and reach might be sorely understated.

All that paled to the real reason she nearly cried out at the recognition of Xander Dyson.

Seven years ago, he had killed her partner and lover, murdered him in the worst way imaginable—a viral death that took days, and gave him just enough time to make it back to her, only to die in her arms. It was a loss that haunted Veronica every minute of every day.

Now, at last, here in the most unlikely of places, Xander was in her sights.

7.

Antarctica: American Drill Site Montgomery-Alpha

Refreshed if not at all rested, Alex felt too snug in his father's sweater, but the casual sweatpants worked fine. His fingers and toes tingled, and the padded loafers felt like little slippers from heaven. As he entered his father's command office again, he felt a sudden crushing weight of guilt. *Tony.* His body, torn and broken, was out there, a few miles to the east, and it was likely they would never get it back, and this icy wasteland would be his tomb for eternity.

"Alex, sit down," his father's voice broke him from his misery, "and grab a cup of coffee if you like, right in the corner."

Shuffling in that direction, Alex never made it that far. His eyes tugged to the window and view of the action outside: blazing spotlights, the cranes in full action, then men rushing back and forth, securing crates and readying a pair of giant ice-rovers with a flatbed trailer, equipped with great chains and harnesses.

"It's going to fit on that?" he wondered.

"It will, I'm told." Marcus stood, stepped away from his desk, and walked to the window. He was dressed a little more professionally, with a dark tweed sports coat and white turtleneck, khakis and a set of alligator skin boots that Alex couldn't recall ever seeing him wear before. Of course, it had been a long time since Alex had spent much time with his father, let alone noticed what sort of footwear the man preferred. When he wasn't busy ignoring his son or his wife, Marcus Ramirez was consumed with writing papers, researching, and giving boring talks at conventions full of equally boring scientists theorizing about everything except what was going on right under their nose.

Alex decided to switch the conversation to an arena where he stood a chance.

"So, heard from mom lately?"

Marcus tensed, and Alex could see his reflection in the glass. Flinching. "Ironically, yes. Just yesterday."

"Oh, how's her health?"

"You know your mother, talks about everyone else's problems. Never her own."

"Well, I can tell you. She's not doing well."

Marcus nodded. "Kind of figured, but how would you know? All she wanted to ask about was you. Appears she hadn't heard from you either, in a year at least." He leveled a glare at Alex. "So, it's not just your wayward father that you reserve your apathy for?"

"That's not fair."

Marcus shrugged. "It doesn't matter. I'm not having this conversation, not now. I told her you would most likely turn up somewhere in custody and needing one or both of us to bail you out again. I just never imagined it would be here." He sighed. "What the hell were you thinking?"

"I was thinking of making the biggest point, the largest splash possible. Given the circumstance. Exposing—"

"Yes, yes, I get it. All the corporate greed and worldwide hypocrisy, but did it have to be here? Now? You have no idea who it is that's bankrolling this operation."

Alex crossed his arms over his chest. "Oh, we were quite aware. How you got into bed with someone who's the worst kind of monster, one who claims to be a philanthropist."

"DeKirk is paying the bills and this… this is good work, damn it. Important work."

"Unlike what I do?"

Marcus closed his eyes and shook his head. "I have no idea what it is you do, son. Other than get in trouble and drag everyone else down into hell with you."

The barb stung, and coming right on the heels of his guilt about leaving Tony, and Alex had no comeback. Instead, he decided to shift back to the unfamiliar arena, where at least he wasn't a target. "So where are the others? The *Cryos* or whatever he called them?"

Marcus pointed to a pair of ordinary-looking shipping containers at the edge of the pit. "Already packed and ready for their trip."

Alex whistled. "They were…in the same condition? Preserved?"

"They were. Flesh-on-bones. Same strata, and I have a theory that the bites and tears what you saw on the *T. rex*? Might have been from these little critters."

"Did you say they were sub-adults?"

"Right, from their bone structure and general traits that's our thinking. Only twenty feet long, a ton in weight. Early Jurassic period, the only carnivorous dinosaur discovered up until...well, our other friend down there. Cryos as you called them, have a crest on the tops of their heads, and are probably capable of color distortion for mating and battle purposes. A real amazing specimen, one I can't wait to explore at length, if DeKirk will still allow me that honor."

Alex shrugged. "Sorry for almost blocking you from playing with your toys."

"Alex—"

"No, listen. I...wait, what's going on down there?" He pointed to the cranes, which were straining, then sharply rocking to one direction, and then the other. The spotlights spun and tracked down, and sharply back and forth.

"Oh shit," Marcus hissed, and rushed back to his desk, eying the monitors, sizing up the situation—a blur of images and faces. The winch cables straining and the body on the platform spinning out of control, as men were tossed from its side and others hung on.

"It looks like a fight," he said, grabbing the microphone.

"No," said Alex, "get your men out of there. Those are—the *others*."

"Who?"

"The things. The Russians..."

8.

"I'm going out," Marcus said, sounding hollow as he tried to follow the blurry and frenetic action on the screens. *What the hell was happening down there?* Some kind of fight. Had the Russians followed Alex over? Now the contest was in earnest for the prize, and *shit*...if they damaged the specimen! His mouth dried up and he found himself frozen to the spot. He wasn't cut out for this, didn't know the protocols. These men, the soldiers... DeKirk, where to start? What could he possibly do in this situation?

In moments, however, the decision was taken from him, and a different instinct took over. "I'm going out there," Alex said, already rushing for the door, and snagging his dad's coat from a hook.

"No, you're not!" Marcus yelled, but the door had already been flung open.

Alex whipped the hood over his head and pulled out the gloves. "No one knows what they're facing but me."

"You? Now you're a combat soldier?"

"No," he said over the whipping winds on the metal stairwell outside. "Just someone with a knack for being in the wrong place at the wrong time."

With that, he was out, and Marcus—after a moment's hesitation—was energized. He rushed to a closet and started dressing in one of the spare jackets and gearing up. Done, he snatched a phone and raced out after his son.

\#

Down at the drill site, Alex rushed around one of the shipping containers, giving it a cautious look, as if expecting something to burst through the metal at any second, with spear-length teeth and snarling jaws.

The sound of gunshots echoing off the glacial walls and splitting through the hissing wind snapped him back to the moment, and he was back, rushing—still in those damn comfortable slippers—through the packed ice, racing for the edge. He yelled and waved his arms, trying to get the attention of the men along the edge, framed in the shifting spotlights.

At least a dozen soldiers stood around the edge, aiming, trying to get clear shots of whatever it was down there.

Then suddenly, Marcus was there, running beside Alex and waving his arms. "Don't fire! You can't damage the specimen!"

Dad, Alex felt like saying, *it's damaged enough already, a few bullets won't make a difference.* Then he thought, if that was the case, how did it move? Those wounds should have killed it—if the millions of intervening years hadn't done the job in the first place.

One of the grunts, decked in a white camo jumpsuit, looked back and aimed his M5 at them both as they skidded to a stop.

"Back off, civilians. This is a military operation now."

"The hell it is," Marcus spat, pointing into the pit. "DeKirk gave me orders, too, and that thing—his investment—better be intact when he comes to collect it."

The soldier made a snarling face and looked back into the pit—where Alex, bending over the edge, could barely make anything out. With the dueling spotlight beams and the twisting wires and lifting apparatus, the makeshift metal scaffolding and the shadowy *thing* on the rising platform, about a hundred feet below, he couldn't make out anything in any kind of focus. At least, nothing that made sense.

Were those *men* on the dinosaur's carapace, climbing and fighting each other? Gunshots intermittently lit up the deep shadows, and as the platform continued to rise, Alex got a momentary glimpse of something that made his heart lurch.

A pair of black-clad figures with scales on their faces and bright yellow eyes…contrasting with the scarlet dripping from their flashing teeth as they tore through an American's jacket and feasted on his insides.

#

"Are you getting this, sir?" the soldier snapped into his communicator.

Marcus grabbed Alex's shoulder and tried to pull him back from the edge.

"No, Dad. Listen, everyone—*stop the excavation!*"

"We can't," Marcus said.

"We won't," the soldier in charge returned.

The platform continued to rise, and now Marcus saw what hadn't been clear before: it was covered with soldiers, men in black fighting those in white, and...blood. Blood everywhere. Not from gunshots so much as... "Jesus, they're *eating* our men..."

"My God," the soldier at his side said. He aimed through his weapon's scope. "Screw this. Alpha Team, fire!"

"No!" Marcus yelled and lunged for the weapon, only to have the soldier swing it back hard and knock him on his back. He aimed it at Alex.

"You going to be a problem, too?"

"No," Alex said, hands raised, "but *they* are. Unless you kill them all."

The man nodded and aimed again. "Oh, we'll get them."

He commenced firing.

Alex could only watch, and Marcus, as he pulled himself up, nursing his bloody lip, looked down in dismay. He flinched with every shot.

"It's not working," he said, seeing the black outfits pierced again and again. Nothing slowed down the Russians in their ravenous attack on the Americans, who were doing their best to find cover around the *T. rex's* body, crawling and climbing across the platform, taking shots with handguns. "Body armor?"

The soldier nodded, and spoke into his communicator again. "Sniper shots, to the head. On my command, go!"

Then the real carnage began.

Fifty feet left to the surface, and the dozen soldiers around the ridge, emptied their clips and reloaded. Aiming and firing, aiming and firing. Marcus winced, watching heads blown apart, brains and gore splattering his dinosaur. Hoping against hope the shots weren't going wild, imagining he'd be extracting bullets from the specimen for weeks.

The Russians were dropping now—and for an instant, Marcus thought he saw something impossible. One of their faces an instant before impact: blurry, but unmistakably covered with thick scales, yellowish and pallid, spattered in blood, and those eyes—then the head exploded and the twitching body pitched off the side of the platform.

The Americans were regrouping. Several fighting valiantly, ganging up on the remaining Russians, tossing several over.

Still the gunshots rang out, taking out the few remaining enemies.

Marcus started to breathe a sigh of relief, along with the Americans, he imagined. Then, the soldier in charge paused in his shooting, listening to commands in his helmet.

"What? But...yes sir. I understand. Copy that."

He raised the weapon again, sighting.

"What are you doing?" Marcus asked, as his prize, the *T. rex*, in all its bloodied immensity, was lifted almost into level view. "You got them all, you can stand down now." *And return me to command,* he felt like adding.

The soldier fired. An American dropped, the top of his head blown off.

Alex screamed and tried to rush the soldier, but Marcus held him back. They both turned. "What the hell!"

Then more shots, from all sides. The Americans were sitting ducks, and in seconds, it was over. Twitching, nearly-headless bodies draped over the triumphantly-raised *T. rex*. A few bodies flopped with the jostling of the platform and fell over the edge.

"Toss the rest back into the pit," the soldier growled into his radio, "and continue with the extraction. He slung his weapon over his shoulder and faced Marcus.

"Your show now, Doctor."

"Why?" Alex whispered, still staring at the bodies as they were tossed unceremoniously over the edge.

"Orders," the soldier said.

For just a moment, Alex had a sudden image of Tony, his skin changing. The gash in his arm...

He swallowed hard, even as Marcus found his voice and was about to argue. "Dad," he said, "let it go, I think they did the right thing. The only thing."

Marcus turned to his son. "Are you mad?"

Alex had turned away, and now approached the platform, getting as close as he could to the giant's cranium and that eye...now closed. Alex shuddered, thinking for a moment. "They weren't wearing body armor, Dad. "I saw it, down there on the other side."

"Impossible," the soldier said.

"But true," Alex replied, "and if they were infected with whatever was in that lake, then…"

He stared at the *T. rex*, its enormous jaws, and the hint of teeth. The overlapping scales and thick epidermis. The knick marks from the bullets that had failed to penetrate.

"You had better have a very cold shipping container, and hope this thing never thaws…"

9.

Aboard Oil Tanker Hammond-1, Erebus Point, Antarctica

"Erebrus Point, eh? Should have named it Windy-ass Bay!" Xander nearly had to yell to make himself heard over the roaring winds that buffeted the entrance to the bay, as he and the captain stepped into the glassed-in bridge from out on deck.

"Just be glad we don't have to go to Icy Balls Bay," the captain said, clearly half in the bag, taking a seat in front of the myriad displays and instruments that controlled the massive ship. He shook with hearty laughter at his own joke as he toggled switches on the control panel. Xander wondered again how much he'd had to drink and what kind of oversight, if any, these sea captains were subject to, and especially ones DeKirk would hire.

"Sounds like a brand of rum, don't it? Icy Balls Bay, a shot a day!" The captain kept going as he looked over his head at an array of instrumentation.

Xander didn't laugh. "Yeah, yeah. Hey, maybe we should focus a little. Is there a dock or something?"

The captain made a sharp exhalation that caused little flecks of spittle to pepper the GPS display in front of him. "Sure, mate, right next to the waterfront pub with the girlies in cute little outfits servin' up trays of Icy Balls on the rocks! 'Cept the girls are penguins, and the rocks are icebergs waitin' to tear this ship a new one." He paused, looking over at Xander to see how he was reacting before continuing.

"No, there ain't no dock. There's a couple small piers here and there around this blasted ice continent, but this bay has none, and this ship is too big to navigate them 'bergs in there, anyway." He pointed deeper into the bay where the ocean's surface became studded with white rocks.

Xander appeared confused. "I thought this was an ice-breaker, made for this kind of stuff?" He waved an arm through the windscreen at the iceberg-strewn expanse of water between them and the rocky shoreline.

The captain pressed a button to release the tanker's massive anchor. "Is that what you thought? Imagine that. DeKirk actually giving a shit about anybody's safety. Look here." He patted the dashboard. "This ship's state-of-the-art, it's new, it's badass, but not in the way you think. You see, this oversized metal tub is faster than shit, for a metal tub, but in order to achieve that speed, something else needed to be sacrificed, and that something else was the icebreaking layer, which is heavy as shit."

"Why would you want that?"

"*DeKirk* wants it so's we can reach the Adranos Island quick-like, as soon as we leave this ice-pit."

"What is this I keep hearing about Adranos—"

The captain raised a hand as his marine radio crackled. "Shush now. Time to get to work so we can get outta here."

Xander muttered something under his breath as the captain engaged in some kind of technical chatter on the radio. The conversation became a little more heated, though, when the person on the other end asked if the captain could bring the ship closer.

"Negative. You bring it out here on the barge. We'll be waitin' with Hell's bells on."

He cursed under his breath as he hung up the radio transmitter.

#

About an hour later, a long, flat vessel motored up to the *Hammond* and tied up alongside. Its deck was littered with shipping containers and industrial equipment. Multiple personnel busied themselves on deck like worker ants in a large colony. On the tanker's bridge, the captain barked orders through a PA system related to operating a large crane to his crew outside on deck.

As Xander watched, an oblong crate was crane-hoisted from the barge to the work deck of the tanker. He recalled with a shiver of excitement the image that he'd seen earlier on the laptop from his quarters. Xander left the bridge while the captain was still hollering at his crew through the PA. He descended a flight of ice-covered metal stairs, slipping once and banging his head on the railing, to a deck that wrapped around the ship's bridge tower. The shouts of working crewmen rang out across the ship. As he looked down on the tanker's work deck, the excavated find was transferred from the crane hoist to a large forklift, a dozen burly men putting in a lot of physical effort to center the crate on the lift.

Xander watched as one man walked up to the crew foreman directing the work team. He looked very much out of place holding a clipboard and without the hardhat or rubber overalls the ship's crew wore. Xander watched as the foreman became irritated with the man and hurriedly pointed in the direction of the cargo hold as the forklift started to roll. Xander also made his way down to the hold, recalling the gigantic chains set into the walls. When he walked through the huge double-doors, currently held open, he saw the newcomer trailing the forklift as it came to a stop well into the hold's cavernous interior.

Xander caught up with him as he stood there gawking at the spectacle of it all, at the huge set of shackles, at the crate now being slid off the forklift, the impromptu living space set aside in the hold. He could see now that he had a Hispanic look about him, and a sort of quiet intensity that suggested either continued awe in the presence of such a find, or more likely—a man scheming for a way to get what he wanted. Xander squinted at the man critically.

The observer appeared almost startled, as though Xander had woken him from a pleasant dream by dumping a bucket of water on his head. He shook it off and extended his hand. "Yes? Can I help you?"

"I'm Xander Dyson, Director of Scientific Research for Melvin DeKirk Enterprises, and you are?"

"Dyson, you say? I'm Dr. Marcus Ramirez, Chief Paleontologist for DeKirk's expedition here."

Xander regarded him coolly, never taking the doctor's hand. Now he was up to speed on who this was, and he recognized a threat, however minor, when he saw one.

"Let's get one thing straight. You're not the *chief* anything here. I'm in charge now, and I believe you'll find your services are no longer required." He pointed at the crate, now being pried apart by six crew with crowbars. "This specimen is the culmination of years of planning and hard work. You were brought on for your expertise in a very narrow area that helped us to achieve this means. Don't forget your place in the food chain, and we'll get along just fine until we reach port, and then you can catch the next flight home, or wherever it is you go when you're not digging around in the ice."

Marcus's face cycled through a few shades of red, settling on a particularly eye-catching crimson hue. "Mr. DeKirk signs my paychecks, not you. This specimen is absolutely my responsibility until we reach the island."

The sound of plywood boards slapping the metal floor echoed in the hold. Marcus turned his head to look, but Xander grabbed him by the arm, pulling him away. "Come with me."

Marcus tried to shake off the surprisingly firm grip. "Let go of me."

"I don't think so. You've left me little choice, so now, let's talk about your son. C'mon." Xander started walking deeper into the hold, beckoning Marcus to follow. The crew was still working on the crate, so he trailed Xander past a bulkhead into the middle section of the hold. He was surprised to see a brig area—a tiny office staffed by one crewman across from a small jail cell lit by a bare bulb in a wire cage on the wall. He was even more surprised to see his son inside it, sitting on a threadbare metal bunk, head in his hands.

"Alex! How the hell did you—?"

Alex snapped his head up at the sound of his father's voice.

"Dad! DeKirk's soldier goons put me in here! What's going on?"

The crewman seated at the small desk across from the cell turned a laptop around so that its screen faced Marcus. DeKirk's wizened visage filled the display as he began to speak.

"I'll tell you what's going on." The entrepreneur spoke forcefully, commanding the attention of all in the room. "Dr. Ramirez, as you probably already heard, but refused to accept from my associate, Mr. Dyson, I am terminating your position as of right now. You will be dropped off at a port in Chile, with your return airfare to the U.S. paid for. Is that clear?"

Xander grinned smugly and crossed his arms.

"No! That is *not* acceptable. I was brought on to conduct research, not to be cast aside like some greenhorn post-doc as soon as an exciting discovery is made so that this...this corporate *misfit* can take over!" He glared at Xander with contempt.

DeKirk's voice boomed through the laptop again. "Speaking of misfits, take a look at your son, Marcus." Marcus glanced at Alex, who shrunk beneath his gaze in the grimy cell.

"His fate is entirely up in the air right now. We could keep him in the brig for weeks—months, even—until we reach a U.S. port in which to turn him over to authorities there for acts of vandalism, international espionage, manslaughter..." He paused, enjoying the look of fear on Alex's face and the distaste on his father's. "Or we could even hand him over to the Russians and see if they have an opinion as to what should happen to him."

"Mr. DeKirk! I respectfully..." Marcus began, but DeKirk rolled over him, holding up a hand on the Skype window.

"Or...we have a third option." At this, Marcus quieted, waiting for DeKirk to continue.

"As I was saying, we could simply drop you and your son off in Chile together, where you both will be free to return home. This would be in return for your absolute silence regarding our operations here and upholding the nondisclosure documents you already signed at the time of your hiring, as well as your acceptance of the fact that you are now merely a passenger aboard my ship, in no way acting in a working capacity."

Marcus looked from Alex then back at DeKirk on the Skype window. "My find...all the announcements and press. The release of the discovery..."

DeKirk shook his head, a slight smirk on his face.

Marcus fumed inside. "You never intended to share this find with the world, did you? You needed me to help you find it, but...not to legitimize it after?"

DeKirk shook his head, eyes never wavering from Marcus'.

"So...what then? What are you going to do with it?"

"That, Dr. Ramirez, you will find out, along with the rest of the world."

He lowered his eyes. "Son of a bitch."

"I'm sorry," DeKirk said. "I didn't hear that clearly with this connection."

Xander, off to the side, leaning against a bulkhead with his arms crossed, gave his own smirk.

DeKirk leaned in closer, turning his head so that his ear was to the microphone. "Did you say you agreed?"

Marcus sighed. He glanced again at Alex, restrained and looking miserable and lost. *Goddamn.* They had him, and they knew it.

"Deal."

It took all of Marcus's willpower not to punch the self-satisfied grin off Xander's stupid face, while the crewman behind the jailer's desk stood up with the key for Alex's release.

10.

Aboard Oil Tanker Hammond-1, Erebus Point, Antarctica

The utility closet in the ship's cargo hold wasn't the most comfortable place from which Veronica Winters had ever conducted a stakeout, which was for sure. Cramped, smelling of oil and rat urine, and full of rusty spare parts, what it lacked in comfort, it made up for with a stealth factor that allowed her to observe the happenings in this part of the hold. Her smartphone, connected via shipboard satellite service, would tell her if the ship's "doctor" was being paged. Until that happened, she would learn what she could about that creep, Xander. *It should be you in that cell, you bastard,* she thought, looking out through the door, slightly ajar.

She would also have to learn a little more about whatever the hell that thing was that had just been loaded aboard in the crate. There was certainly a high degree of fuss about it, but that was secondary to nailing Xander. She watched as he told the paleontologist that he should feel free never to call him for a reference while he looked for a new job, and then Xander walked out of the brig area toward the main cargo hold where the crate was. She heard shouts from in there, as if something was happening. It sounded like it should keep Xander busy for a little while.

Peering out from the closet, she saw the jailer call after Xander. Heard Xander say *follow me*, and he, too, left the brig area. She nudged the door just wide enough for her to slip through, praying it wouldn't creak, and then, while the father was telling his kid something about having a serious talk, Veronica slipped out of the closet.

She made a right turn, away from the commotion surrounding the crate, and tip-toed past the Ramirez reunion deeper into the cargo hold. As the ship's supposed doctor, she had been required to know the tanker's layout well, since she was expected to get to any part of the ship quickly in case of a medical emergency. To this end, she had studied the ship's diagrams and blueprints given to her by the captain, and now this prior familiarization with the ship was coming in handy, because while Xander was preoccupied, she would find out what the hell he was doing here by ransacking his quarters.

She knew his room was private—a rare luxury at sea—and located not in the hold, but on one of the bridge tower levels. She could get there by traveling through the long hold which ran nearly the length of the ship, which would also keep her a little more out of sight.

She crept past mostly empty, cave-like spaces that were dimly lit and stocked with unopened shipping containers—the kind that occasionally fell overboard and released their precious cargoes of Nike shoes and plasma TVs. She doubted the ones here contained mundane consumer items, though, knowing DeKirk, but right now that wasn't her concern.

Veronica kept moving, sticking to the shadows and staying low between the storage containers when she heard the voices of crew nearby. For the most part, it was easy going and after a while, she reached a circular stairwell leading up. She ascended, adopting an official air about her as soon as she reached the outer deck, as if she was headed somewhere on business and had to get there fast, no time to chat.

She knew there was a corridor of quarters for VIP guests, meaning that other than the captain's quarters, they were the nicest accommodations on the ship, and private rather than spaces crammed with triple bunks. She pounded up more flights of metal stairs, traversed a couple of wire mesh catwalks, and then pulled a door that opened into a short hallway with doors spaced at even intervals on both sides.

Guest quarters. She had taken a look earlier at the room assignment chart and knew Xander's quarters to be one of these, #412. She found the marked door about halfway down the hall on the right. She tried the knob.

Locked. As the shipboard physician, she did have keys to certain areas but the private rooms were not among them. Years of field work as a CIA operative certainly had its benefits though, and so Veronica looked both ways down the hall and then removed a lock pick from the medical bag she carried. She defeated the simple lock within ten seconds, opened the door, and slipped inside. She eased the door softly shut behind her.

Xander's quarters consisted of a single ten-by-ten room with an adjoining closet-sized bathroom, which she checked and found to be empty. In the main room, there was a single bed, a simple desk, and dresser. By the looks of things, Xander travelled light and did little but sleep in here, and probably not even much of that. She searched the dresser drawers—completely empty. She saw a duffel bag at the foot of the bed and rifled through it. Just clothing, nothing in the pockets. She saw a single shallow drawer in the desk and went to it, sliding it open.

A white MacBook Air lay closed inside.

A smile eased its way across Veronica's lips as she set the machine on the desk, flipped it open, and lit the thing up. She was immediately greeted with a password prompt, not unexpected, but she knew some rudimentary CIA hacking tricks, restarting it in safe mode, gaining administrator access, bypassing the security altogether, and accessing the root directories.

Biochemists, she thought with a smirk.

In moments, she was looking at Xander's programs and files. There were the usual office productivity applications, but also some specialized programs as well. Her brow furrowed as she read a few of the names: Matlab, Stata, ChemPro, GenTrack, and SequenceGuru...

What the hell were these programs? She clicked one at random.

The title of one of the panes read, *Gene Mutation,* and beneath that were twin columns of data with values like, Tac-1, Pep-4, etc. Veronica had heard the shipboard rumors of dinosaurs being pulled from the underground lake, but she figured they were just boring bones. Why would Xander—or anyone—be working with genes already if they didn't have any actual dinosaurs yet? *Wishful thinking?* Did they find a way to clone them from bones that still had some marrow left?

Suddenly, she felt a vibration in her pocket and pulled out her smartphone, reading the text on screen, a red exclamation point accompanying the message: URGENT: SHIP'S DOCTOR

REPORT TO AFT WORK DECK IMMEDIATELY FOR CREW INJURY WITH HEAVY EQUIPMENT!

It was the first such page she'd received since boarding the tanker in South America. Just as she was beginning to think shipboard doctors had it easy...*Crap! Who would have thought these at-sea M.D.s actually has to work?* Her cover was predicated on the fact that statistically, a few days on board should be incident free, meaning that all she would need to do was fill a few prescriptions from the infirmary. *So much for that.*

Skimming rapidly through one of the other panes on the screen, she saw a table of electron micrographs depicting the inner workings of various microbes, none of which meant anything to her, as well as what looked like an X-ray with the caption, *Cross-section of Cerebellum Post-injection.* A block of dense, jargon-laced text with terms like, *weaponized* , *Mesozoic viral load, reptilian host, cross-species vector*...Realizing she had no time to take all this in now, she used her smartphone to snap a picture of the screen.

Veronica hurriedly closed the app and shut down Xander's Macbook. She put it back in the desk and stepped back to look at the entire area to make sure everything looked as it had before she got here. *Check.*

She put her ear to the door, listening for a moment to make certain no one was coming down the hall. *Clear.* Then she opened the door and slipped into the hallway, closing the door softly behind her.

She checked the handle to make sure it was locked and then proceeded down the hall, holding her phone out in front of her as though she were a busy doctor just receiving an alert.

11.

Aboard Oil Tanker Hammond-1, Erebus, Antarctica

Marcus looked up from embracing his son to see the crewman who'd acted as his jailer return from the adjacent part of the hold, staring at them, hoping for a good argument that could entertain him, as he whiled away the rest of his shift at the shabby little desk. Marcus pointed toward the end of the hold where the crate was.

"Let's go to my quarters where we might find a little privacy." He glared at the guard, and then he and Alex walked out of the brig and into the section where the crate had been delivered. It was busy with workers now wrestling a huge, adult dinosaur body onto a specially constructed wheeled platform where it could be laid out in all its frozen glory.

Alex stopped walking as soon as he got a glimpse of the incredible sight. "I still can't believe that's a..."

"*Tyrannosaurus rex*? Believe it."

Marcus waved his son onward and they walked up close to the spectacle. Xander was standing nearby, pointing toward the makeshift large-scale laboratory, a worker then trundling a cart laden with electronic equipment in that direction.

Xander looked over at Marcus when he saw him approach and gave him a dose of stink-eye before looking away. Marcus couldn't help but hear a couple of crewmen talking about a serious injury out on the work deck.

"Dad, we should be careful around this thing." Alex sounded genuinely nervous, not simply trying to make a scene for the sake of attention.

"Calm down. It's remarkably well preserved from the below-freezing temperatures of the freshwater lake—but it's dead as a doornail, a stiff for millions of years."

Alex rubbed his forehead. "Why do I feel like we're in a horror movie and no one fucking believes me?" A crewman put his bare hand on the animal's tail and attempted to drag it onto the platform where it flopped back onto the floor. It proved too heavy and stiff for one man, though, and another came to his assistance, the two of them together wrangling the wayward appendage fully onto the platform.

Marcus put a hand on his son's shoulder. "Alex. We need to finish our conversation. My quarters." He pointed to the opposite side of the hold, about the width of a football field, where his divided-off area was. "Now!"

Alex shuffled off toward his father's room. When they got there, Marcus indicated for him to walk around the divider and take a seat on the military-style cot that served as his bed. He also had a folding card table for a desk and a single chair, a small transistor radio, along with a few books on Antarctica, and assorted field guides about flora and fauna.

"Nice place you got here," Alex joked, flopping onto the cot and crossing his arms behind his head as he stared up at the high ceiling.

"Sit up please."

Alex grunted with the effort of pulling himself to a sitting position. "C'mon, Dad."

"Alex," Marcus thought about his next words, but couldn't stop himself, "shut up and listen for once in your life!"

His son's eyes widened a little at his sharp tone. He remained silent.

"This time you've gotten yourself into one hell of a situation. Maybe more than you bargained for." He saw Alex about to reply and put his arm up, palm facing out.

"Don't talk. Listen. Don't think for a second that just because you're out of that cage for the time being, it means your troubles are over."

"Aren't they? Thanks a lot for getting me out of there, Dad. I'm sorry for what it cost you. I know it was a cool job, working with dinosaurs and all, and that's what you love..."

Marcus shook his head vigorously. "No, you still don't get it, Alex! Look around you. At this ship..." He waved an arm at the rust-streaked metal walls soaring high above them where racks of fluorescent lighting kept the space from being in the dark. "...Outside is *Antarctica*, Alex, one of the most forbidding places on the planet. We are *far* from civilization. My point is that you have absolutely nowhere to go from here. You're entirely at the mercy of DeKirk's people. I got them to release you from the brig for now, but they know you can't really go anywhere! At any moment, they could change their mind, decide they need a favor from the Russians, and turn you over to them. You got people *killed*, Alex, do you understand that? We're at their mercy now, and let me tell you, after working for them—that's not a good position to be in."

Alex held his head in his hands. "I know I screwed up, but you have to admit, the conditions here were pretty freakin' unbelievable. I mean, who knew—"

"Even coming down here at all was a ridiculously stupid stunt, much less what you did after you got here. The question now, is what are you going to do about it?"

"Well, I just plan to lay low until they drop us off in Chile, I guess, and then..."

"No, Alex. I mean with your life. What are you going to do to make sure this kind of thing never, ever happens again? Because this might be Antarctica, but you pull something like this back in the States, and there won't be anything I can do to help you, Alex. Do you understand that? You thought it was bad standing over there for a few hours? You want to go to prison for the rest of your life?" He raised his voice. "Because that's where you're headed, damn it!"

Alex looked down at the floor. Marcus, seeing that he had finally managed to make an impact, pressed on.

"What else can you direct your energy toward besides activism? Because nobody's going to pay you inadvertently to kill people and destroy property, I don't care how pure your motives are. I understand where you're coming from. I really do. You wouldn't believe the number of times I've been out in the field on a dig in some remote, beautiful place, and find all kinds of trash left behind by careless campers, or even worse, industrial waste dumped by companies who can't be troubled to dispose of it properly. It disgusts me, but I don't blow up their campers or poison their food. I just do my job in the hopes that the more I can tell people about the amazing history of life on our planet, the more respect for the environment they'll have."

Alex wiped his eyes and looked up at his father. Marcus was certain he saw something there he'd never seen before. *Was that respect?*

"Um...I can fly."

Marcus wondered, *is he high on drugs?* "What?"

"Flying lessons. Summer three years ago. I didn't tell you, but mom knew. She paid for them."

"She did? Great, I guess I know why she kept that quiet. Yet another summer break spent goofing off while the rest of the world worked."

Alex took a deep breath, as if pushing back a reply he might regret with a blast of incoming cold air. "Okay. Not going to argue, but what I was saying is that I finally finished. I actually saved enough money on my own to go back and finish the lessons. I just got my prop plane license in the mail from the FAA two weeks ago."

Marcus studied his son's expression. "That's great, Alex. Congratulations, but honestly, I don't see what that's got to do with your situation right now."

Alex held his hands up. "Dad. I can be a pilot! I can take people on eco-tours in small planes. My instructor told me he can hook me up with a guy who certifies for float planes, and then I'd be able to..."

"Alex! Really—"

He cut himself off as they heard the sound of the tanker's humungous anchor being winched back into the ship.

"What?"

"I just don't think—" Again, Marcus stopped himself short. *Now is not the time to talk about being realistic,* he told himself. It wasn't realistic to be stuck on an oil tanker in Antarctica with a frozen dinosaur after you've just been shit-canned from the most rewarding job a paleontologist could ever hope to find, either, yet...here he was. *Let it go.*

"Never mind. We'll discuss it further when we get back home."

Alex shrugged. "Okay. Well, it would make Mom proud, don't you think?"

Marcus looked at his son. Yet another uncomfortable subject between them. "All your mother wants from you, Alex, is simply to hear from you now and then. She's dying of cancer and you haven't seen her in over a year."

"I thought it was in remission?"

"It was. For a while. It came back about six months ago."

"I sent her an email."

Marcus gave a sage nod. "So you send your dying mother an email on Mother's Day and now you've fulfilled your obligation, is that it?"

"Oh, come on!" Alex stood up from the bed.

"A real Son of the Year. Yeah, that's you."

"And you're Husband of the Year? This is why I can't ever talk to you!" Alex got up and ran around the divider, and out into the main cargo hold.

"Where are you going?"

No reply came.

"I'm proud of you for getting your license!" Marcus called out, but he wasn't sure if Alex heard it. He stood from the chair and walked out of his living area. Didn't see Alex, but the crew had cleaned up the last of the crate mess and was now driving the forklift away. There was a cluster of people on the far side of the hold, in the lab area. Alex could not possibly have gotten all the way over there yet. Marcus looked right down the long way through the hold, then left and saw him, almost to the stairs leading to the aft deck.

He started after him and then halted. *Let him go. Give him some space.* Feeling like he'd gotten his point across for the most part, Marcus' growing curiosity over the dinosaur got the better of him. He started walking over to the lab area as he felt the ship's engines vibrate the hull beneath his feet.

They were underway.

12.

Aboard Oil Tanker Hammond-1, En route to Chile

Alex walked out of the cargo hold onto the aft work deck, not looking for anything in particular other than to be as far away as possible from his father right now. Soon, he came across a small crowd gathered in a tight circle. He heard shouted instructions like, "Put some pressure on it!" and, "Does anyone have a belt?"

Edging up to the gathering so that he might see what was going on without bothering anyone, he got a peek between two bodies of a crewman lying on deck, writhing in agony, clutching his right leg. His rubber overalls had been severed at the knee and copious amounts of blood soaked through. A piece of heavy machinery Alex couldn't identify lay toppled on the deck nearby.

"Where's that damned doctor!" somebody yelled.

"She's been called," returned another.

Since there was nothing he could do to help, Alex thought it best if he stayed out of the way. He climbed the staircase of the ship's looming bridge tower. When he reached the top, he stepped out onto a perimeter walkway that surrounded the tanker's superstructure. He didn't see or hear anyone up here so he paused at the rail, looking out over the water. The sun was setting over the field of icebergs they were leaving behind. He was numbed to the spectacular view, though, as well as the biting wind that pummeled its way through the slightest opening in his parka. Watching the Antarctic coast recede into the distance, he thought about his friend. Tony's body was still down there in that horrible place. *Because of me, and those Russians...what were they?*

He couldn't stand to think of it anymore and turned away from the view of the coastline. Suddenly, he couldn't take being outside where he could see the place where everything had gone so horrifically wrong for him. There was a door in front of him. Didn't know where it went, but he didn't care. He flung it open and stepped into a short hallway—then stopped.

He was surprised to see a person walking toward him down the hall. He was even more taken aback to see that the person was female, and an attractive one at that. Her haircut was a little weird, cropped short but not in a stylish way, and her outfit wasn't much to look at, either, but hey, this was a working tanker ship at Antarctica, not Spring Break in Cabo San Lucas. He judged her to be about thirty. Her sea green eyes were fixed intently on the screen of her smartphone, but he saw them flick upwards at the noise of the opening door. The black medical bag she carried, as well as the Red Cross and Caduceus symbols sewn into the front of her frumpy sweater, told him that she was the ship's doctor.

"Hi, uh...excuse me," Alex began.

She looked him briefly up and down, probably to see if he needed urgent medical attention, although Alex preferred to think she was checking him out for different reasons. Their eyes met and Alex felt something stir within him beyond the tilting of the ship and the crisp air tingling the flesh on his neck. The sort of spark he had only felt very rarely before, but this wasn't some eco-girl back home that he could comfort after watching *Blood Dolphins* or *Blackfish* and see where it led. An older woman, and a physician to boot. Smart and good-looking. Probably out of his league, but then again, so was this entire misguided trip.

"What is it?" She asked, looking past him.

"Oh, just taking a walk." *Great, that's a brilliant opener.* "Oh, but hey—I was just down on the work deck and there is somebody hurt bad down there. Not that I'm a doctor or anything." *Real smooth, dumbass.*

Veronica looked at her phone again and then back up at Alex and gave him a chilly response. "Yes, I've been alerted. Listen, would you mind…"

"Oh, I'm sorry." Alex bowed his head and stepped aside.

"No," she said, her tone softening, "I mean would you mind taking me there? I'm still new to the ship and time is of the essence with these kinds of injuries."

Alex looked up, a slight smile tugging at his lips. "Okay, sure. It's this way." He led her back out the hallway through the door he came in and then along the platform outside. "My ex-girlfriend is pre-med," Alex said, making conversation as they descended a series of ladder-like stairs. "Got into U.C. San Francisco and left me."

"Sorry to hear that."

"Oh, no worries. I'm way over it by now. Where'd you go to med school?"

A pause, then: "UCLA."

"Oh, wow! I used to live in Westwood, right there. I didn't go to the school, but I grew up there, so I totally know the area. What street did you live on?"

She didn't respond, and for a few seconds, he heard only the pounding of boots on metal stairs. They reached a landing and made the turn down the last flight of stairs that would lead to the main deck.

"I don't remember the name, sorry. All I did was study. It was, you know, pretty typical for student housing kind of thing."

"Isn't med school like six years?"

"Eight, actually, counting the residency. I had a few different apartments while I was there."

Alex frowned. *Shut up, stop making her uncomfortable.* The wiseass in him couldn't resist. "So you don't remember the name of a single street where you lived for eight years? That must have been some—"

Veronica's phone chimed and she held it to her ear. Alex could hear a frantic voice emanating from the other end and then heard her say, "On my way. Almost there." She pantomimed *which way* to Alex when they reached the lower deck walkway. He pointed to the left and waved an arm for her to follow as he took off at a jog toward the work deck.

When they ran up, the crew parted for the doctor like the Red Sea for Moses.

"Right here, Doc," one of them called out. "A davit motor busted off the rail under heavy load. Too damn cold probably, and landed square on his right knee. Crushed it pretty bad. We tied a tourniquet on his thigh to stem the bleeding."

The injured crewman was in bad shape. Someone had given him a piece of wood to bite down on, but his anguished cries still filled the air. His knee had been severely crushed. Alex noted that even the doctor seemed to be squeamish around it. He saw her face wrinkle in revulsion as she moved in for a close look at the wound. A few seconds passed and she still had said nothing.

"Doc?" one of the crewmen pressed.

She shook her head back and forth, as if snapping out of it. "Good work with the tourniquet. Seems like most of the bleeding has stopped. We can't do anything else for him here. I need to get him to the infirmary. You two, can you lift him?" She pointed to two beefy crewman standing nearby. They looked at their wounded associate's crumpled knee and then exchanged confused glances.

"Whoa, wait a minute," Alex said. As a long-time adrenaline junkie and X-games sports enthusiast, he'd been treated by emergency responders and ER doctors for more than his fair share of various impact injuries. "Doesn't he need splints and a stretcher to move him?"

Veronica looked confused. One of the crew gave Alex an angry stare. "This the kid who should be in fuckin' jail? Why the hell should we listen to you?"

"He's right, though," another said. A murmur of agreement could be heard in the huddle of men surrounding their fallen colleague.

"Okay," Veronica said, somehow mustering an air of authority behind the word, "who can get me the splints and a stretcher?"

The victim continued to moan in agony on the deck.

"Doctor, don't you have splints in the infirmary? You didn't bring them? I thought they messaged you a crush injury notice?"

Veronica gave the man a stern look. "I wasn't coming from the infirmary. I thought perhaps there might be a trauma station closer by than the infirmary."

"Ask the patient if he cares," somebody said, pointing to the man writing in pain, clutching his ruined knee.

Another man quickly waved him down. "Not now, man. He needs her help."

Veronica stood up from the victim and threw her hands up. "You—" she pointed at Alex— "Can you come to the infirmary with me to get the stretcher?"

"Sure."

"Let's go, and you *gentlemen*, keep that tourniquet tight."

They watched her leave, many shaking their heads.

"I don't know where the infirmary is," Alex said, realizing he was leading Veronica.

"This way," she said, breezing past him. They passed by the staircase they'd used earlier, remaining on the main deck. After what seemed to Alex like a long walk, they made a right turn through a door into a small structure. A door on the right had a large red cross painted on it. Veronica pushed it open and they walked into the ship's infirmary.

The room was packed with shelves, drawers and cabinets full of medical supplies and equipment. Alex spotted a pair of stretchers hanging from a rack against a wall and quickly picked one of them up. He hefted the stretcher, ready to start moving, but when he looked over at Veronica, she was looking around, not moving.

"What's up?" he inquired.

"Just looking for the splints..." Her gaze shifted around the room.

Alex gave her a look and rolled his eyes. "You sure it only took you eight years for your degree?" He quickly scanned the labels on the cabinets, searching for recognizable groupings. "First aid in that one there," he said, pointing to a cabinet with his free hand. "Splints got to be near the bandages."

Veronica went to the cabinet and opened it. He saw her arm reach out and then withdraw from the cabinet clutching a bag of splints. She tucked them under an arm, ready to go.

"This is it, now for the stretcher." She moved toward the exit.

Alex remained standing. "Hold on."

She looked at him expectantly, her hand on the door handle. Alex looked her directly in the eyes. He lowered his voice.

"You're not an M.D., are you?"

Her mouth dropped open and hung there for a moment, as though she was going to say something, but then she closed it without having spoken.

Alex thought of the real doctors he'd been treated by as well as known personally, as friends of his family. The air about her just wasn't right. He shook his head, not even saying anything. He didn't need to.

She let go of the door, then moved in closer, staring him down. "You don't want to press this issue. You're just some troublemaker kid, the son of the paleontologist who just got fired.

Yes, I overheard all that, so you'll forgive me if I don't take too kindly to your inquisition here."

Alex raised his eyebrows. "If you knew half as much about treating injuries as you do about what's going on with DeKirk's personnel, you would have been fine with your...disguise, or whatever game you're playing here."

"Listen, you little—"

"No, you listen!" His tone came out sharper than he'd expected, and he was surprised to see her shut her mouth. He continued. "The guys down there are already suspicious, I'm sure. It wouldn't take much," he threatened, but then softened his tone. "Just...listen, please. Even if you're not a real doctor, I'm sensing your heart is in the right place, and what's more...we might be on the same side."

"And what side is that?"

Alex shrugged. "Not that Xander guy's, and not Melvin DeKirk's. If that's a safe bet, then I'm willing to help you, and my guess is that right about now, the way things are going, you're going to need all the help you can get."

Veronica sighed heavily, staring back at his eyes, gauging his sincerity. "You win. You're right, you're going to have to help me, or we're both in deep shit."

13.

Aboard Oil Tanker Hammond-1, En route to Chile

The last thing Marcus wanted to do was stand in the same area of the ship as Xander Dyson, but the allure of the dinosaur was too strong. A flesh-and-bones *T. rex*! If he wasn't seeing it for himself right now with his own eyes, he'd never accept it. After a career full of teasing glimpses of this mighty prehistoric beast, in books, in computer simulations, and movies of course, or if he was lucky in actual bones or teeth—now he had the chance to see a whole one close-up and in the flesh. He pushed his way past a couple of drilling technicians gawking at the dead beast from another era.

The air was still frigid, and his breath spooled out in clouds. He walked up to the wheeled, stainless steel platform that the once mighty beast was strapped to so that it wouldn't slide off due to the ship's motion and be damaged. It was about forty feet long and twenty wide. The dinosaur's long hind legs nearly protruded over the edge of the platform, one of its sharp, black toenails curling over the side. Marcus stood in front of the creature's chest, near the two upper arms that appeared almost comically small in proportion to the body of the mega-beast. He was drawn to this part of the body that was most heavily damaged. There were gouges, cuts, and bullet holes riddling the rest of its flesh, its sides and back, legs and torso, but this area... At first, he thought it might be from the drilling operation to exhume it, but then he doubted that notion. When he bent his knees so that he could peer up into the gaping wound, it was clear that, although it looked okay externally, the body wasn't whole. He stood up straight and addressed a worker standing next to him.

"Did our crew do this?"

The man shook his head emphatically. "No, sir, it was there already. We were as careful as a doctor pulling out a splinter with a pair of tweezers."

"Not our doctor, though," another member of the crew joked.

Someone cleared his throat. Xander came over, appearing as if he'd been lurking in the shadows, waiting. At first, Marcus was afraid he was going to ask him to leave in front of all these people, but instead he said, "I've been assured that this is the precise state in which the animal was brought up. Not too bad for fifty million years, right, boys?"

A chorus of affirmations went up from the crew around them. When it died down, Marcus spoke.

"Sixty-five," Marcus corrected with some satisfaction, "and did you happen to notice the obvious?"

"What's that?"

"It's missing the heart?" He bent down again to look back into the body. "And most of one of the lungs."

He stuck his head farther into the ragged cavity, wishing he had a flashlight. The smell inside was beyond awful but surprisingly, he recognized it while forcing himself not to retch. Xander would like that way too much. One time in a college chemistry lab, Marcus was looking for supplies and came across a bottle of a chemical called putrescence, and sniffed its contents out of curiosity. It was a lab-quality perfect distillation of the exact organic compound produced by decaying flesh. This was that smell, he was absolutely certain of it. Only a thousand times more powerful than what he'd experienced in the little bottle.

"Why don't you keep crawling until you plop yourself out of its ass?" Xander suggested. "Maybe you could write a paper about it in all your spare time now."

A round of raucous laughter ensued. Marcus was offended but at least Xander wasn't ordering him to leave. He could put up with the indignity—and the smell—in order to get a look at this magnificent specimen. He slid out from the animal's putrefied insides, ignoring Xander as he walked toward the *T. rex's* head.

Marcus' eyes drank in the details of the reptilian skin, its intricate scales, how they overlapped...It didn't look right, though, if a dinosaur's skin was supposed to look like the skin of today's reptiles that is. A layer of slimy, yellowish mucous oozed from between the scales. Here and there an actual bubble of the stuff cropped up like a thin membrane and popped. He supposed it must be due to the moisture still there from thawing and the sudden change in environment after so much time in the lake. The skin in general, when viewed up close, was riddled with tears, slashes, gouges, and the occasional bullet hole—although the hide was so tough in several places, he could still see the flattened bullet lodged only an inch or so down.

He gave the entire body another look. In short, though, this was a messy, smelly corpse, not the pristine specimen he'd dreamed about finding one day. Still, a *T. rex* was a *T. rex*.

Now he continued the visual inspection, concerned that at any moment, Xander would enforce the full terms of his recent deal and banish him from this area altogether, maybe even confine him to his quarters until they hit shore. He needed to make the most of this, and wished he had the freedom to take his time—and take pictures. He reached the partially open mouth, where two other drill-team men stood, marveling at the sheer immensity of the jaws and the impressive rows of five-inch long curved teeth that were bone *white*, not the dark or black color of the fossilized ones Marcus was used to working with.

He sucked in a breath and held it as he stared into the mouth, his eyes agog with trance-like wonder while the specimen's were closed.

Hello, Tyrannosaurus rex!

Marcus tentatively reached over and laid his hand on the snout, just behind the nostrils.

I'm touching...hell, petting... a T. rex! He flashed on his life with the extinct reptiles up to now—receiving a pop-up book of dinosaurs as a five-year-old boy for Christmas, watching the movie *Jurassic Park* as a teen, digging up his first *T. rex* fossil in North Dakota as an undergraduate biology major, earning his PhD in Paleontology with a thesis entitled, *Reflections on the Obligate Scavenging Hypothesis for Tyrannosaurus rex...*

Moreover, here he was feeling the actual *skin* of a remarkably preserved *T. rex*.

"Dr. Ramirez," Xander called, "kindly keep your fucking hands off the merchandise."

"Just think of this sexy beast like a stripper," one of the crewmen added, "look but don't touch!"

"Unless you spring for the VIP room..." Another began.

Marcus could not hide the look of irritation that took over his features. Keeping his hand on the dinosaur snout, he turned his head toward Xander, about to lay into him for whatever that would be worth, knowing it would lead to repercussions for him and his son, but he didn't care. He still burned with the indignation and the injustice. This was *his* find, his glory, his moment. His whole entire life, in fact, came down to this monumental discovery. He had given up so much—his family, his wife's health, his own for that matter. It had all been for this and the hell with it all, he wasn't going to let this asshole, or any other, take it from him.

The action that happened next was so unexpected, so otherworldly that it caught everyone by surprise, especially Marcus. The *T. rex's* eye *opened*, revealing a black, moist orb with angry red streaks beneath its surface.

It raised its head, and a guttural, groaning-creaking sound emanated from its esophagus.

"Look out!" one of the crewman called, but it was too late.

Marcus, still directing his fury and full attention at Xander, suddenly felt his hand drop off the dinosaur's skin and into an open space. He thought someone had wheeled the platform away from him so that he couldn't touch the specimen anymore. He opened his mouth to yell back at them, the first words meant to be, *What the fuck*—?

Instead, what came out was a blood curdling scream that he was sure came from someone else, not him. No way such a primal sound could come from his throat.

He felt a terrible crushing sensation—more like his wrist was in a vice than being sliced by sharp objects—and was dragged toward the table for a second. Then, as quickly as it started, the sensation stopped. He no longer felt the pain. He felt nothing.

Marcus turned back to look at the dinosaur in time to see its head flopping over to the other side. His mind registered the open, red and black eye, and then he noticed that he was missing his left hand.

A stream of blood geysered from his open wrist.

Then the giant lizard's head swung back in his direction again, jaws snapping (and was that his chewed up arm lodged back in its throat?), and he felt hands on him pulling him roughly backwards. He toppled to the floor as all hell broke loose, the men leaving him while they went to tighten the straps on the Tyrannosaur's body. Those restraints weren't meant to contain a live animal, though, just to hold the corpse in place, and one of the ones on the upper body snapped as the *T. rex* whipped its head to and fro, faster now.

Alex was right, Marcus thought, as he dimly heard Xander shouting in an absolute frenzy, "Tranquilizer!"

The paleontologist forced himself to tip his head up while his vision faded around the corners. He didn't have the energy to maintain the position and he slumped back to the deck, but not before seeing, between the weird spots dancing across his retinas, Xander loading giant syringe-like ammo into what looked like a spear-gun and grinning like a Cheshire cat.

The last thing he heard before passing out was a sound not heard on Earth for millions of years—the vocalization of a *Tyrannosaurus rex*, like a wailing banshee, piercing the night.

14.

Aboard Oil Tanker Hammond-1, En route to Chile

In the infirmary, Veronica and Alex both looked up at the sound. Some kind of screeching noise from another part of the ship.

"What the hell is that?" they both asked almost in unison.

"No idea," Alex whispered. "Except... I've got a bad feeling."

Veronica stared back at the bag of splints for a moment. "Okay, let's move, and listen...I can't tell you exactly who I work for, but you're right. I'm not a doctor. I was placed on this ship by the people I work for—powerful people—who are investigating DeKirk for some serious criminal activity."

Alex digested that for a moment. "My father was just fired unexpectedly for no reason. Yeah, yeah, I'm sure having me around wasn't exactly a plus for him after the stunt I pulled, but it wasn't that. He said DeKirk wants everyone who knows anything about the dinosaurs, taken from Antarctica." He lowered his voice and leaned toward her. "We saw soldiers down there deliberately *killed* for no apparent reason! That doesn't exactly fill me with confidence that he'll be happy with a simple non-disclosure agreement."

"That would be a concern of mine too," Veronica admitted. "Watch your back, always."

Alex shook his head. "What's he really up to with all this dinosaur shit?"

Veronica shrugged. "I don't know, not exactly, but I've been following him for a long time—many years—and believe me, whatever it is, he never does anything small-time. DeKirk is involved in all sorts of illegitimate business practices and shady dealings. Rich as hell, though, so he can throw up a lot of walls and red tape. Hard to get to. This is the closest I've been to him in a long time and I'm still not even sure where he is, physically, right now."

"On this island you're going to after he drops me and my Dad off in Chile, what do you—"

At that moment, Veronica's radio blared with an urgent voice. Alex recognized it as Xander's.

"Cargo hold to physician, cargo hold to physician. Please acknowledge!" The shouts of several other men were heard in the background of Xander's transmission.

Veronica brought the radio to her mouth and keyed the transmitter. "Physician here."

"We need you down here in the cargo hold lab immediately! Bring tranquilizers, sedatives, and a trauma kit. Hurry!"

"I was just on my way to the work deck injury."

"That can wait. This is worse!"

"On my way." Veronica returned the radio to her belt and looked at Alex, then around the infirmary. "Tranquilizers?"

Alex gave a brief expression of exasperation before dropping the stretcher and springing over to a locked cabinet. "The good drugs will be in here. You have the key?"

She fumbled around in her pockets.

"Hurry!"

She blanched, looking flustered, but came up with a ring of keys. She sorted through them, held a couple together and handed them off to Alex. "I think it's one of these two."

He tried the first one without success and then inserted the second key into the cabinet lock and turned it. The door opened and he was looking at racks of syringes, ampoules, and pill bottles.

"Bring your bag over here."

Veronica ran over to Alex and held her open doctor's bag beneath him as he dumped in various drugs. When the bag was full, he spotted a stack of larger red plastic cases and handed two of them to Veronica. "Trauma kits."

While she tucked them under an arm, Alex grabbed a couple of bottles of pills, quickly eyeballing the labels. With a shrug, he put them in his pocket. "These might come in handy, too. Let's go."

He picked up the stretcher again and they exited the infirmary, running down the hall out to the walkway.

"I can't be in two places at once," Veronica huffed as they flew down the narrow staircase toward the deck. "What about the guy on the work deck?"

Alex negotiated the stretcher around a stair landing. "We'll just drop off the stretcher and the splints. They can stabilize him and get him to a bed. Then we go to the hold lab."

After jogging across the ship, they emerged on the aft work deck. The group of men was still huddled around the man with the devastated knee, who still moaned in excruciating pain. Alex ran up and set the stretcher down next to the man.

"What the hell took y'all so long?" one of them asked in a southern drawl, looking at Veronica.

"There's a situation in another part of the ship," she explained.

"So? Tell that asshole to get in line!" somebody said.

Veronica was just standing there, preparing to argue, so Alex grabbed the bag of splints from her and held it up. "It's called triage. Look it up. Here, you guys get him onto the stretcher and splint him up? Get him to a bed inside, and the doctor will be back to see him as soon as she can."

One of the men nodded, taking the bag from Alex.

"Take the trauma kit," Veronica offered, handing off one of the red plastic cases she carried.

Alex reached into his pocket and pulled out one of the pill bottles. "Give him two of these every couple hours for the pain. No alcohol with 'em, though, unless he wants a really good time."

To everyone's surprise, the injured man on deck opened his eyes and said, "Thanks, kid."

Alex looked at him for a second, nodded, and turned to leave.

Free of the stretcher, he could run fast now, and Veronica struggled to keep up as they made their way toward the cargo hold. As they got closer they heard the noise again—the screeching that they'd heard only faintly up in the infirmary. Now it was much louder, a repetitive grating sound that reminded Alex of dragging fingernails across a chalkboard.

The big double-doors to the hold were closed now. He ran up to them and pulled on the handles, but to his surprise, they were locked. *Xander keeping out prying eyes?* He remembered someone mentioning a ladder entrance. They climbed up one flight of stairs and found a circular opening that dropped into the hold with a ladder.

Alex slid down the ladder that led into the hold the way he'd seen some of the crew do, not using the rungs but just wrapping his hands and feet around the outer poles and letting himself drop. Veronica used the rungs, but was quick about it, and they followed the sounds of chaos into the cargo hold. Alex looked over to the right to see the dividers marking off his father's quarters, but didn't see anyone over there. To the left, though, was pandemonium.

So ethereal was the scene before him that he stopped in his tracks despite the urgency of the situation. He simply stared, attempting to process what was unfolding in their midst. Veronica did the same, the medical bag slipping from her fingers and hitting the floor as she stared agape at the ungodly spectacle.

The *T. rex* lay on the steel platform, most of the straps that had been holding it in place broken and swaying in the air, but it was...*moving!*...thrashing its gargantuan head back and forth while pedaling its tiny forelegs uselessly in the air. Alex noted it had what looked like a serious injury to the chest region and wondered if Xander's men had somehow done that to the beast in the process of trying to contain it after it woke up, or if it had happened in that fight he saw down in the excavation pit.

As he stood there frozen, one of the dinosaur's thrashing movements brought its head around, jaws snapping, and a large protruding tooth just nicked one of the crew, gouging into his shoulder, and clean through. The man screamed and whirled around, clutching the wound and then backing into a wall. He looked at all the blood and the total shock, and fear sent him toppling forward into unconsciousness.

"Come on!" Alex yelled, hoping to galvanize Veronica into action. She scooped up the medical bag and they ran to the fallen man. The bodies of the two crewmen rendering aid blocked his view, and at first, all Alex could see was a bloody arm with no hand on the end of it. *Jesus.* One of the men was cinching a belt around the forearm as a tourniquet, but still blood erupted from the open wrist.

He sprinted over to the *T. rex*, which was writhing now, slower, grumbling lethargically after the third tranq dart thudded into its thigh.

"Go down!" Xander hissed, loading up another dart. "Shit, that's enough to drop a whale and it's still moving!"

Two men struggled to avoid the still-snapping jaws and loop a cargo tie-down strap over the animal's neck, and that was when Alex got his first look at the face of the man with the missing hand.

His father.

Alex slid onto the floor next to Marcus. "Dad! What happened?"

The face of the crewman administering aid assumed a softer look when he recognized Alex. "That thing came to life while your Dad was standing over its mouth, looking at it, and the next thing anybody knew, it snapped his hand clean off!"

The man then looked down at the wound, which was ragged-looking with a couple of long skin flaps hanging off, and the skin a sickly gray hue with disturbing yellow streaks. "Well, not all that clean, really. We need to get this fixed up. First priority to stop the bleeding, so…"

"Hey! About goddamn time you got here, Doc!" Xander's voice pierced the conversation as he finally lowered the gun, satisfied that the beast was stilled for now.

"What about his arm?" Alex wanted to know, looking around as if it might be lying on the deck somewhere. He'd heard they could sometimes be reattached if they were kept on ice. The man applying the tourniquet shook his head slowly and pointed to the dinosaur, now lying still as the crew cinched another tie-down strap around its snout for good measure.

"Listen up!" Xander bellowed. "I need everyone out of here right now except for the physician. Including you." He pointed at Alex.

"This is my Dad!"

Xander widened his eyes at his crewman, cocking his head at Alex, a silent command. "Let the trained professionals handle it, kid. The doctor here will take great care of your father."

"But—"

"Doc," Xander continued as Veronica walked up to the carnage, holding her medical kit in a daze, "It looks like the tourniquet's fine for now. What I need is for you to draw a blood sample from this man, *stat*, and then return it to my lab on the main deck, is that clear?"

Veronica knelt by Marcus. "I heard you, but, his hand... that's the first priority. Why a blood sample?"

"Just do it," Xander repeated, with more authority.

Veronica set the bag down on the deck and opened it next to the paleontologist's unconscious form. She opened her bag and removed a syringe along with a bottle of pain pills and sedatives.

Xander wheeled around and headed for the *T. rex*, calling out over his shoulder. "Everybody else besides me and the doc, out *now!*" He looked to the body of the crewman who had been kicked and gouged in the process by the great beast. "Get that dead man out of here, now! Secure the area!"

Alex dug in his heels, determined not to leave his father's side, but a crewman grabbed him by the shoulders. "Kid, move it, now. Don't make me have to drag you outta here, I don't wanna do that. There's enough crazy shit going on as it is."

Reluctantly, Alex stood up. He made eye contact with Veronica just before he turned around. "Smelling salts and adrenaline shots are in the trauma kit—they might wake him up," he said, and began walking toward the exit. "Only if you have to." He looked at his dad's peaceful face. *Maybe let him sleep, might be his last peaceful dream for a while.*

"I'm sure the doc knows what she's doing." The crewman smiled at Veronica. "Everybody's an expert, right?" he said with a small laugh after Alex was out of earshot.

She looked down at Marcus' bloody stump, and then the syringe in her other hand, as Xander folded his arms, watching impatiently. "Uh, yeah. Right."

15.

Aboard Oil Tanker Hammond-1, En route to Chile

Veronica watched Xander usher the last of his personnel out of the lab area, leaving only himself, Veronica, and the unconscious Marcus, and the unconscious *T. rex*, which Xander had shot full of enough sedatives to kill a herd of elephants. He walked over to Veronica, who had so far done little more for Marcus than to don latex gloves and clean the blood off his wrist and arm with antiseptic wipes.

"Blood sample?" Xander squinted his eyes at Marcus' handless arm and looked away quickly, scanning the shadows against the hull as if to make certain no one else remained.

Veronica looked down at the syringe she hadn't used yet. "One track mind. Just hang on." She made a couple of more swipes with the antiseptic and then tossed the blood-soaked wipe on the deck.

"We're in a hurry, here! In case you haven't noticed, Rex Van Winkle over there just woke up after a sixty-five million year slumber and bit this man, and we kind of need to know how it affected him."

"It doesn't take a genius to see how it *affected* him. He's missing his left fucking hand! He could bleed to death or die of infection if you don't allow me to get to work on him."

Veronica's indignant response was surprisingly genuine. She didn't know crap about medicine, but she did know one thing, Xander was a grade A asshole. The only thing he cared about was his own agenda. She started to flash on her ex-lover's untimely death at the hands of this arrogant...*stop it, you'll blow your cover.* The M.D.s she'd been around did have pretty big egos, though, so she figured her little outburst probably put her in character—a doctor who wouldn't take any shit and would always put the interests of her patients first. Still, she would need to take it down a notch or risk being kicked off the ship when they got to Chile, before she learned where DeKirk was.

Xander's voice helped to bring her back to the moment. "Now that you mention it that wound does look like it could be infected," he said, gazing with intent curiosity at the jagged aperture where

Marcus's hand should be. The skin nearest the bite had a sickly pallor about it. Veronica held up the arm so that he could get a better look, and then quickly brought it down again. As she watched, a partially clotted blood globule dumped out of his wrist, despite the tourniquet, and splashed apart on the deck, causing her to flinch and Xander to back up a step. He made the same expression one might have if they discovered maggots on leftover food when they opened the trashcan. He acted the same way, too, wanting only to close the lid on it.

"Okay, leave me with one good sample and then you can take him to the infirmary. I'll test the dinosaur myself."

Veronica hadn't even considered that she would be asked to draw blood from the extinct reptile. Or *extant*, as the case may be. Whatever. The fact that Xander would rather deal with that smelly, knocked-out beast *by himself*, knowing that there was no such thing as an expert in Tyrannosaur anesthesiology and that it could awaken at any moment, was telling. Veronica gazed down at Marcus' face. Eyes still shut. Still breathing shallowly.

"Okay. I'll need you to get me two men and a stretcher to get him up to the infirmary."

Xander picked up his radio and snarled into it. "Peterson? Get a stretcher and two men into the cargo lab, ASAP. Two men only!" They heard a clipped reply of "Yes, sir."

Xander gave Veronica a what-are-you-waiting-for look. She picked up the syringe and Xander trotted back over to the *T. rex.* Veronica had never taken blood before, but she'd had it done to her enough. Taking a deep breath and gritting her teeth, she waited until she was sure Xander wasn't about to look her way and then jammed the needle hard into Marcus' good arm, her best guess at fitting into a vein. She winced while she looked at his face to see if he felt it. No reaction. She pulled the plunger back, watching the syringe turn dark red as it filled with the paleontologist's blood, and then withdrew the needle.

"I've got it!" she called to Xander, who stood near the base of the *T. rex's* tail with a hypodermic of his own, only his was substantially longer and thicker. He held the hypo up to the light and then jogged over to meet Veronica. He handed her the syringe filled with the Tyrannosaur's blood, which had sort of a brownish hue to it with small particles floating around. It reminded Veronica of looking into a backed up toilet.

"Get both of these blood samples to the lab—actually scratch that. Leave me the samples, I'll analyze them myself. You just go straight to the infirmary and get ready for your patient." Without waiting for her reply, he turned and strode back toward the *T. rex.*

"Okay." Then, under her breath, *"Yes, sir, right away Sir Asshole, Sir!"*

Then her brain pulsed with the idea that she could take this guy out right here—walk up behind him, put him in a choke hold, and rake his miserable throat across that monster's huge teeth. Then just leave and let everybody connect the dots. *T. rex* ate Marcus' hand. *T. rex* tried to eat Xander's head. *Or—she could slam the T. rex hypo into Xander's neck and inject one monster with another monster's blood.*

She opened her medical bag, withdrew a multi-tool, and opened its three-inch folding knife. She hid it up the sleeve of her sweater and began walking toward Xander, who was now facing away from her, punching keys on a laptop.

She concentrated on silencing her footfalls. As she closed to within ten feet, she let the knife slip down into her hand. *It's just you and me, now, you sick sonofa—*

She saw the Skype window pop up on the screen just in time and spun around on a heel as Melvin DeKirk's face filled the monitor window. *Can't let him see me, who knows how much he knows or how good his intel is about who's after him?*

She slid the knife back up her sleeve and walked toward the medical bag.

"Are you still here?" she heard Xander heckling. "Get to the lab now, Doctor!"

Veronica reached the bag, scooped it up, and then headed for the ladder exit at the end of the cargo hold. "On my way," she called out, trotting off.

#

Xander turned and watched her legs—shapely even through the layers she wore—disappear up the ladder, before turning around to resume his video chat with DeKirk. His boss sat in front of a wall that was plain white, save for the painting that Xander knew to be an original Picasso.

"So," DeKirk began, "how's my prize? Let me get a look at him. Or is it a her?" He laughed as if that was the funniest thing he'd ever heard. Xander's expression remained dire.

"We haven't been able to sex it yet." Xander turned the laptop around so that DeKirk could see the *T. rex*, now unconscious and strapped to the platform.

"Why not? Surely it's thawed by now? I'd like to know exactly what we're dealing with, here, Xander—male, female, hermaphrodite?" At length he added, "Wow! That is *fantastic*! Walk over to it for me, would you? Give it some scale. I could be looking at a toy model for all I know."

Xander moved to the *T. rex* and stood in front of it, wearing a there-are-you-happy-now expression.

"My *God*! Simply astounding! Only question…why does it have a fucking harness around its jaws?"

Xander walked back to the laptop and sat down in front of it. "Um… just to help keep it secure."

"Xander. I'm going to need you to elaborate upon your answer."

Xander rubbed an eye before continuing. *No point holding back, he's going to find out.* "If I look a little funny it's because…fuck it. I just witnessed a *T. rex* wake up and attack everything in sight."

There was a moment of confused silence followed by DeKirk starting to laugh in fits and starts until he guffawed heartily. "Oh, Xander my boy. That's priceless."

Xander waited for him to get the last few cackles out of his system before continuing.

"I'm not kidding." He leaned in close to the screen. "It *came to life* when it was just barely thawed! It would be thrashing around and destroying this ship right now if we hadn't thought fast and sedated the hell out of it."

DeKirk's expression darkened. "It doesn't look very alive. Do Tyrannosaurs sleep on their sides?" He chuckled at his own joke.

"He doesn't look it because I emptied the ship's medicine cabinet into it, *Melvin*. Knocked it out with a collection of sedatives that would be the envy of Michael Jackson's doctor."

DeKirk was speechless for a lengthy pause. "You're serious? Because let me tell you, Xander, if this is some kind of practical joke—"

"Here. Look." He turned the laptop around so that Marcus' inert form was visible in the background.

"Who's that?"

"That's your former paleontologist."

"Marcus? What happened, he have a heart attack after we fired him?"

"That *T. rex* chomped off his hand when it woke up, because he happened to be standing right at the mouth admiring the thing like some kind of obsessed fan boy. He passed out from shock and loss of blood. Got men coming with a stretcher to haul him to the infirmary."

"Oh." DeKirk let out a chuckle. "Well, at least he won't be able to claim worker's comp, since we fired him before it happened."

"Will you get serious for a second?"

"Whenever you're ready to get serious, so will I. A *T. rex* pulled out of a frozen lake, undisturbed for millions of years, woke up, and bit a guy's hand off? Really?"

Xander picked up the laptop and walked it over to Marcus. He knelt down with the machine and pointed the webcam at Marcus's blood-caked stump.

The tone of DeKirk's voice changed to a sort of raspy monotone with a certain intensity about it. "Xander, listen to me. If what you say is true..." He broke off in thought for a few seconds, then resumed. "You have to get the captain, tell him to turn the ship around."

"What? We're going to Chile, remember? To drop off Marcus and his punk kid who sabotaged the drill site."

DeKirk shook his head strenuously. "Change of plans. No, this is...beyond incredible! We have to study this development. Top priority, it changes everything." He sat back and Xander could tell the little wheels in his brain were spinning like crazy, deviously calculating, having gone from disbelief to acceptance, now to making plans to capitalize on something far more significant. DeKirk was a man who didn't get his billions from luck, but from the ability to adapt *fast* to his surroundings and changing events.

"I've taken blood samples of both the dinosaur and its human victim. I'll analyze the samples myself and after the tests are run—"

"No, Xander. A frozen *T. rex*, revived after millions of years on ice? To get the answer of how that's possible, you're going to need more than the facilities you have at hand."

"You're probably right. Especially since there's one more little fact you're not aware of. Not only did it revive itself, somehow, but it doesn't even have a heart."

DeKirk blinked, and his face floated closer to the camera. "Say again?"

"Before he lost his hand, Marcus—well, I was really the one who noticed it, but he corroborated it—saw that the *T. rex* had a gaping chest wound and is completely missing its heart. No heart. It's not there. One of the lungs is gone, too."

"Oh great, so he *was* working after all. Why'd you let him in here?"

Xander looked away from the webcam for a second before responding. "I made it clear to him that he was no longer in an official capacity. He just walked up to the *T. rex* in the middle of the crowd of workers. By the time I noticed him, he had his head up to the wound, talking about the missing heart."

"I thought you said it was you who first noticed the missing heart?"

Xander forced himself to bite back an acerbic reply. He took a deep breath. "What difference does it even make right now?"

"Since I'm not actually there, I'm relying on you to tell me what happened. It's important that I can trust your account."

"I still don't see how—"

"You know what I think, Xander? I think Marcus is the one who noticed the missing heart, and that you just tried to pass it off like you discovered it first. I know Marcus. He's a damned good paleontologist. I know we thought we didn't need him anymore, but now with this development, I have to reconsider. He knows more about dinosaur anatomy than anyone, especially you. So stop lying to me, Xander. Because if I can't trust you..."

Duly chastened, Xander dropped his head a little, eyes downcast. "Okay. I apologize." Xander threw his hands up. "Can we just move on please? I guess we could use Marcus—*if he lives through this!*"

DeKirk stared at him a moment across the Internet, the eyes of the abstract figure in the Picasso right along with him. He paused to light a cigar, and exhaled a cloud of blue smoke at the lens.

Xander, not liking the silence, added: "No idea how long this thing'll stay out for." He turned around and peered over at the *T. rex* as if checking it for signs of stirring.

"We need to figure this out, and fast."

"No shit. So what—?"

"Order the Captain to reroute the ship to Adranos. Marcus can be properly evaluated at Adranos. My facility there is state-of-the-art and fully operational."

"How come I was never told about what you've got at Adranos?"

"Xander, don't press my patience."

"How far away is it? Can you tell me that much?"

"It's far, but the ship is fast."

"So I've heard."

The video image dissolved into a mess of pixels and DeKirk was gone, leaving Xander to wait in uncomfortable silence for the men with the stretcher, to wait with a dying man and a slumbering ancient predator...

16.

Aboard Oil Tanker Hammond-1, En route to Adranos Island
Marcus felt like he was coming off the worst bender of his life. Except that he hadn't gotten drunk in the last twenty years, since his college days. The lights of the ship's infirmary began to come into focus as he brought a hand to rub his throbbing temple...and felt only a smooth lump of bandage drag across his skin. Making his headache worse was the incessant yapping of the ship's doctor. *What's her name...?*

Veronica Winters stood in the corner of the infirmary, about as far away from Marcus as she could get in the little room, talking furtively on a satellite phone that Marcus hadn't seen her use before. Usually, she carried the smart-phone that worked via shipboard satellite, or else just the two-way radios. He closed his eyes again, not wanting her to know just yet that he was listening.

"...certain that DeKirk isn't on board. No. If you'll just let me explain..."

She talked very softly, with just enough air behind the words to keep them from being a whisper.

"No, we *were* headed to Chile, but the course has been changed to go to some island. Adranos something. Listen, if you don't want me to compromise my cover, I've got to get going and try to patch this guy up somehow. I'll initiate contact at this number from the island and give you a sit-rep. Out."

Marcus heard her stash the sat-phone in her medical bag and then take a measured breath. He opened his eyes. Turning his head, he watched her take a smelling salt packet from a trauma kit. She then turned around to walk over to him, stopping in her tracks as they made eye contact.

Dropping the smelling salts, she nervously approached him where he lay in the cot. He dimly remembered the *T. rex*, the crushing pain in his hand. He looked down, saw the bandaged stump, and the gauze soaking through with spots of pus. He did his best not to lose it. He wiggled his remaining fingers and toes. Those that were there seemed to work, but he didn't feel good, and that was for sure. The headache. The general feeling of malaise, like something he couldn't put a finger on that was just...*not right at all.*

His wrist hurt like hell, too. "What medications have I been given?" He stared expectantly at Veronica.

"Oh, good, you're awake!"

"I asked you a question, Doctor."

"So far...ah...nothing."

He tried to sit up in the bed, but the sudden movement caused a sharp pain in his temples as his blood pressure dropped, and he eased himself back down. He turned his head sideways to look at her while he spoke. "Nothing! Why?"

"You seemed to be recovering well and I thought it best you get some rest."

"What? Wait a minute. You mean I haven't even been given antibiotics yet?" He looked down at the bandages over his stump and their muted rainbow of malodorous discharge.

She looked at him blankly.

"This is preposterous!"

"Do you want something to drink?"

"Something to—" He started, but had to stop when a bolt of pain shot through his head. One of his eyes itched and he scratched at it, the finger coming away with a copious amount of viscous, mustard-colored goop.

Frustrated and scared, he held the finger out towards her, taking satisfaction in her shock as her eyes opened wider while she backed up, but at the same time, realizing that he was not in capable hands.

"Where exactly did you study medicine?"

"I..." She broke off as though receiving new instructions from her brain. "Look, I can see now that you've got an infection. It hasn't been that long since you were bitten. Let me give you something for it."

"Like what, *Doctor*?"

"Well, this is an unusual case since I've never treated anyone who was bitten by a dinosaur before, but—"

"Look, I don't have time for this bullshit. Do you have any broad spectrum antibiotics in here? That'll at least take care of the bacterial stuff. I hope." Clearly, if he was going to survive this, he would have to take matters into his own hands.

"That's just it, Mr. Ramirez. We…"

"*Doctor* Ramirez."

"What?"

"I'm a Ph.D."

"Oh. Right. *Doctor* Ramirez, my bad."

Marcus sighed. "So at least there's one actual doctor in the room, right?"

She blushed, but chose to ignore the accusation by continuing the conversation. "As I was saying, Dr. Ramirez, whatever came out of that ancient lake wasn't meant to interact with modern biology. I have no idea what to treat it with. No one does, how could they?"

"Consider that later. Now, let's start with the antibiotics. Where are they in here?" He looked around the room as his son had done, reading the labels on the cabinets. Only he found that his vision was failing him. He could still see for the first few feet, but beyond that, everything got blurry. While Veronica walked to a cabinet and opened it, Marcus continued.

"Setting aside for the moment the era of the biology that's infected me, what I want to know is how could *any* era's biology explain how a complex, multi-cellular animal could not only be alive after all this time, but alive without major organs?"

His excitement at the uniqueness of the situation proved too much for his frail body and he vomited down the side of the cot—a yellow substance streaked with green, so foul-smelling it caused Veronica to retch.

"Here! I found some!" The degree of surprise Veronica displayed at actually finding a common medicine in her own infirmary only solidified Marcus' fears, but right now, he needed antibiotics.

"Great. Bring them here, please."

She brought him two bottles of pills, presenting them both to him so that he could make his own choice. Marcus read the labels and picked one. She opened it for him, gave him a cup of water and he downed twice as much as the recommended dosage.

Then he lay back on the cot again, the exertion of sitting up for the pills having worn him out. He looked over at Veronica, who was staring at the streak of weird-colored puke dripping onto the linoleum floor, but all he could think of now was one thing.

"Where's my son?"

17.

Aboard Oil Tanker Hammond-1, En route to Adranos Island
Alex backed away from the porthole above the cargo hold, which afforded him a position to look down on his father and Veronica. He waited until the men arrived with the stretcher, and then he stepped away, further out into the bitter wind and the cold.

He stood there on the deck, shivering, unsure of what to do next. He felt change in the air temperature though, just enough. It had warmed slightly as they escaped the frigid Antarctic zone, but now the winds swirled angrily and collided with a warmer front from the north. The stars were swallowed up with a thicker darkness and ribbons of lightning streaked in the distance.

Storm coming, he worried. Still hesitating, he pulled up his hood, glanced around, and ducked farther into the shadows, behind an exhaust vent, and waited.

He didn't have to wait long, as Xander emerged shortly, carrying a small leather bag. Inside, Alex knew, were the blood samples from the *T. rex,* and from his father.

Follow the blood, or follow his dad?

Alex shivered. The fake doctor—as much as he didn't trust her skills—at least was on the right side of this mess. He could trust her with his father, but this Xander...Alex needed to know what he was really up to, and why he wanted to test that blood. Certainly, it wasn't out of concern for his father, so there must be something more sinister and far-reaching at work. Alex needed to find that out, and fast. His time was running out—and possibly his father's as well.

Xander ducked his head into the wind and strode right past Alex's hiding spot.

Hood up, Alex followed at a safe distance, not concerned about the noise his boots were making on the slick metal stairs, as the biting wind drowned out everything but its own insistent howling. Xander made his way efficiently to his cabin, #412, but as he unlocked the door, he was met by the captain coming from the opposite direction. The big hulking figure, having lost his coat and braving the winds with just a turtleneck, seemed to have something urgent to impart to his newest passenger, and Alex, turning and blending back with the shadows, waited for an opportunity.

He'd only get one shot, and as it was, this would be beyond crazy, but really, given the stakes, his father's condition and everything Alex had done already that had all but ensured his fate, couldn't get any worse, why not risk everything? A moment later, as Xander followed the captain a short distance away, where the big man pointed at aft over the railing and shouted something Alex could barely make out as related to the approaching storm, he moved swiftly. Ducking inside #412, Alex gave the quarters a quick glance-over: desk and laptop, cooling unit and flat screen TV, bed and closets…

He had to move fast, hearing the clanging of a pair of returning footsteps, and chose the farthest set of closet doors. Nothing inside except hangars and a safe, Alex ducked in, closed the door and crouched low in the shadows, peeking through the louvers just as Xander stormed inside his cabin. The door closed behind him and Xander placed the black bag on his desk, and then tapped some keys on his laptop before he shrugged out of his coat and kicked it to the floor.

I should have done the same, Alexander mused from his hiding spot. Still breathing heavy, he felt overheated in the warm cabin. Soon, he'd be sweating and having more trouble breathing. Xander better make this quick and get back outside—or take a leak so Alex could get those samples and get out.

He realized it was better than nothing, but hopefully, he'd learn something first, and Xander didn't disappoint. All business, he went to a cabinet, opened it up, and came back with a supply bag—and a case he must have brought along. Inside, Alex recognized the device—a centrifuge, and then a microscope came out.

Okay boss, get to work.

#

Xander completed the first round of analysis, focusing on the slide with Marcus's sample. Better to ascertain whether he had been infected with anything first, before checking out the *T. rex* blood. God only knew how he was going to figure anything out there, not being a paleo-biologist. If such a thing even existed. Hell, probably the only one who could really figure that out right now would be the guy whose blood was on the slide, and he was in no condition to help.

Suddenly, a Skype window popped up, and DeKirk's face leered back at him.

Damn that connection, Xander thought, wishing the storm the captain warned him about was already here and blocking the satellite linkup.

"Xander?"

"Yes sir, no results yet. Give me a minute, please!"

"We don't have that luxury of time. I'm tracking that storm too, and I don't want excuses—or blackouts. What have you got?"

Xander shrugged and looked into the eyepiece after taking a drop from the centrifuge sample. "Well, as you said, I'm not equipped here with the facilities to properly analyze, but I should be able to…"

He dropped off and his mouth hung open.

"Xander?"

He stared and stared, then pulled his eye away. Blinked and looked back to the screen and DeKirk. "We've got a serious problem."

#

Alex heard all that and had to hold himself back. He wanted to burst out from his spot, tackle Xander and run for his dad, but he needed to listen. Xander was rambling non-stop, in a frightened voice, about some kind of cellular breakdown and simultaneous infection from the invading cells that strengthened the existing structures—while apparently feeding off of them. Something about energy manipulation and strangulation of mitochondrial forces.

Whatever it all amounted to, this conflict of prehistoric DNA meshing with modern genetics, the billionaire guy on the other end seemed thrilled by it all. He stopped Xander in a few places to ask more specifics, then he cut him off altogether.

"The *T. rex* sample! Load that in and let's see if it bears the same virus markers."

Xander shook his head. "What are you talking about? Didn't you hear me, what we just saw was the *T. rex*'s living cells, transferred through the bite, and they were attacking—"

"I'm not sure you're qualified to make that conclusion."

"But..."

"Just load up the slide, hook up the imager, and let me see and download the visuals."

Xander grumbled, but did as he was told. "I don't know what you're looking for. It's not as if..." Then he paused, thinking, and suddenly moved faster, switching out the slides and drawing up the new samples. "Shit. You might be right. The lack of its heart, the continued mobility. Cellular energy self-sustaining... Jesus, what if—?"

Alex got a glimpse now of the laptop screen, and saw the man on it nodding. "Now," said the billionaire, "you're reaching the shore I already landed on minutes ago. You see the potential?"

Xander nodded and straightened his shoulders before prepping the slide for a visual inspection. "We've gone from a monumental discovery of an extinct specimen, a collector's piece and find of the century for sure, to a potential biological... I don't know what to call it. The uses are staggering. A cure...?"

"For mortality," DeKirk said. "Perhaps, but certainly..."

"*A weapon*," Xander whispered. "A terrifying weapon."

#

He fit the slide in and gave it a look. Unrecognizable prehistoric biology for sure, but similar cellular structures as he'd expect. Biology was biology, especially when it came to reptiles and mammals, once you ignored the general size and shape differences and compared things only on a microscopic level.

This... this still wasn't right. The virus—for that's surely what it was—was present here too, except much more advanced. Parasitic almost, grafted to the sub-cellular structures of the *T. rex*'s DNA. Xander absently plugged in the adapter so DeKirk could reach the same conclusion, but first...

Something else had been bothering him. From the moment he had walked into the cabin. Something not right, and then he saw it.

On the rug, alongside the wet indentations of his own boots—another set, faint, but he could just make them out now, drying in the heat.

Another set of prints, leading to the closet.

He wasn't alone.

Reaching back into the bag with his equipment, his grip settled on a silenced 9mm. He had a feeling he knew who had tracked him in here. That doctor…something wasn't right about her, and he had a feeling he had seen her before. A feeling he would have acted on if not for the mayhem in the cargo hold.

Well, he'd remedy that mistake right now.

"Hang on Mr. DeKirk. Something I need to take care of while you study our friend's blood sample."

#

Before he knew it, Xander was at the door and Alex could only brace himself. One chance. Based on the angle and his positioning, he might get the edge.

The closet door ripped open and a gun barrel aimed, but Xander met his eyes and had a moment of shock. *Not who he thought*, Alex realized, just as he understood that gave him a split-second advantage. While Xander hesitated, he launched himself up and under Xander's aim.

He struck, thrusting the top of his head into Xander's chin and hearing the satisfying thunk as the man was knocked backward. Alex landed hard on him, rose up, and threw another punch to the face before Xander could recover.

Hoping that knocked him senseless, at least for a moment, Alex jumped to his feet, got to the desk and slapped the laptop off it in one clean motion, hoping DeKirk didn't get a good look at who was now messing up the works. Alex considered the bag and the blood samples, grabbed both, turned, and raced out the door—

—right into the chest of the Captain, rounding the corner. It was like smashing into a rock wall. Alex bounced off, staggered. The captain's eyes widened with surprise, then anger when they flashed to Xander, struggling to rise off the floor.

Alex swore, turned and slipped through the door and started to run when a big hand caught his hood from behind and yanked him backwards.

He landed on his back.

"Hey, wait a sec…" he started, but a huge fist slammed down between his eyes and everything went black.

18.

Aboard Oil Tanker Hammond-1, En route to Adranos Island
"Alex is safe," Veronica assured Marcus. "I saw him, even though he was escorted away during your...incident, he should be fine."

"Check...on him later?" Marcus was still shaking and Veronica looked around and grabbed a blanket.

"Of course. Now, you need to rest. You're in shock, and I don't need a medical license to figure that out."

Marcus groaned as she covered him and he held the stump of his arm, looking at the bandages. "It hurts...Oh God, it's like a colony of ants gnawing away at where my hand used to be, and I still feel every bite."

Veronica stood up, shaking her head. "I'm sorry, I just...I wish I could help more but I've got another mission, as you must know."

"A different sort of license, I imagine." Marcus nodded, and motioned to the door. "Go, I'll live. I think."

"Okay, but I'll be back."

"And if you see Alex..."

"I'll send him over, trust me."

Marcus let out a long sigh, garbled with fluid. "This... You have to stop them. If that *T. rex* really is alive and if it's...I don't know, carrying something. A plague or..."

He held up his stump again. "You have to call in the major players, here, Doc. Army, CDC at least. Who do you work for? Please tell me you have connections."

She looked at him, and her expression darkened. He was right, of course, but making her handlers understand that there might be something even bigger than the DeKirk target here? "I do, but just what do I say? There's a very-much-alive dinosaur drugged up on a boat here, headed toward some island for god-knows-what purpose?" She frowned a moment, thinking of the programs she had seen on Xander's computer. "Shit, maybe he wants to go all *Jurassic Park* on it, and clone the thing and create—"

"An amusement park? Unlikely," Marcus said, "doesn't seem DeKirk's style."

"It isn't. I was going to say, either he creates a preserve and sells them off to rich bastards like Kim Jong II, collector types who would spare no expense, tossing chump change to board a flight to the moon or hop on a living dinosaur..."

"That's one possibility."

"Yeah, the somewhat more benign one. The other is that he somehow weaponizes this thing, a plague as you said, or a clone army or just... hell if I know. I know DeKirk hired Xander, and Xander has a history of using bio-agents for nefarious purposes, but still, I need to think about what to say to get help out here."

"Make it up," Marcus said, coughing up a little blood on the blanket.

"What?"

"Make something up. Say—and this might not be far from the truth—that someone on board got infected with what might be a strain of never-before seen virus, and for now, it's contained on this boat, but for the fate of the world, etc. etc., it can't be allowed off until everything's been analyzed."

Veronica thought for a moment. "You're right. It's our best bet, because shit, everything else just vaulted way above my pay grade."

Marcus nodded, his eyelids flickering. Coughed again, then looked like he was about to pass out as Veronica went for her bag—and the satellite phone—when all of a sudden, the ship's alarm rang out.

Shrill and penetrating, Marcus almost screamed and Veronica jumped as the intercom crackled in between alarm pulses.

"Attention all *crew, prepare for major storm bearing down from the southwest. High winds, high seas expected. Brace for impact!*"

19.

Aboard Oil Tanker Hammond-1, En route to Adranos Island
Alex awoke as the freezing rain pelted his face, and he felt the strong hands dragging him along the upper deck. He shook his head, tasting blood. Hopefully, his nose wasn't broken and he didn't have a concussion, but that fist hurt like an anvil to his skull. He struggled but found his wrists were tied together with a plastic tether.

"Damn," he muttered, shaking off the rain to see through the gloom of the meager flickering lights on deck. They were passing the cargo hold—the doors closing now in advance of the rain. One more glimpse of the monstrous thing below, still tranquilized and motionless except for the rocking of the ship, and then the men hauled Alex past, and up to another level. He glanced over his shoulder, past the two goons carrying him.

"Ah, Captain!" He spat out blood and rainwater. "So, what's it to be, back to the brig? Or..." He eyed the ledge. "Is this a plank walk?"

The captain's face lit up in a shrieking bout of lightning. "Option B. Sorry, mate, you don't get any second chances after the stunt you pulled."

Alex tried to laugh. "Okay, so maybe it's like the old days, and I'm to be sacrificed to the ocean spirits to stop the storms and save the ship."

"That too," the captain chuckled and nodded to the others, who pressed Alex against the ledge. He looked out over the blackness beyond, and with his eyes still stinging from the lightning strike, he couldn't make out anything.

"Any chances we're close to that island y'all have been steering toward?"

"Not close enough for you," the captain shouted back over the peal of distant thunder. "No hard feelings, but—"

Just then, a horrifying, primal scream cut through the wind and the storm. It came from down the next stairwell, the stairs leading to the cargo hold. Everyone froze, and the captain took a step into the well. The light down there flickered, and then went out, just as gunshots fired out.

"Shit!" the captain yelled and pulled his own sidearm. "Leave the kid," he ordered, "and get over here!"

The goons shoved him into a wall where Alex crumpled.

He shook it off and then stood, rooted to the spot in fear. Saved from a watery grave—for the moment—but what was down there? Horrific screams and rending sounds split the air, and then more gunshots and cries of panic.

The captain's voice echoed from below as Alex took a tentative step forward, enough to peer down into the gloom. Lanterns or flashlights must have been in use, at the far end perhaps, where the *T. rex* (hopefully) still slumbered. Whatever this was, Alex thought, it was definitely smaller and less catastrophic than a rampaging dinosaur, but chillingly, it might be just as deadly.

He backed away as he saw something with yellowish scaly skin and bloodstained teeth dart into the path of the light for just a moment, and in that moment, Alex recognized the features—it was the crewman who had been trying to restrain the *T. rex*, the man who had been gouged and kicked across the room.

The dead man.

He came into view and snapped his head up and around, as if sniffing the air. His eyes settled on Alex—and he snarled, tensed, and then leapt for the stairs.

Alex rocked back, slipped and fell hard on the slick grating as the crewman launched himself to the top stair. A double split of jagged lightning tore across the clouds to his right and over the crewman's head, highlighting for Alex his first full-on bright view of what he had seen down in the Russian pit: *Zombie* was all he could think, all his mind could fathom, but even that didn't do it justice. This was no run-of-the-mill Romero or *Walking Dead* shambling thing, this was a prehistoric-skinned mash-up between human and reptile, with yellow, slitted eyes, a tough-scaled almost leathery skin, sharper, longer teeth, and fingers the size of Ginsu knives. The talon-like nails clicked and scraped on the metal banister. The mouth—with extra rows of incisors bursting through the bloody, stringy gums and flesh from a recent kill—opened and hissed, the long tongue protruding and tasting the rainwater.

I'm dead, was Alex's second thought as terror flooded through his veins and rooted him to the spot. The thing tensed and was about to leap onto him when two gunshots rang out and holes burst through the zombie's chest, exiting and striking the railing right over Alex's head.

The creature paused and looked down at its wounds, snarled and turned back toward the staircase.

The captain's voice shouted up—pained and gargled as if coming from a ruptured throat. Alex imagined the captain dragging himself along, getting off a few more shots before—

The zombie hissed and darted incredibly fast back down the stairs, its clanging feet reverberating in the hold. Another gunshot, a cry of pain and then...

Silence.

Thunder rumbled and the rain beat down harder. Alex finally found his energy and crawled forward, sliding across the pooling water, brushing it away from his eyes as he followed the source of the light, down in the hold, past the stairs where a few lanterns and flashlights lay unmoving.

He found a vantage point, held his breath and strained to see.

Nothing at first, just an outline or two that resolved into bodies. One, the crewman he had just seen, lying sprawled on the last few stairs—all but his head, which had been nearly blown off, just a grisly mass of gore seeping from the top half after what must have been a headshot from the Captain.

The captain, *where*—?

Alex saw movement not too far from the dead zombie thing. The big form of the captain shifting, sitting, getting up from a prone position. Rising.

Alex couldn't see his face, only the body. The arms at his side. One hand still holding the gun, but only for a moment as it listlessly slipped from fingers that suddenly and quickly flexed and cracked and appeared to grow in length.

A hissing sound came from somewhere in that darkness, and before Alex could think of backing away, the captain moved in a burst of inhuman speed and was at the bottom of the stairs, looking up at him, sniffing the air.

His now-yellow dragon-like-like eyes focused and sharpened, and his mouth, over the gaping gash and bite marks in his neck, opened wide, revealing immense teeth and a ragged tongue. He gripped the railing and vaulted up in seconds, reaching for Alex.

20.

Aboard Oil Tanker Hammond-1, En route to Adranos Island

Veronica raced out into the storm, holding up her waterproof satellite phone and hoping for the best, but knowing that out here, in this weather, it wasn't going to be possible to get a signal. She'd have to rush to the bridge, get help from the captain and hope to raise someone on ship-to-shore communications, but before she could take another step, and then she saw activity near the cargo hold.

"Alex?"

Speaking of the captain—there he was now, lurching out of the cargo hold stairwell, moving...damn fast for a big guy, and bearing down on Alex who appeared to be bound at the wrists.

What the hell...?

She ran, shouting, and then vaulted over a railing onto the deck. She saw Alex get in a double-fisted punch at the captain's face—which apparently had no effect, and then he ducked and rolled away from a backhand swipe that instead connected with the ship's metal ductwork, denting it severely. The captain's head spun around—to Alex, and then to her—his nostrils sniffing the air. Veronica froze. A lightning burst riddling the sky lit up his features, revealing nothing like what she had expected: thick, putrid scales on his face, seething yellow eyes and a mouthful of razors dripping crimson.

She felt a pit of primal fear open in her throat, rooting her to the spot. No weapon, nothing except for a syringe and a bunch of bandages. She was dead, she knew. Only option was to run, but...

"Hey!" Alex shouted over the thunder. He had maneuvered back around and was half in the stairwell, a length of broken metal piping in his two handed grip—banging it on the floor. Distracting the captain.

It worked, and saved Veronica, but in the next instant, the captain had moved effortlessly fast, closing the gap and reaching for Alex. The kid dropped just in time down into the hold, and the captain—or whatever he was now—leapt in after him.

Veronica paused only a fraction of a second before her training kicked in. *Assess. Adapt. Improvise...*

She had promised Alex's father she'd look out for him. Anyway, she kind of liked the kid.

\#

Alex struck the ground hard just beyond the gore from the first crewman's head, then rolled into the shadows and out again, toward the light. A flashlight was on its side, and in the beam of light—the captain's sidearm, a big hefty .45.

Alex lunged for it even as he heard the captain landing on the floor behind him, his feet crunching with a sickening sound into the other body.

Hurry...

Alex grabbed the gun, felt it slip in his bound hands, and heard the pounding footsteps. *Notgoingtomakeit...*

He rolled again and again, then got on his back, straightened his grip and fired toward the shadowy, snarling blur. Two hard recoils and deafening retorts.

The captain, only a foot away, staggered with each impact. Straightened and took a step back. In the dim lantern's glow, Alex saw that both shots had connected, but not where they needed to be. His shoulder and his sternum had big bloody holes punched through them, and maybe for a moment, the captain—or what was left of his consciousness—recalled that *this should hurt,* but it didn't and when it didn't, he growled and tensed and—

Alex saw a blur behind him, a flash of blonde hair and a whistling sound as Veronica swung hard and down with the metal piping Alex had dropped. It connected hard across the captain's skull, spinning his head around.

It didn't stop him. Veronica backed up, pipe raised in a two-handed sword grip. The captain shook his head, drooled another thick line of syrupy blood, and then advanced. Veronica swung and clocked him again, dodging out of the way as she caved in his nose. He turned and just growled and shook his head, and opened his jaws wider, revealing even more jagged incisors.

"What the hell are you?" was all she could yell, as fear and incredulity lowered her guard. The captain saw his chance and leapt at her—

He never made it. One shot. Alex had it all lined up, and this time he didn't miss, blasting a perfect hole into and through the captain's right temple. The big man dropped, lights out, as if he had been a robot and someone had just killed his power supply.

The body twitched once on the floor, face down in front of Veronica, and then lay still. In a moment, gathering her wits, she stood up, glancing around nervously. "Any more of those fuckers?"

Alex waved the gun around, looking at the three other bodies. One with brains exploded, two others with so many bite marks and rabid devouring it looked as if the first zombie had nearly eaten every last bit of exposed flesh—including cracking open the skull and eating the prize inside.

"I think we're good," he said, "for now."

She stared at him, lowering the metal rod. "Zombies?"

Alex nodded. "Goddamn *prehistoric* zombies."

"How?" she whispered.

Then they both stopped and turned, looking toward the slumbering *T. rex*. Alex thought about telling her about the lake, the microbes, and the floating dinosaur submerged in the muck with all those primitive microorganisms for millions of years, but figured he'd leave the speculation to brighter minds, like his dad's.

"I think," Veronica said, pointing at the gun, "you'd better shoot that thing in the head now. Just to be sure. No idea how long those tranq's are going to last, and I don't know about you, but I have no wish to be up against an undead one of...whatever those are."

Alex nodded and moved closer, taking aim at the T. rex's head. He paused, and considered telling her there were two more big reptiles—the *Cryolophosaurs*, somewhere around here in a shipping container. Probably in the next hold. "Wish my father was here. I have no idea where the brain is in this thing's head."

"Heard it's small, like a walnut," Veronica said. "At least, that's what I remember from high school."

"Great." Alex shrugged, eyeing a head that was the size of a compact car. "What if I miss and it just wakes up pissed off?"

Veronica took a few steps back, toward the stairs, just as a wave pitched at the ship. The metal joints creaked and the *T. rex* slid hard, platform and all, into the side wall. It stirred, groaned, and turned its snout.

"Now," Veronica called. "Do it…"

Alex regained his balance as a flood washed in over his feet, spilling in from the stairwell and the splitting joints. Water suddenly burst from a seam behind the creature, and then another spout erupted from his left, blinding him.

"Shoot!"

He squeezed the trigger, and a section of the thing's snout blew out. "Damn." He aimed again, a little higher. "You know it would help if you could cut my wrists free." He took a breath and tried to steady his aim. "I also just had a bad thought. With the captain dead, who's piloting this thing…?"

He turned back in the silence, and saw why she hadn't answered.

Veronica's back was to him, her hands raised in the air. "Uh, Alex…"

Xander was on the stairs. Holding an M5 submachine gun on them. "Drop the gun, kid. If you take one more shot at my prize, you and her are dead meat."

Alex swore and was about to drop the gun when the boat pitched again. He saw Veronica lurch backward while Xander held on for dear life. The *T. rex* groaned and Alex heard something that sounded like breaking chains just before the tortured grating noise of the hull splitting open. He was thrust across the room into a wall that suddenly broke apart as he struck it—letting in thousands of gallons of ocean, swirling, pulling, and tugging him under and out.

Everything spun into the black maelstrom and his thoughts drowned with his screams.

21.

Adranos Island—Dawn

Marcus woke on a rocky shore that reminded him of his honeymoon in St. Lucia. A black sand beach and a sky full of angry clouds punctuated with flecks of weak sunlight from dawn's cautious appearance.

He blinked, coughed, and felt a hundred bruises and pains, and a surge of something else, vitality maybe, coursing through his veins. He shouldn't, couldn't feel this good, not after his trauma, a shipwreck and all the drugs that fake doc had given him, but still… something must have been transferred in that bite…

He groaned and sat up. His head spun and hurt like apocalyptic hell. Everything was blurry and he should have been freezing, but instead felt an agonizing fever, and there, splashing out of the pounding surf… that doctor, the fake.

Dripping wet, shivering, but pretty, resolute and angry.

She carried a gun.

#

Veronica splashed over to Marcus, but slowed as she came closer.

"You've got it," she said over the surf, as the rumbling thunder chased the clouds away to the south. She leveled the M5 at his head. Not sure it would still fire, waterlogged as it was, still she felt better for holding it.

"Got what?" Marcus said with a gasping, raspy voice.

Glancing away from his jaundiced skin, already tightening and scaling, away from those haunted, changing eyes, she looked up and down the shore. The *Hammond* was crashed upon a rocky incline fifty yards distant, its midsection split open, cracked like an egg, its contents expelled into the sea. Boxes, crates, and debris littered the shore.

"Hello?" Marcus coughed again. "Can you see…Alex?"

"No," Veronica said, sweeping her gaze around, now farther out to sea. "Not yet. I'm sure we'll find him."

"No you're not." Marcus coughed again, then rolled over, trying to get up. "How could you be?"

"You're right, but I'll look for him. I promise."

"Thanks," he said, grimacing as he stood up, holding his stump, "but I can manage."

"I doubt that," Veronica said, aiming the gun at him again. "Although you do seem healthier. More energy." She took a step back.

He eyed her. "You seem far too cautious of me." He cracked his neck, flexed the fingers on his remaining hand, and then looked at his nails intently.

"There's something you should know."

Marcus opened his mouth to reply, then groaned and doubled over, suddenly spitting out blood—and bits of white teeth. "Oh God..."

"Yeah," Veronica said, "you might be...changing. We've got to—"

Suddenly, the water erupted in a human-sized splash of arms and legs and coughing, a crashing wave that brought Xander rolling onto the shore. He gasped and shook his head and jumped to his feet, only to meet the barrel of the M5 aimed between his eyes.

"I'm not second guessing fate," Veronica said. "Especially when it's delivered you right to me."

Xander blinked away the water from his eyes. "Knew there was something about you. CIA spook, right?" He spread out his arms. "Congratulations, you got me. Although you don't really have me."

Veronica tensed her finger on the trigger. "Sure looks like I do."

"No evidence of anything." He thumbed over his shoulder, toward the wreck. "Are you just going to shoot me and deliver up a body to your bosses? Never knowing what I was really up to, never being able to unravel all the sticky threads of my supposedly criminal web?" He grinned. "You have no idea."

"I don't need the details," she said defiantly. "This isn't part of my assignment. They send me after the big fish. You...you are only a blessed coincidence. A chance for perfect revenge." She had him at last. All those years of anguish came down to this. One pull on the trigger could erase all the pain.

Xander narrowed his eyes. "Ohhh. Wait, now I know. Edgars, wasn't it? Your...*partner* maybe? Or was he something more?"

She paled, tensed. Aimed lower. "You're going to suffer, just like he did."

Then Xander turned his head slightly, listening. He smiled. "Oh, I don't think this dish of yours is yet served cold enough."

He lowered his arms, and then waved with a motion like a conductor calling for a new instrument to join the chorus. Seven Jeeps bounded over the ridge and tore onto the beach, bearing with them several dozen soldiers in green woodland camouflage.

"DeKirk's men, I imagine," Xander said, stepping forward, hand out for the M5. "Come to save the day."

Veronica kept her grip on the gun, even as Xander walked right into it, smiling, but she couldn't take her eyes off the men and the weapons trained on her, the soldiers leaping out, surrounding them.

"Welcome, boys." Xander grinned. "Glad you brought reinforcements. We'll need to sweep the shore and locate our prized cargo, but in the meantime, Marcus here has to be secured and brought to the lab for further analysis, and this one..."

"Drop it," one of them said, approaching Veronica, but she didn't need to reply, as Xander, in one quick motion, disarmed her and used the butt of the gun to bash her on the side of the head.

22.

Alex woke as a crashing wave kicked black sand and rugged shells into his face. He tried to get up. Wrists still bound, he gathered himself and stood, looking down: clothes tattered, flesh scraped and bruised but overall, no deep cuts or (God help him) bites. He looked around the windswept volcanic sand beach. Far to his left, he could just make out the ship crashed up on the shore. It didn't look much damaged from this vantage point, but it surely wasn't a gentle landing.

He wondered about the cargo hold. About his father's fate. About Veronica, and…

Just then, around the bow of the ship came roaring three Jeeps, launching into the air and crashing down. Bearing toward him. Four men in each vehicle, each in camo outfits carrying machine guns.

Damn it, Alex fumed, standing wearily. *Out of the furnace…*

He tried to raise his hands, but they were still bound with that damn plastic. He winced against the sun and another crashing wave that almost knocked him forward, but as the Jeeps roared to a stop in a semi circle in front of him, he noticed something unusual. The men weren't pointing their guns at him, but at something over his head. Something huge, something rising and dripping.

Something that roared and expelled a putrid gust of breath, like millions of years of delayed decomposition.

A shadow fell over him just as the bullets flew.

Alex didn't need to look up or back. He knew from the screams of the men and the intensity of the slamming footfalls behind him, on either side of him that he just needed to run.

#

Forward, then ducking left and banking right, Alex burst out of the ocean, scrambled onto the beach and took off for dear life at an angle away from the soldiers and…

He risked a backward glance and had to freeze in his tracks. There could never be a more surreal and absolutely incongruous site: a beached cargo ship as the backdrop for a battle between armed mercenaries and a prehistoric marauding zombie *T. rex.*

Men were out of their Jeeps firing, running and shooting, screaming at each other and the beast as it moved incredibly fast (were *T. rexes* supposed to be that fast, Alex wondered, or were they plodding hulking things that you just wanted to avoid at all costs?) He wished he could ask his Dad.

He watched, lingering on the beach as the dinosaur tore through the first wave of men. It lurched its giant head and snapped one man clean in half, shook, and flung the lower section back into the sea before leaping and crushing another soldier beneath its huge foot. Bullets sprayed its neck, its jaw, into its chest cavity, but it just kept roaring, lunging, and swiping its jaws. Onto the beach now, it bit down onto a Jeep with a driver still inside. Lifted the Jeep, crushing it like it was a metal toy and crunching into the man inside. Shaking its head again, the vehicle parts fell out and just the dangling legs of the soldier remained, kicking as the *T. rex* chewed again, crushing the bones and gulping down the rest.

More bullets sprayed into the monster's back and up its head, and Alex had a moment's hope—but if anything the skull seemed thicker, or the scales around there tougher, and nothing got through to the brain case.

The *T. rex* howled, its bloody snout raised skyward, then it raked its talons into a man who crawled on the beach, leaving a crimson trail. Punctured his back, then withdrew, and the *T. rex* launched itself to the side where it chased down two soldiers who were firing from the cover of another Jeep. It used its snout to flip the small truck end over end, over their heads, and then chomped down, eating one man whole and gouging the other straight through the ribs and nearly taking off his leg.

Alex backed up now, ascending a ridge, still watching the carnage. Just two soldiers were left firing, emptying clip after clip into the creature's hide until they ran out and just seemed to stand still, accepting their gruesome fates, which the *T. rex* mercilessly delivered.

In moments, the beach was a bloody patch of gore and crimson sand. The dinosaur, it seemed, was still hungry. *Probably after not eating for sixty-five million years, the thing worked up an appetite.*

Of the five or six corpses lying on the rocks or in incomplete pieces in the surf, the dinosaur merely sniffed at them. Then lowered its head, grumbled, and made a strange sound. Sniffed again, and then lifted its head and—appearing to look right at Alex—it roared in frustration.

Alex shivered, unable to look away during that bone-chilling sound, and he was glad he didn't, or he never would have believed it.

As if woken from a slumber, the dead men stirred.

They slowly moved, raising their heads, lifting themselves up. They stood, wobbling, and approached the *T. rex*. It lowered its head, now making a low purring sound.

The zombie soldiers grabbed on, one by one, and climbed. They ascended the head, down to the neck and attached themselves to its body where... they began slowly to chew.

Feeding...

Hungrily like pups to their mother.

Alex almost retched, but held it in as he backed away farther, over the ridge where he finally turned and looked out over the descending terrain. He took in the jungle foliage that gradually gave way to rocky outcroppings, flat dry lands and a long stretch leading to a facility set in a valley, surrounded by steep cliff walls and rising hills that eventually after several miles, converged into a larger peak. A smoking peak.

A volcano lording over some sort of military installation, and a lone road that now Alex could make out weaving out of the jungle area. Two Jeeps way in the distance, roared toward safety along that road.

Dad's on one of those Jeeps, Alex felt with certainty.

He focused on the facility, knowing he had to get there, and fast, if he had any chance of saving his father. Then he glanced to his left, toward the chilling thumping that reverberated through the earth.

He wasn't the only one with his sights set on the installation.

The *T. rex*, its snout high in the air, sniffing like a bloodhound after the departing prey, carrying its six zombie riders like over-enthusiastic children, roared and raced ahead, tearing in to the jungle.

Reluctantly, Alex started to follow, and then looked back to the beach.

One Jeep left, not crushed or eaten.

Engine still running.

Smiling, he broke into a run, leapt inside and first, dug around in the glove compartment and found what he needed: a utility knife.

Finally free of the wrist bands, he flexed his arms and cracked his knuckles, then settled his hands on the wheel.

Time to chase after the monsters, he thought, and save his father.

23.

Veronica woke in the back seat of a Jeep with guns trained on her. She sat dangerously close to Marcus, also in the back. Far too close, she thought, watching his eyes, which came in and out of focus. He seemed to marvel momentarily at the foliage, the landscape, the jutting cliffs and vistas peeking out from the dense wood, and then the jarring drive would seem to have the opposite effect and lull him to sleep. Veronica, meanwhile, tried to keep away from his stump and from the drool and the fear of any sudden movements.

"It's spreading," she said to Xander, who was in the passenger seat.

He donned mirrored sunglasses as the sun peeked out from behind a ridge. "That's why you're in the back with him."

"You know what he's turning into, don't you?"

Xander sighed as they drove again into the woods, careening through a shaded area littered with protruding roots and jutting volcanic rocks. "I got a glimpse of the dear captain while he was topside, attacking your friend here's son. So I can guess."

"Then we have to do something." She glanced back at Marcus, lolling in the seat and moaning. A golden patch of spider web veins had moved up his bad arm and encircled his neck, throbbing in places. "And fast. This thing can spread, and quickly."

"Oh, and is that your *medical* opinion, doctor?"

She gave him a glare. "Fine, then you ride back here with him."

"And give you another chance at me? No dice, Miss... Winters, isn't it?"

She gave a start, and then composed herself. "I guess you did your homework."

He leveled his gaze at her, and she could imagine his eyes roaming over her body behind the mirrored lenses. "So you came all this way, all that effort with the aliases and sneaking on board, and you got this close...and it all came to nothing. Just that short of revenge for your little friend Edgars, who if I recall, held up quite well before the end."

She clenched her fists. "I'm not through yet."

Xander laughed as they rushed up a hill and around a bend that gave them their first look at the lone installation on the island—a barbed-wire enclosed square area consisting of multiple connected white walled facilities and a lone tower.

Veronica pointed out, "If you had been my target all along, we wouldn't be having this conversation."

That stopped Xander's mood cold. He looked back at her. "DeKirk?"

"Tell me," she said, pointing to the facility, "what do you know about what he's really doing here? How much of this..." she pointed to Marcus, "...is his plan?"

Xander thought for a moment. "Honestly, I don't know what he planned versus what was simply a tremendously fortuitous coincidence."

"What, like that dinosaur you just lost back there?"

"Not lost yet."

"It's probably at the bottom of the ocean."

"DeKirk's men will find it. If it doesn't wash up, then it's down there waiting for a crane and a sub and a little elbow grease." Xander shrugged. "It's not like the specimen hasn't been used to an underwater environment for sixty-five million years. It can wait a few more hours."

Veronica thought for a second. *Have to keep him talking, try to figure a way out of this.* She was sure she could choose her moment, jump free from the Jeep, and lose them in the woods and the terrain, but then what? And just leave Marcus? Bad enough she lost his son—who was most likely drowned out there, but now she couldn't save the doctor either, but if she ran, she might lose her only chance to get closer to DeKirk, to unravel his plans and stop what she had come to believe had to be some sort of biological weapon. There were still too many questions.

"It's a virus," Veronica said, risking a gambit. "A prehistoric one—something we most likely have no defense against."

The soldier driving the Jeep cleared another ridge and now they were out in the open, in the rising sun as the clouds rolled away and cleared a path to the facility. The Jeep picked up speed as the road leveled.

Xander looked back at her. "You say that like it's a bad thing."

"In DeKirk's hands? Don't you know who his clients are?"

"I have a good idea, yes."

"Then think it through. You may be a cold-hearted murderer, but you're not an idiot."

He grinned at her. "Now you're hitting on me?"

"Shut the fuck up. Listen, he's going to weaponize this, and probably use you to do it." She pointed to the facility, looming up fast now. "He'll probably promise you the world, and when you deliver, you'll be of no more use to him. Think about that."

His grin faltered slightly, and then turned to a smile as he leaned in toward her. "I can handle myself, and I'm no one's lackey. Now, shut up and enjoy the ride. We've got some big plans for you and the other 'doctor' here once we get to the lab that DeKirk has promised is more than sufficient to prepare what I need for the next phase."

"So you are involved, and you know what he plans?"

"His plans and mine are... evolving, but given this turn of events, given that we've found living specimens...the possibilities are staggering. DeKirk may be thinking about living fossils and dinosaur attractions and sales to world leaders, while maybe, dear, I am the one with more far reaching plans."

He licked his lips, then turned and put his feet up, content to enjoy the rest of the drive.

24.

Adranos Island

The Jeep followed roughly in the path of the other tracks, and Alex had no trouble keeping the trail despite the lack of a true road in more than a few places, as the Jeep tore in and out of foliage, around great roots, jutting stones, rockslides and muddy creek overflows. It was sometime around the twentieth minute, just as he narrowly avoided tumbling over a ridge at the scenic vista overlooking the valley and the distant volcano that Alex had an unsettling thought.

He slowed and considered the vista, at once feeling like Frodo gazing off toward Mt. Doom, and feeling just as lost and inconsequential in this impossible quest. He stopped the Jeep and over the low idling, he listened.

Where was the T. rex?

Did it move that fast, carrying its human-zombie cargo? Were they already down there somewhere, hauling across the open land, or...

He shivered and looked back into the overgrowth and the woods, the hills covered with hiding places. Maybe it had found other prey, local denizens and wildlife to consume. Was it just a ravenous killing machine, did it need blood or meat to keep its energy up, or was biting and chewing just a byproduct of the virus? What were the microbe's methods of transference and reproduction?

Alex didn't know, but there was one thing he was sure of, one thing that kept nagging at the back of his mind.

This *T. rex*—it didn't need oxygen. No heart, no lung functionality. Underwater? No problem. It did have a voracious appetite and an insatiable drive for mayhem. It had broken free when the tranqs wore off, and it came looking for food. *So then what about...*

A rustling brought Alex's senses into focus, and his head twisted back toward a section of the forest. A tree bending. A branch snapping. A scrambling sound.

What about the other dinosaurs?

#

Without even being aware of it, Alex shifted back into drive and eased off the clutch. He saw something weird and out of place. A color shift of something that looked like a giant leaf: green one moment, shifting to reddish ocher the next.

What was it his father had said about the other species they had found? The *Cryolophosaurus*? That it had some ornamental feature, like a crown, something that could mimic the color surroundings, or served a more basic function besides being ornamental—like used for attracting mates, or possibly even for combat?

He floored it and the Jeep took off, an instant before something burst out of hiding. Something with a flurry of swiping talons and snapping teeth. Alex got a glimpse of jet black eyes, ancient and unfeeling, driven purely by hunger. Another glimpse of ragged flesh, huge chunks taken out of the thing's hide, protruding ribs and glistening organs.

A stench came with it, old and retching, foul beyond anything he had ever smelled, like frozen, virulent death had just warmed over.

It swiped at the Jeep with its massive jaws, much smaller than the *T. rex*, but wickedly fast. The rear bumper shattered and sparked. The vehicle lurched, skidded, but held, the front wheels digging into the earth as Alex shifted and turned the wheel into the rise. The Jeep cleared the ridge and then launched into the air. It landed hard, spinning just out of the way of a boulder, finding purchase on a short stretch of open path, and tore ahead.

Alex glanced up to the rear-view mirror and saw what he feared: the creature hauling ass after him.

Suddenly, the Jeep felt like it was dragging, the speedometer struggling to break thirty, and then the path narrowed and banked and he had to slow to avoid another wall of rocks and a gnarled old tree. The passenger door scraped along a rock wall, kicking up sparks and breaking off the side mirror.

A fetid breath, chillingly cold, exploded over Alex as another of the creatures—a little smaller, with more rugged features and a broken set of teeth just above a slashed bite wound in its neck—burst from a higher vantage point. Its skull lowered and it rammed the driver's side. The Jeep flipped up on two wheels, then crashed back down as Alex swerved, dug the wheels back in and spun hard, banking and accelerating. A glance back and the Cryo had lost maneuverability, rocketing forward with its momentum, crashing headfirst into a tree and backing up. It shook its head, bellowed a challenge, then looked toward its departing prey and started after him.

Moments later, its friend appeared, careening out of the woods and slamming into it. They both screeched at each other, then turned back to watch the Jeep. They took off after it like a pair of Olympic track stars.

Oh come on, give up!

Alex swore and shifted gear again, finally locking it in and stomping on the accelerator as the trail flattened out and then gradually declined. Finally, getting the *mph* up past sixty, the creatures now were just dwindling blurs, screaming and roaring in frustration.

Okay, he thought. That's everyone present and accounted for, *and we're all gunning for the same destination.*

He had to get there first.

25.

Inside the DeKirk Enterprises Adranos Facility

Marcus Ramirez stood inside a room within a room. Crouched was more like it, really, as he had his knees flexed while he whipped his head to and fro, occasionally licking his cracked lips. Xander had deposited Veronica in a glorified holding room, telling her he'd be back for her after dealing with Marcus. Then he had taken Marcus here, to this interior lab room designed to contain specimens. It was a sterile environment, all white tile flooring and bright fluorescent overhead lights. A wheeled stainless steel table occupied the middle of the space while an industrial sink was set into one wall. The room had but one window, a wire mesh affair set into the upper half of the only door.

Xander now peered intently at Marcus through this portal. Two hulking men stood beside him, both well-paid soldiers in DeKirk's private army who looked to be in their late twenties, sporting buzz cuts with elaborate razor designs shaved into the sides, physically fit and well-armed. He wasn't sure of their background, whether they were ex-Navy SEALs or just street thugs, but either way, he wouldn't want to mess with them.

As far as Xander could tell, this place was well stocked, more like a small city than a mere lab. He had counted literally a hundred and fifty personnel so far—about half of those soldiers or internal security, armed just as heavily as the guards outside. Then there were battalions of support people—medics, janitors, cooks and administrators, all working alongside several dozen researchers and scientists.

Xander observed Ramirez for a few more seconds. The paleontologist was squinting up at the lights, facing away from the door. He shuffled his feet as he stood, leaving a wet, sticky residue on the floor. Xander wasn't sure, but thought maybe that it was his skin sloughing off.

"What's wrong with this guy?" one of the soldiers asked. All of Marcus' visible skin was yellow and gray, with alarming clusters of pulsing, orange veins or arteries clumped around his neck and face.

"Looks insane," his associate added, and covered his mouth. "Like the plague or smallpox."

As they watched, Ramirez jumped high into the air, and his arm that still had a hand swiped at the ceiling lights. As he landed, he crouched all the way back down, then sprung himself upwards again from a squat. On his next jump, his fist smashed through one of the glass panels for a light fixture set flush into the ceiling.

"C'mon." Xander pushed the door open as a cascade of clear shards rained down on Marcus's upturned face. He didn't even blink.

"Marcus?" Xander forced his tone to be upbeat, as if talking to a dangerous animal that could sense and would react to fear. How's it going?"

Marcus Ramirez whirled his body around so fast it was almost a blur, but his head moved very slowly as he gave Xander and his paid warriors the once-over, as though he was a sloth poked with a stick. He began to blink a lot, but said nothing.

"How do you feel?"

In response, Marcus took an interest in a long piece broken of glass protruding from his cheek.

"Marcus?"

Blood oozed from the paleontologist's mouth and dripped from his chin onto the floor as he stared at Xander. They could hear the little splatters while they waited to see if he would speak.

"Can you talk? Say something."

The noise that escaped his lips caused the two hardened soldiers to take involuntary steps backward. "Aaaaaaaaaaaaaaaaaaaleshhhhh!"

It was barely recognizable as a word, so off was the enunciation, the vocalization sounding more like someone gurgling water than a human voice.

"What'd he say?" one of the henchmen asked.

"His son's name." Xander took a step closer to Marcus and spoke slowly.

"He's not here yet. He—" He started to say he was missing, probably drowned, and then thought better of it. Before he could come up with something else, Marcus shook his head in frustration, spitting out the piece of glass which landed on

Xander's boot along with a thick piece of oddly gray, decomposing cheek flesh.

One of the soldiers looked down in horror. "I think this guy's *rotting*, man. Fuckin' rotting alive!"

The other soldier turned to Xander. "Is this like leprosy or Ebola where your body parts drop off?"

"Not sure yet. You two just keep an eye on him, please, while I do some work."

Xander moved to one of the lab cabinets and removed a digital camera. He began taking video of Marcus, slowly circling him to capture his transforming body from every angle. Suddenly, Marcus spun around and looked directly into the lens.

"His eyes aren't right." One of the soldiers said.

"Looks like snake eyes," his colleague agreed.

"Will you two please shut up? I'm documenting the specim—I mean the patient—and I don't need your jibber-jabber in the background. Do your damn jobs."

The soldiers shrugged it off and contented themselves with slowly backing away from Marcus, hands unsnapping the safety catches on their pistol holsters.

"Marcus, can you describe for me how you feel?"

Alex's father had no reply.

Xander let the camera drop to his side as he took in the horrifying details of Marcus' condition. *That goon is right. This man is rotting alive, in some sort of accelerated state of decomposition. There must be a unique biochemical reaction behind it that I'll have to elucidate later, but fuck me if he's not rotting alive in response to a prehistoric virus transferred during the dinosaur bite. Maybe it triggered some kind of exaggerated autoimmune response...*

Still, he seemed to be fighting it, changing slower than the others—the crewmen aboard the *Hammond*. The fake doc had given him antibiotic, maybe that was slowing things down.

Marcus looked at the bandaged stump and clawed at it with the fingers of his right hand, a compulsive, reflexive movement like scratching a sudden, bothersome itch. The motion caused something to fall from his stump onto the floor. Something white that blended in with the tiles, making it hard to discern at first.

Xander thought it was pieces of the soaked-through gauze, but as he watched, he saw the pieces moving on the floor.

Maggots. Writhing maggots falling out of the bandage, squirming around on the floor as they sought the warm pocket of decaying flesh they had just been shaken from.

Xander felt the bile rise into his throat and tried to force it back down, but it made it all the way to his mouth. He looked over at the soldiers to see if they were looking at him. Their eyes were on Marcus. Xander tried to swallow his puke back down without them knowing, but he retched uncontrollably. The soldiers watched as he wiped his mouth with his shirt sleeve, looking embarrassed despite the situation.

Xander composed himself and strode to the door. "I need to get a chem-test kit. Wait here, I'll be right back."

The soldiers appeared concerned but said nothing, only eyeing Marcus.

As Xander pulled the door open, something—perhaps the incoming rush of fresher air from the main lab—disturbed Marcus, who began raising and lowering his head in a hyperactive motion. He reminded Xander of the lizards he'd seen exhibiting the same behavior, and for some reason, he found that extremely disturbing, because he knew that lizards made those kinds of head movements in order to pass air more forcefully over their sensory organs. *Could Marcus be doing that?*

No sooner had this thought completed itself than Marcus leapt toward the two soldiers with a feral hiss. Xander watched, stupefied, as Marcus proceeded to bite the shorter soldier on the collarbone, the one to Xander's left. The second soldier attempted to pull Marcus off of the man, but it was no use. His teeth were latched on tight to the collarbone of the soldier, whose mindless shriek conveyed searing pain.

While the three of them were locked in struggle, Xander slipped out of the room and eased the door shut, locking it. He stood there looking through the window as the scene unfolded in the inner room.

The larger soldier yanked Marcus off of his colleague, but his jaws never opened. Marcus was flung across the room, a hunk of flesh and—*is that bone?*—clenched between his bloody teeth.

Xander was stunned to find that he could hear the soldier screaming through the thick, nearly soundproof door as he clutched his ruined collarbone.

The second soldier drew his pistol. He aimed at Marcus's chest and gave him a double-tap, sending two rounds into his heart. Marcus' body spun from the impact, but somehow he remained on his feet, stumbling as if in a dance to music that only he could hear. The soldier fired again, the single shot connecting this time with the target's midsection. Xander winced. A gut shot.

Remarkably, Marcus kept coming, even as blood fountained from his abdomen. He fell upon his bloodied victim with what seemed to Xander like real zest, and proceeded to whip his head to and fro over the soldier's wound like a shark in a feeding frenzy. Blood sprayed the floor and the cabinets nearby, some even flecking across the ceiling.

Xander gazed into the horror chamber, the camera in his hand completely forgotten, not even on.

The other soldier tried his luck again with the pistol, this time firing into Marcus' back. Xander saw the flesh pucker as the bullet penetrated his skin, but the attack went on unabated. If anything, the ferocity of the assault increased, with Marcus applying his fingers to the soldier's open wound as the trained operator flailed his legs uselessly into the blood-streaked floor. It looked like Marcus was trying to pry the collarbone out of the way in order to stick his face deeper into the exposed meat.

The soldier with the gun turned and looked back at Xander, mouthing something that meant, *get help right fucking now.* That was a mistake, because all Xander did was check to make sure the door was still locked. Meanwhile, the wounded soldier was able to kick the monster that Marcus had become off of him, sending his assailant across the room toward the other soldier, who turned around just in time to be beat in the face with Marcus' messy stump. Gouts of yellowish pulp exploded into the air.

Xander was stunned at the speed with which Marcus moved, especially given his condition. Suddenly, the face of the soldier who'd been shooting Marcus was pressed up against the glass, Marcus' hands keeping him there, but he didn't really think of this inhuman thing as Marcus anymore, did he? He saw Marcus' mouth open and those jagged teeth descend into the soldier's neck.

The soldier's uncontrollable movements in response to the bite caused him to knock into the thick safety glass so hard that his teeth fell out of his mouth, sliding down the glass. Xander had never seen such a violent attack, not anywhere, not even in the movies. His mind was somewhere else, floating above this hell as if in a trance. It was a productive trance because he knew one thing, and one thing for sure, as he witnessed the now dead soldier's face press into the window.

This was the bio-weapon of the century.

Imagine these...these creatures, not stopped by bullets...turned loose in the cities or battlefields of an enemy state...How much would America's enemies pay for such a tool of destruction? First, Xander needed to convert it from the raw force of nature it was now into controllable technology.

As his mind flipped around the possibilities, he peered over at the first soldier who now lay apparently unconscious on the floor on his back, what was left of his collarbone protruding from his open neck.

Then the soldier at the window was shoved down to the floor and Marcus was gaping at Xander through the window. He pressed one of his eyes right up to it, peering at him through a smear of blood with one of the soldier's incisors somehow wedged into a crack in the glass. Marcus' eyes were yellow and black. Distinctly reptilian, but at the same time, without even the suggestion of life that a normal reptile had. Dead, cold eyes, with the barest flicker of recognition.

Xander wondered if Marcus' mind was still there, if he could remember anything, like being fired and tossed aside. Wondering if revenge was even a factor in his changed brain. He didn't think so.

He sure hoped not.

26.

Adranos Facility

Xander watched through the window while Marcus knelt over the soldier with the exposed collarbone. He couldn't see his face, but he didn't need to, didn't want to. Marcus—*but he wasn't Marcus anymore, was he, no way, no how*—gorged himself on the flesh of the unconscious soldier. The mercenary was still alive, though. Xander could see his belly beneath his shredded shirt, rising and falling with very shallow, labored breaths.

Marcus Ramirez—the talented paleontologist who had once given Xander pause as to his own job security within DeKirk's enterprise—was *eating* a living man's flesh.

He was, for all intents and purposes, Xander thought, a zombie. He stared into the room at Marcus wolfing down hunks of raw human flesh. That's what he had turned into, but definitely, this thing shared none of the characteristics of the shambling, lurching, slow-moving creatures in most movies. This was…raw power, mixed with speed and ferocity.

A saurian zombie… He pictured the worker who'd been nicked by the *T. rex*.

The applications for this discovery were limitless…What would Marcus—it was time to stop calling him that, he told himself. What would the creature—the *zombie*—do once it exhausted its food supply in the lab? Xander supposed that, like any organism without sustenance, it would eventually die. He wasn't certain about that, but he didn't want to risk it. The dinosaurs—a *T. rex* and two Cryos—were loose on the island. What if he couldn't create any more zombies? What if DeKirk evacuated his people when he arrived and was overwhelmed by the horrific spectacle of it all? He was used to watching things from afar in the comfort of his remote mansions, after all. In that case, this would remain his only zombie specimen.

Xander had a lot of work to do in the lab before he could be first mover on this new bio-weapon. He needed to concentrate undisturbed. He looked over at the zombie, still feasting on the soldier. Xander's gaze traveled up the wall to a vent shaft door in the ceiling. He recalled seeing the switch for it in the main lab. It looked large enough for a human—or zombie—to fit through.

He turned and ran back into the main lab. It was time to find out just what kind of mayhem these prehistoric zombies were capable of. Call it an early field test. He walked over to the wall switch for the vent shaft door, flipped it, and jogged back over to the inner door.

Inside, the Marcus-zombie stared up at the open vent shaft, ragged hunks of dripping meat hanging from its open craw. Again, it started with the head movements, detecting the flow of air through the vent. Just as Xander began to wonder if it would try to escape (maybe it had enough food supply in there for now?), it jumped onto the stainless steel table and crouched, looking up at the grate.

Then it sprung—*Marcus sprung*—disappearing into the overhead space.

Xander peered in at the mangled human bodies on the floor. *What a mess.* He turned to leave but motion caught his eye. Unbelievably, the soldier Marcus had been feeding from the most—the one with the missing section of collarbone—*sat up.* Then he began to nod his head rapidly back and forth and after that, he got to his feet.

Impossible! Xander thought, but he knew it wasn't, and he was thrilled to witness this firsthand. The new zombie stood and looked around, limping a bit, his severed collarbone protruding obscenely, and his service pistol still clutched in his right hand. He looked down and the jagged, raw bone impaled him beneath the chin, causing a new trickle of blood to fall from his neck.

A hand flattened out on the glass in front of Xander's face before springing off, leaving a bloody palm print. Xander watched as Collarbone looked up at the ceiling, after Marcus.

Xander was flabbergasted. These men were undergoing the same transformation that had befallen Marcus, and were turning into zombies before his eyes—even after death. The change had been much more rapid, though. *Perhaps because they were bitten by a human-zombie instead of a dinosaur-zombie?* Xander didn't know, but he fully intended to find out. There was big money—the kind of money lasting empires were founded on—in finding out.

Then Collarbone turned around and Xander was mortified to see a revolting gash in his midsection through which a waterfall of blood flooded—no, *dumped* out along with his intestinal mass. *Zombie Marcus must have done that!* The pale coils unraveled onto the wet floor as the man—no longer could that word truly describe him, though—shuffled toward the table. He made grimacing facial gestures with each step, as though in pain. He tripped once on his own intestines and stumbled headlong into the edge of the table where his gun struck the surface and discharged.

The errant round struck the zombie-soldier in his good shoulder, the left. He slowly rose from the table, both of his arms now dangling limply by his sides, unable to be supported by his decimated upper musculature. He abandoned his gun on the table as he tried to jump to the vent. Unable to raise his arms fully, he couldn't grip the edge of the vent to pull himself up, and so repeatedly jumped, poking his head far up into the space before falling back to the table. Xander left him there, a zombified pogo stick yearning for the warm flesh to be found at the other end of the vent.

Xander pulled his attention away at last. He exited the lab, trotted down a long, tunnel-like hallway with a polished concrete floor, and subdued LED lighting. He reached the door to the holding room and gazed in at Veronica through the small window. She'd sat next to Marcus—to that *thing*—the whole Jeep ride over, but no, he thought, as he stared at her while she pecked her phone. She looked good. Hell, he'd still do her.

He put a key into the door, causing her to look up immediately, and he pulled the door open. He entered and she shrunk back from him before giving him a death glare once she realized he obviously wasn't planning on killing her, at least not yet.

"What the hell do you want? What's going on out there?"

"Good times, Veronica. Good times!" He backed out of the room, but left the door open. "Why don't you go see for yourself? You're now free to move about the compound."

27.

Adranos Facility

Veronica watched Xander leave the holding room. He turned left down the hall, back the way he had come. He'd seemed distracted, in spite of the control he now wielded over her. She'd thought he would have lorded the situation over her more, knowing who she was, but it was as if he didn't even care, and he was just letting her out? Something more important had to be going on, and she had to find out what it was.

She had to find DeKirk, too. Was he here yet, or still on his way?

Veronica stepped out into the hall. She looked both ways and saw only Xander way down to the left, jogging. She struck off to the right. In here, the place was eerily quiet, but outside in the distance she could hear shouting, and peppered gunfire. She cursed the fact that she'd lost her medical bag in the rush to escape the ship. Not because it had medical supplies—the jig was up on that by now—but because it had her tools of the trade, her operative's field kit hidden below the false bottom. The multi-tool, her service pistol...Her sat-phone! All she had now was the stupid smart-phone. She'd tried in the room back there to get a signal but couldn't, no surprise there. There was a wireless Internet connection here, probably satellite based, but she hadn't been able to get past the encryption, so as of now, she had no way to contact her CIA handlers.

So here she was, walking around the island with little more than the clothes on her back, trying to hunt down a ruthless bio-weapons dealer on an island with dinosaurs running around, and some kind of disease turning everyone else into murderous, marauding zombies...

Gusts of powerful wind buffeted her body as she neared the end of the tunnel, open to the outside. She hunched forward and burst outdoors, now feeling the pelt of rain on her face. A Jeep lay overturned off to the left, no sign of anyone near it. It could be the one she'd rode in on, but she wasn't sure since they all looked the same—completely open with no doors, no windows. One of the tires still spun in the air.

To the right was a dirt embankment overgrown with ferns. She heard a commotion in that direction. She climbed the small hill, swearing softly as leaves and branches whipped across her face, spitting out pieces of plant matter. She rounded the top and stopped in her tracks.

A soldier was engaged in hand-to-hand combat with another man, only as she looked closer it was clear that his opponent was not a man, or at least he wasn't anymore. She recognized the tattered jumpsuit as belonging to one of the ship's crew, and even recalled the face, but it was his face no longer. Gaunt, gray, with yellow streaks and strange vein clusters behind tight scales. Eyes that were mostly black with yellow, elongated irises.

It looked like whatever Marcus had progressed into after his bite, but it wasn't Marcus, which meant that whatever this...this *plague* was that those idiots had dredged out of that Antarctic subterranean lake, it was spreading.

She stood there shivering behind the curl of a fern leaf while the fight played out not ten feet from her. The soldier had an automatic rifle slung over his back, suggesting that the zombie had surprised him, perhaps jumping out of the very foliage in which Veronica now hid. DeKirk's man did have a fixed blade knife in his right hand though, slashing with it when he got the chance. She watched as he opened a tear in the zombie's side, releasing a crimson sheet that soaked his jumpsuit.

The zombie had both arms outstretched, hands on the soldier's arms as the mercenary sought to push the beast away long enough to sling his gun around, but each time he wrenched an arm free, the former crew member would latch onto him again. At the same time, the zombie continually thrust its head toward the soldier's neck, making anticipatory biting motions that snapped at the air.

The rain came down harder, blowing horizontally in the forceful wind. Veronica shrunk deeper into the plants, terrified.

The soldier pulled his right hand, the one with the knife—one Veronica recognized as a U.S. Marine Corps issue Ka-Bar—down sharply so that it broke free of the zombie's spastic grasping. One of the zombie's fingers was caught under the blade in the process and the severed digit went flying, eliciting a grunt from the quasi-mindless attacker. The soldier backpedaled but the zombie pressed forward in a surprising burst of speed. Veronica thought about the classic zombie movies she'd seen, how they always walked so slowly. This one started slow, but it also seemed to store energy in reserve for the occasional quick burst. Like a reptile, she thought. A cold-blooded reptile that needed to lay in the sun for a while to build up its energy...

A breathy gasp issued from the zombie's lips, tearing Veronica from her speculation. The soldier had parried and thrust until his seven inch blade was buried to the hilt in his foe's chest. Left side.

He's dead now, Veronica thought, brushing a horsefly off her cheek as she watched the soldier deliver a powerful kick to the zombie's chest just beneath the protruding knife, sending it rambling backwards until it tripped over a raised root and landed on its back, splashing into the muddy earth.

DeKirk's trained fighter cocked his head to the right and keyed a radio transmitter fixed to his shoulder. "Bravo to Alpha, Bravo to Alpha: one tango neutralized, Sector 2. I repeat..." While he turned and squinted into the distance, looking for signs of his associates, he failed to notice that the zombie sat up.

Veronica felt her throat catch as she saw the living dead man rise to his feet, seven inches of steel still piercing his heart, a black stain soaking through the fabric of his outfit. She wanted to warn the soldier (*He's getting up!*) but she was scared that he might spray her position with bullets in a knee-jerk response, so she remained silent. She heard another voice say something unintelligible in reply over the soldier's radio, and then he turned around and saw the zombie rising, stumbling.

The soldier's mouth dropped open in absolute incredulity. He swiped his auto-rifle around to the ready position. Raised it. This time he aimed for the head. The zombie fell into a shambling motion that was ungainly, yet nevertheless, resulted in forward progress.

The soldier stood his ground and cut loose with a full-auto bullet hose. The zombie's face, teeth, eyeballs and brains, crashed through the back of its exploding skull along with the slugs of lead. A small, unseen animal skittered out of the way as the wet matter strafed the ground along with the rain. The zombie's near headless form hung in a standing position for perhaps a second longer and then it buckled at the knees, crumpling to the dirt.

Behind the ferns, Veronica was shaking. She'd shot people before, killed them, sure. In her line of work as an operative, you did what you had to do, but they were clean kills and proper assassinations with discreet amounts of firepower. This...this was just not right. The degree to which this—this *being* who had once been a man—had been so hideously butchered...so thoroughly deconstructed....was threatening to unhinge her. Even the soldier was unsettled, she could see. He practically tip-toed over to the massacred form, unsure if perhaps it might rise yet again. He stood there grimacing, then his radio blared again, something about half a click southeast, and he was off running.

Veronica waited until she was sure there would be no more movement from the zombie. As the rain let up, she cautiously emerged from her cocoon of greenery and approached the puddle of wasted flesh that had once been one of DeKirk's men. It looked like part of its lower jaw might still be there, or was that the spine sticking up? She didn't know, but the knife still jutted from the thing's chest.

She went over to it and wrapped her hand around the handle, which, even in the falling rain, was sticky with blood. Pushing against the ground with her feet, she yanked the knife free of the zombie's chest cavity. It slid out with a wet sucking sound. She eyed the zombie with trepidation. If this thing moved now that it had no head, she would lose it for sure.

It didn't move. She wiped the blade off with some plant leaves because the zombie's clothing was already sopping with blood everywhere, and she wasn't about to stain her clothes with that diseased, rotten blood, no way in Hell.

She looked around. Where to now? She spotted the entrance to the tunnel. This experience having soured her on the great outdoors for now, she set off back toward the complex.

She had made it about halfway there when she saw a vaguely familiar human form walk—or more like stumble—around a concrete abutment. *Zombie or—?* She wanted to be sure. A cluster of industrial pipes surfaced out of the ground nearby. She ran to them and ducked behind one of the large ones. She saw the figure stop and sniff the air.

Yeah, definitely Zombie!

She froze, clutching the Ka-Bar in her right hand, even though she couldn't imagine having to get close enough to the thing to use it, like that soldier did. She wasn't sure she could do that, and then it hit her—the realization that this zombie... It was missing the hand on his left arm. Marcus Ramirez!

Would he recognize her if he did see her?

She doubted it. He was pretty far gone even on the drive over here, but maybe there was still some fight left in him. Maybe the antibiotics she had given him were somehow fending off the virus. Her curiosity made her want to get a closer look, though. She needed to gauge how far he had progressed, or maybe *regressed* was a better word for the transformation brought on by the primordial infection. Either way, she had to see it for herself. *The Regression of Dr. Marcus Ramirez.* If only she had some popcorn to watch the show with, she joked to herself. The humor kept her going in dark moments. She'd learned that about herself long ago, the only way she had managed to survive after what Xander did to Edgars.

Remaining stock still in the cluster of pipe work, she held her breath as Marcus The Zombie shuffled toward her. When he drew near enough, she looked closely at his face.

Oh God.

It was now sunken and gray, cadaverous, all shrunken and shriveled. He was missing front teeth, too, although, she supposed, they could have been knocked out due to trauma as opposed to falling out, but somehow she suspected the latter. She recalled her confrontation with him in the infirmary when he had accused her of not being an M.D. *In my non-expert, non-medical opinion, Marcus, your goddamned gums rotted out from under your teeth, and that appears to be the least of your problems.* New rows of sharp-edged incisors were coming in, pushing out the old teeth unsuited to their new function.

She waited for the zombie to walk far enough away. Then she bolted for the entrance to the facility. Even hanging out with

Xander in there was preferable to this. At least she'd confirmed one thing, she thought, improvising a holster for the knife in the waistband of her jeans.

It took a headshot to kill those things.

28.

Adranos Facility

Marcus Ramirez wandered up to the dead zombie slain by the soldier. He crouched eagerly, animal-like, pulling the corpse so that it remained upright in a sitting position. He felt waves of revulsion as he sniffed the corpse.

Revulsion that was quickly overcome with another feeling. A *need.*

Hunger…

So intense. His jaws opened and snapped. His tongue came out and licked the edges of the new teeth. He wanted to lap the blood pooled in this corpse's open neck, like a drunk guy at a wedding sipping directly from a champagne fountain. Wanted to sink his face into the dead one's right bicep, but instead, his belly aching and rumbling, he stood and sniffed the air in the direction of the facility.

He sniffed the air again. Something else, something… better… was around.

He set off in that direction, the vacant mind filling with vague purpose like a pinball bouncing from one target and seeking the next. Marcus's remaining hand scratched reflexively at the now open stump while he stumbled along, the bandages long since having fallen away. A cloud of flies buzzed about the raw amputation, the zombie's personal air force.

The light of the tunnel stood out from the rest of the storm-battered island and the Marcus-zombie gravitated toward it. In the distance, he heard a large animal vocalizing, causing him to turn his head but not to stop walking. A high-pitched squealing sound, and it was almost—but not quite—alluring enough to call him toward it, but for some reason, he fought that call. For some reason, he turned right instead of going inside, walking around the outside of the complex. On this side of the building, the ground sloped away sharply, causing him to adjust his shambling gait with one leg higher up than the other.

When he came upon an open doorway set into an alcove in the side of the enormous structure, he paused, the sounds of a human struggle piquing his dulled senses. He turned and walked inside the open concrete bay, some kind of receiving station meant for vehicles to back into. Two still-functioning Jeeps were parked inside.

He shuffled past them into a narrow entrance vestibule, a sign overhead he could no longer comprehend reading, MEDICAL UNIT. This area emerged from that into a small hospital-like room, which led in turn out into the same large hallway he had walked through earlier, although he had no recollection of that. Wheeled cots, defibrillators, various medical machines, supplies, and equipment filled the space.

He paused, drooling, and stared ahead.

Feeling the hunger surge, his stomach rumbled and he licked his lips in anticipation.

#

In this room, two of DeKirk's doctors—genuine research physicians—both wearing white lab coats, struggled to keep two of the zombified ship's crew at bay, keeping a wheeled table between themselves and the reaching attackers.

"I thought you said they were dead!" One of the men said to the other, his mind struggling to accept the impossible.

"They were! They were dead on arrival. I'm sure of it! I took their pulses myself. They were flat lined, I swear it! That guy is the one who had his leg crushed by the crane on the ship. The other one drowned, his body washed up on the beach."

"Steve..."

"We need to get some help." This doc, a pudgy, bald man in his fifties, let go of the table and rushed to a handheld radio docking station on a counter, but froze when he sighted The Zombie Formerly Known As Marcus standing there at the back of the room. Marcus was dripping a cornucopia of bodily fluids and rainwater onto the tile floor, sounding like a mini-percussion ensemble as the steady drips intermingled with the occasional *plop* of an abscess releasing its cargo of smelly pus.

"Good Lord," the other doctor said, ducking away from the reach of one zombie. "Get back here and help—" Then he saw the Marcus-zombie.

The one who'd been going for the radio considered their situation. Three zombies, although he didn't yet think of them as that, occupied what until now had been their comfortable little work area where they'd treated the occasional workman's injury during the construction of the facility. He turned to the newcomer. Maybe it was the unreality of the situation, or it was just his mind's way of breaking away from the terror of imminent violent death, but he spoke, as professionally as possible.

"Hey...uh, you require some urgent attention?"

No response came from the zombie. From any of them.

Meanwhile, the doctor in the corner faced off against two slow-moving but relentless zombies. The nameplate pinned to that doc's coat read, Felix Alvarez, M.D. Alvarez was clearly not a fighter, awkwardly attempting to fend the zombies off with timid arm gestures. One more shove of the table against his hip caused him to notice behind him the enclosure on the wall containing a fire extinguisher next to a red-handled axe. He stood there looking at it for a moment too long, before the nearest of the zombies suddenly launched itself over the table.

"Get off me! Get! Off!"

The attacker only sunk its teeth into Alvarez's upper back, eliciting a blood-curdling scream from the man.

"Get it, Steve—" Felix, lying on the floor, pointed with a spasming hand. "—the axe!"

Steve, meanwhile, continued to stare at the motionless, newly arrived zombie. He noted the missing hand and the hopelessly gangrenous, abscessed wound there. *That entire arm will have to be amputated*, he couldn't help but think, before mentally chastising himself. *Stay focused!* He'd heard the whispered rumors of some of DeKirk's "experimental" endeavors and wondered if this could somehow be one of them. *There were those blind tissue assays Melvin asked us to do last week...*

Felix managed to get to his feet, one zombie still feasting on his back, the other shoving the barricade away and lurching toward him. He reached the fire implements on the wall, the zombie riding him, now trying to take additional bites from the smorgasbord of his back. The semi-tough lab coat material was the only thing making it difficult, but it wouldn't be long before the monster took a real bite.

Marcus suddenly jumped, and came toward Steve fast.

Steve tried to summon the Judo skills from the classes he'd taken decades ago as a teenager and never followed through on. He kicked out awkwardly with his right leg and connected with Marcus's gut, knocking him back a few steps but also winding up on his back on the floor in the process. He shot to his feet. *No more of that crap*, he told himself. The zombie he'd kicked was just recovering. He'd bought a few seconds. He moved toward Felix, now cornered by two zombies, one still clinging to his back, repeatedly jabbing his mouth onto him, while the other still sought access to the potential meal.

He had to help Felix out. Steve ran up to the lagging zombie and gripped it by the shoulders. He jerked it backwards, sending it flying to the floor. Looking back, he saw the zombie with the missing hand start to walk toward them, his left foot dragging across the floor. Steve turned around to face this threat.

At the same time, Felix got a hand on the axe and ripped it from the wall, knocking himself in the lip with the butt of the blade in the process. He caught a glimpse of his face in the reflection of the fire extinguisher case and saw the blood running from his split lip. The zombie on his back became even more excited, crawling higher in order to feverishly lick and sniff his at his face like some kind of hyperactive, rabid dog.

Hunched over with his attacker sprawled over him as he was, Steve had no way to brandish the axe. The only direction in which he could strike with it was directly in front of him. He had to keep shaking his head from side to side to avoid a facial bite from the zombie, but he was able to thrust the axe into the fire extinguisher case. Shattered glass dropped from the housing. He let the axe fall to the floor and reached out for the extinguisher as the zombie took little nips from his skin, now frustrated at not being able to sink its teeth more deeply, like a toddler unable to bite into a whole apple.

Steve circled around the Marcus zombie. As a doctor, he'd dedicated his life to relieving human suffering, and even though he was a threat, the details of this person's condition had a sobering impact on him. His skin had congealed to form a scale-like dermis. The edges of the scales were rimmed with blood. He was covered in festering abscesses, terrible infections that would require lengthy intensive treatment, if it wasn't too late for this poor soul already.

He found that the zombie wasn't able to track him so well when he circled in this way. Its head turned much too slowly, although when it decided to adjust its position it moved very quickly. As Steve circled he got a look over against the wall at how Felix was doing. It wasn't a pretty picture. The zombie that Steve had thrown to the floor was now back on its feet and lumbering over to Felix's left side. The other zombie still straddled the physician high on his back, assaulting his face with a barrage of quick, vicious little bites.

"Get him off you, Felix!" Steve yelled his encouragement, but there was little more he could do. He wasn't about to turn his back on this one-armed monster, which now became more aggressive, lashing out alternately with its stump and its whole arm when he thought Steve might be in range.

That's when the Cryolophosaurus hopped into the room.

A small dinosaur by ancient reptile standards, it was no *T. rex*, but still, when a reptile twenty feet long and a dozen high hops into a room, people—and zombies—pay attention.

A reddish, feathered crest sat atop its slim head, which it lowered order to fit into the space. Its two clawed feet clacked on the floor as it pushed further inside, aware that the ceiling was far too low for its usual loping gait. Its beady black eyes gave away nothing as its nostrils flared while it jerked its head up and down.

Steve couldn't tell what the creature was looking at. To say his mind was blown simply did not do justice to the utter detachment from reality he felt at that moment. *Dinosaurs? Zombies? Did DeKirk leak psychoactive drugs into our water supply?*

As Mr. One Arm took advantage of his lack of attention and threw itself at him, Steve knew beyond a shadow of a doubt that the situation he now found himself in was all too real. So real, in fact, that it wasn't just another part of his life, it represented an entirely new existence for him.

Zombie...zombie...zombie... He flashed on a vacation to Haiti he'd taken many years ago, during a pocket of political stability there to indulge his adventurous first ex-wife's penchant for exotic travel. They'd stayed in some fluffy beachside resort but took a day trip into a genuine village to see a real life witch doctor. She was an old, superstitious woman who, in a Creole accent told him about spirits and voodoo and zombies while he drank something of the Earth...He was a man of science, a physician, but the essence of her message had never left him. *There is more to this world than you can see...* He pictured her leathery, lined face now, heard her rhythmic chanting...

In the distraction served by the dinosaur, the Marcus zombie leaped across the space between them and closed its jaws around Steve's throat, clenched in a spray of blood. *My blood,* Steve thought indistinctly. Struggling to breathe, struggling against an onslaught of such pain he could never imagine. He felt drained, the strength sapped out of him along with the image of the witch doctor.

Next he knew, he was on the floor and staring up. He felt his larynx pull free into the monster's mouth with a sickening snapping sound and a burst of blood. With a bizarre form of objectivity, he mentally pictured the anatomical parts of his throat that had been removed, exactly where the tendons, nerves and blood vessels had been severed, picturing the full color plates from Gray's Anatomy that he'd pored over for countless hours all those decades ago.

Then he watched the Cryo rush at him. Sadly, he welcomed it. He wanted the monster to step on him, to bite his entire head off, to end his life quickly... far better than to asphyxiate on the floor while this subhuman brute ate the rest of his throat and face.

As the dinosaur pushed further into the room, the high point of its back wedged into the ceiling, halting its forward motion. Stretching its neck out, its head reached a couple of feet shy of the zombie dining on Steve's throat. It squealed in frustration, but the zombie bent over Steve only gave it a passing glance before returning for another feeding session.

Steve's vision faded to black.

The last thing he heard was the strident hiss of a fire extinguisher.

29.

Adranos Facility

Alex Ramirez shifted the Jeep into four wheel drive and flipped on the fog lights. The weather intensified, the wind and now the rain increasing in force. Finally, he could see lights a hundred yards or so through the jungle. After standing in place in the driver's seat, looking around for signs of dinosaurs or zombies, he rolled the Jeep down a steep, muddy incline toward the facility.

Xander would be here, along with Veronica. He had to admit that he wouldn't mind seeing her right now, and his Dad. Alex had no idea about his health or his condition, and he feared the worst.

The Jeep's right front tire bounced off a volcanic rock and he corrected for it, coaxing the vehicle back on course. The land flattened out at the bottom of the incline and he followed the muddy track out of the jungle into a clearing, at the opposite end of which lay the lighted facility.

He looked around again, half expecting the *T. rex* to come barreling out of the forest, racing to devour him, but there was only open space between him and the building. He pressed his foot down on the pedal and ate up the distance, rolling by the corpse of the soldier Veronica had taken the knife from without noticing it. He parked the Jeep in front of the tunnel entrance and got out.

He could hear shouting now, and sporadic gunfire. Definitely not coming from inside the tunnel, but somewhere close. In the tunnel, however, he could hear an alarm of some type, not unlike the fire alarms he'd heard during school drills. He took off at a jog inside the structure, glad to be out of the rain. He tried the first couple of doors he passed but they were locked. He was about to call out when he heard it.

A prehistoric roar.

Not the *T. rex*. More shrill, and chilling in its simplicity. *One of the Cryos?*

He continued down the hallway, the braying alarm growing louder until he reached an open door on his right. A current of cool air passed from it into the hall. His eyes narrowed as his gaze caught on a blood splatter pattern extending into the hallway floor.

He darted to the wall on the same side as the open door and flattened himself against it, listening.

A shuffling and clopping sound, like a large four-legged animal walking, emanated from far into the open room. As he listened that sound grew fainter, as if moving away. Alex slid along the wall until he couldn't be any closer to the doorway without being in it. The shuffling continued away from him, so he poked his head around the doorway.

He'd never seen a floor with so much blood on it. That was the first thought to strike him. The second was that the room had a strong metallic odor to it, like copper. His gaze was riveted to that shimmering, red floor. It was like a lake of blood, there was so much, although it did thin out toward the opposite end of the room, where the shadows were thicker.

Against his better judgment, he stepped into the room—obviously a medical facility of some kind. He crossed the lake of blood over to the right side of the space, where it was even deeper. His shoes splashed in the stuff with each step. He saw a busted BREAK GLASS IN CASE OF EMERGENCY fire alarm on the wall. On the floor, he saw a raised outline of an axe. He almost missed it because the axe was red—a fire axe—while the floor was red with blood. A burst of adrenaline bloomed in his abdomen and spread to his fingertips and toes in half a second. Something god-awful horrible had transpired in here, and not very long ago.

A fire extinguisher also lay on the floor, its black funnel spray nozzle hung up on the handle of a cabinet door. Looking up, he followed a trail of white chemical spray that went from the wall near the fire case on up to the ceiling—random zig-zaggy swathes of discharge that suggested whomever had used it had been under great duress and not aiming steadily. Which one might expect in a fire situation.

Looking around, Alex didn't see any signs of a fire. No charred areas, no smoke damage, no lingering smell, and of course, most fires didn't leave behind a lot of liquid blood.

He splashed further into the room, glad for the fact that he wore "old school" leather sneakers, not the new ones with that fabric mesh crap. Full-on shit-kicking boots would have been even better, but he had what he had. Alex reached the vestibule area near the back and ventured through it.

Two Jeeps in good shape were parked here, a bloody handprint on the hood of one of them. Lesser amounts of blood compared to the medical room streaked the concrete floor. He passed through this area to the outside, where an unpaved access road led away from the building and curved off to the right. He traced its path with his eyes but saw no activity there. Then he looked off to the left, out toward the tree line that marked the edge of the jungle, and he spotted it.

A *Cryolophosaurus* stalked the perimeter, shaking its head back and forth. Its snout was bloody. It had fire extinguisher residue plastered to its right flank, giving it a most unnatural white stripe down its side. Although Alex wasn't sure how much, if anything, about this monstrosity could be called natural.

He shifted his weight and a thin branch snapped under his foot. The Cryo stopped moving, and then it whipped its head around in Alex's direction. The creature's nostrils flared, and then it jumped—not ran, but leapt in a single bound—three-quarters of the distance to Alex, who whirled back around into the vehicle area. He bolted between the two Jeeps, through the vestibule and back into the medical room, home of Blood Lake. He heard the dinosaur's feet pounding the floor through the Jeep area. Alex was making his way across the slick floor when he sighted something in the corner he hadn't noticed on his first trip through.

A human leg, severed at mid-thigh. Ragged chunks missing from much of it. He stared a little too long and slipped on the blood, the side of his face pancaking into the liquid floor. He heard the Cryo bashing its way through the vestibule.

Panicking, Alex pushed off the floor but the heel of his right hand slid out and down he went again, bruising his chin and soaking the front of his shirt. The beast behind him snorted as it entered the medical room. Alex craned his neck from the prone position and saw it coming for him. Maybe two or three of its gigantic strides away, and that's without jumping.

I'm dead.

He tried to push up again, anyway. *Ain't going out like that,* but he was going out like that, with a twenty-foot-long dinosaur about to trample him or eat him, or trample him and then eat him. Either way, he was done. It was at that point, as he was just beginning to rise to a standing position from his hands and knees that he heard something happening to the ceiling. Like it was being ripped apart, the fiberboard tiles shredding. A precipitation of plaster dust rained down on the room, settling on the blood like snowflakes on iron-rich soil.

Alex turned around to face his fate, but the Cryo's back was wedged into the ceiling, impeding its forward progress. It could advance no further into the room.

Alex locked eyes with the hideous dinosaur. Black, lifeless eyes streaked with red, and the body—he hadn't noticed it outside—but it was ravaged with wounds. Whitish bulbs of what appeared to be entrails protruded from several slits in its underside, a couple of them dripping copious brown slime. Open flesh pockets festered from neck to tail. Alex almost felt caught in that soulless gaze and felt a fleeting sympathetic bond with it: remorseless and icy-cold, as if the countless centuries in the frozen lake had destroyed any sense of warmth or emotion. Then it passed, terror and self-preservation took over and he rolled, got to his feet and ran for his life.

A large section of ceiling tile came down as the monster thrashed, and Alex took a couple of steps and slid, coasting through the blood to the door.

The reptile gave ear-splitting bird-like screeches as Alex ran from the room.

In the hall, he saw no one to the left, the way he had come, so he continued to the right. It was empty but there were sporadic smears of blood here and there. He kicked something small that made a metallic ringing. His eyes followed it, seeing a shell casing to a small caliber weapon. Swallowing hard, he turned suddenly, terrified he'd see the Cryo bearing down on him, but there was nothing behind him.

Just then, as he was about to take his first relaxing breath in a long time, the lights in the tunnel began to flicker, casting it into intermittent darkness.

Holy shit. He had no flashlight on him, or gear of any kind other than the blood-soaked shoes and clothes on his back.

Deciding there was nothing he could do about any of that at the moment, he pressed on, running through the flashing lights.

Before long, he heard a dramatic struggle playing out in a room up ahead on the left. Objects smashing or being thrown. Guttural hissing noises, and a woman's voice. Screaming.

Veronica.

Alex set off at a full-out sprint until he arrived at an open door. He paused, then dashed inside and stopped short as he saw Veronica Winters in the grasp of those *things*—this one had on the green-camo paramilitary uniform of DeKirk's soldiers, but it was clearly no longer a man. She slashed at it with a huge Rambo knife as she tried to keep its jaws from snapping anywhere near her.

Another of the zombies was coming for her. This one wore a white medical coat and had huge chunks of flesh torn out of its throat, and ragged bloody teeth marks on its back.

"Veronica!"

The closer zombie heard Alex and turned its head and Veronica, cooler than Alex would have ever expected, took advantage of that. She jammed the blade of the Ka-Bar right through what was supposedly the softest bone in the body—the one on the side of the skull—and then twisted it savagely, churning the thing's brains into disorganized mush that oozed out around the blade.

She gripped the hilt of the Ka-Bar as the zombie attacker fell to the floor, dead, brandishing the brain-covered weapon as she turned to face the approaching white-clad zombie.

Risking a glance over her shoulder, she gave him a once over. Literally soaked in blood from head to toe, he realized with an unsettling start that she easily could have thought he was one of *them*, and if she had a gun instead of a knife she might have simply shot him in the head on sight. Others might, too—the soldiers. He would have to clean himself up. He thought about the rain outside.

"Alex? You good? Any…bites?"

"Uh, no. Fine, I slipped in a mess back there, and—look out!"

"I got him," she assured Alex, sweeping the knife back and forth in front of her to keep the fresher medic zombie at bay.

Alex noted the physician's outfit and guessed he was part of the fun at Blood Lake back there, and wondered how anyone could possibly have escaped from that little piece of Hell. As he appraised his condition, though, he realized that he most certainly hadn't escaped. He barely had time to process the irony of it, that Veronica, the bogus doctor was now being assailed by a real one who was no longer among the living.

Dr. Zombie growled at her and lunged. Veronica slashed its throat, opening a wide gash and slicing into the cheek, but still it came at her.

Alex looked around the room for anything he could use to help. It was some sort of computer lab, but not the kind he'd seen in school. Stacks of Cray supercomputers, servers and appliances lined the walls, humming and whirring and blinking to do God only knew what. He saw a high-backed swivel chair on wheels and ran to it.

He waved and yelled for Veronica to step aside. She rolled smartly to her left, leaving Dr. Z hunched over in mid-strike. Alex took a running start with the chair and rammed it into the zombie's backside. It flopped right into the seat and Alex gave it a full-strength shove, sending it past Veronica and toward the wall of Crays.

A flash of sparks and a hiss burst out of the terminal. On the screen, rolling lines of code started scrolling and scrolling, along with diagrams and molecular schematics. The back of the zombie's head slammed into a control panel before its body crumpled out of the chair in an uncoordinated heap. It was very slow to get up but still moving. Alex and Veronica closed in on it, Veronica apparently more concerned about whatever was still outside. She glanced back at the door even though it was shut.

"What do you think is out there?" she wondered.

Alex tried to listen and identify the sounds, responding: "One of two possibilities. Zombies, or it's that nasty little zombie dinosaur that's been trying to get in here in the worst way. Almost had me back there."

"Let's hope for the human variety." Veronica turned and rather calmly closed in and ended Dr. Zombie's illustrious career with a knife implanted firmly to the brain stem. "Much easier to deal with. At least when they're alone."

Suddenly, the door behind them bulged in its frame as something kicked on it. Then several more thumps simultaneously crashed onto the other side.

Veronica withdrew her knife from the corpse and wiped it on her pant leg. She looked at Alex, who had been drawing nearer to the keypad, trying to look at the lines of code and hoping to piece together anything about what DeKirk was doing here.

"Forget that," Veronica said, "we've got company—a lot of company."

30.

Adranos Facility

"Door's locked, right?" Alex kept his eyes on the door handle, hoping... but then his heart leapt as he saw it turning—the full 90 degrees.

Veronica brandished the knife and crouched, preparing for the fight of her life.

"Someone's unlocked the door!"

"Impossible."

"Goddamned, Xander!"

The door rattled, the handle slid back up, and more thumps hit the other side. Alex was suddenly a blur in Veronica's vision, rushing to the large filing cabinet beside the door. He shoved, but it wouldn't budge...

The door jammed, rattled, and then the handle turned again...

"Alex..." Veronica would never get there in time to help.

"Hang on." He turned, pressed his back against the cabinet and shoved backwards. It tilted, and with one more surge, if fell back, toppled and landed with a huge thud just as the door started to open. A couple of inches, and bloodied, scaly fingers emerged in the crack, pushing.

Alex regained his footing and joined Veronica. "That won't hold them long."

"Already working on a plan."

"Does it involve something other than us getting eaten?"

Veronica kept scanning the room, trying to keep her attention away from the door—and the increasing number of gruesome-looking hands appearing to join the others pushing, shoving. "I think I might be able to arrange that."

She rushed to the left side of the room, leapt over a desk and bent down beside a vent grate. Brought out the Ka-Bar knife and fit it in the first screw slot. "You've got to buy me some time!"

Alex nodded, but said without a lot of confidence: "Yeah, I'm on it."

He rushed the door, shoving against the cabinet just as the door buckled with a fresh surge from the other side.

This wasn't going to be fun.

\#

After minutes that seemed more like hours, and just as Alex felt his muscles giving way, Veronica shouted, "Done!"

The crack between the door and the frame had widened to an almost two-foot fissure, and snarling demonic faces in a frenzy of snapping teeth tried to push through.

"Get in there," Alex yelled. "I'm right behind you."

He shoved against the barrier one last time, then spun and ran. Her feet just kicked out of view as he leapt over some debris, stepped on the grate and ducked to get inside—

Just as the barrier was thrust away and the sea of zombies flooded in. Alex gave a glance to the grate and debated whether he could possibly grab it and wedge it sideways in the vent to stop their pursuit, but terror quickly dissolved that idea.

He barely had enough time to dive in and scamper forward, yanking back his legs just as he felt fingernails scraping for purchase on his boots. He kicked back, heard something squishy crack, followed by a snarl, and then he was scrambling right up to Veronica's feet as she crawled ahead.

"Hurry!" she shouted as she disappeared around a bend.

"We've got a crowd following us!"

"Figured that! Here, go that way!" She pointed to the left side of the T.

Alex crawled around the bend, awkwardly twisted his body, and suddenly fought a massive bout of claustrophobia to go along with the terror of zombie pursuit. He pulled his feet back just as the first undead soldier—sporting a crew cut above the reptilian scales and ridges along the center of his forehead—wriggled into the opening. It was so focused on its prey—Alex—that the zombie didn't notice Veronica around the other corner, ready with the knife. She brought it around in a backhanded sideways jab, directly into the forehead ridge, so the tip speared out the back of the thing's skull.

It jittered and gasped and made a sound like a snake's hiss, and then seemed to deflate and just sag to the ground. She pulled out the knife, squeezed herself past the body and joined Alex.

"Uh," he said, "the others are—"

"I see 'em." Veronica brought up her knees and kicked the dead creature's shoulders, shoving the body back and having it buckle upwards. The next zombie charged into its dead brother and tried to reach around it. Snarling, it thrashed, pushed, and scrambled for a few inches.

"That won't hold them," Alex said.

"Give me some credit," she replied as she kicked out again, shoving both of them back, and then pulling back her legs and leaning forward, readying herself. The zombie, enraged, pushed back again expecting resistance, but now tumbled ahead over its mate. It slid and landed headfirst, its body over the other corpse, and now face down.

"Too easy," Veronica said, bringing the knife around sideways, crunching through the zombie's left temple. She twisted one direction then the next for good measure, and then withdrew the knife. She wiped it clean on the soldier's sweater.

Alex's head appeared next to hers and they both watched through the gaps of the dead bodies as the pursuing zombies tried to get in, squeezing into the vent single file. The next lead zombie was up against the barricade of its two fallen brethren, and couldn't force its way through or get around the limbs and torsos lodged in the narrow ductwork.

Alex cleared his throat. "Think they're smart enough to back up and pull out the bodies?"

"Negative," Veronica said. "They're going to keep bashing up against this thing till eternity comes or they run out of juice."

Nodding, Alex looked away from the spectacle and back the only way they had left to go. "Where does this lead, do you think?"

Veronica shrugged. "Somewhere better than the way we've just come, and that's all that matters." She gripped the knife, slid around Alex—pleasantly close, until their faces were just inches apart and their eyes met for a brief second and he felt her sinewy body glide over his—and then she was past him.

"Let's move," she said. "Tight spaces bother me."

Alex watched her body wriggle ahead into the darkness. He swallowed hard, and for a moment the sound of furious clawing and growling and hissing behind him vanished in the thumping of his heart echoing through the ventilation corridors.

\#

Veronica almost forgot Alex was there, until the scrambling sound of his boots and the buttons on his jacket scraping the metal made her turn and hiss, "Quiet!"

As he froze, she peered down again through the slats, into a large chamber that looked like a control room. Multiple monitors, some of which Veronica could barely see from this vantage point, revealed images of the compound's exterior and interior. Computer terminals and gauges and monitors, and there at the center, leaning forward, madly searching the screens—stood Xander Dyson.

Her heart leapt and her blood seethed.

He was studying the screens, checking one then another. On the larger monitor, cameras tracked a firefight in the courtyard— where four soldiers pinned behind a makeshift barrier were blasting away at a horde of fast-moving zombies that had once been their colleagues. Before the screen shifted, Veronica thought she caught a glimpse of something enormous moving in the foliage behind the fence at their backs, something with javelin-sized teeth and a gaping mouth.

Another monitor with split screens showed various scenes from the inside of the facility: blood soaked walls, empty corridors, a lone white-jacketed zombie furiously butting its bloody head against an unyielding door. Another screen showed a woman—one of the administrators no doubt—spread-eagled on a table, being rapidly devoured by six feasting coworkers, while it seemed she was still alive, mouthing silent screams.

Xander impassively hit a button and changed the screen again.

I bet I know what he's looking for, Veronica thought as she brought the knife around slowly and started to work on one of the two screws for the grate.

"Screw that," Alex whispered, and Veronica paused at the horrible pun. She looked back and saw him turning himself just enough to curl his knees to his chest. "Get ready."

"What, no—!"

She glanced down, even as Xander cocked his head. *He's heard, now we're screwed...*

In the next instant, as Alex's boots kicked at welded seams in the vent, it was like gravity had just kicked in on a shuttle mission and they both tumbled back and dropped as the duct broke apart in the middle and spilled them out into the control room.

Veronica, twisted up in her own legs, landed hard on her side, cushioned only somewhat as the duct worked like a slide to dump her out behind the main desk. Alex wasn't so lucky, crunching hard onto a flat monitor, hitting his ribs on the edge of the desk and slamming to the floor.

He grunted and tried to get up fast and get the jump on Xander, except—Veronica beat him to it. She slid over the desk and in a flash, had a knife at the scientist's throat...

He had a sub-M5 pressed against her gut, and a smile on his face.

"I hate when unwanted guests drop in, but in this case I'll make an exception. Saves me the trouble of making sure the zombies finish you."

31.

Veronica still could have taken him, she was sure. Maybe suffered a reactionary gut shot in the process as she slit his throat, but she could have taken him. Still, she hesitated. Again and again, she lost. In a heartbeat, Xander spun his free hand around and disarmed her by twisting her wrist and squeezing the bones in her hand so hard she dropped the knife.

A backhand slap sent her reeling. She collided with Alex as he tried to stand.

Then the gun was trained on them both.

"Stay," Xander commanded, like he spoke to a pair of unruly puppies.

"What the hell are you going to do?" Alex asked, his hands on Veronica's shoulders, keeping her from falling, and helping himself up. He gingerly put weight on his left leg. "In case you hadn't noticed, things have gone to hell pretty damn fast around here."

"Your boss won't be too happy," Veronica added, pointing to the screen. "His investment here, I'd say, is pretty much fucked."

Xander never lost his smile. Then he shrugged. "Oh, I don't know about that. I think with these cameras rolling and recording, we've just got ourselves some major top notch marketing material, showcasing exactly the extent of our product's capabilities. Prospective buyers couldn't ask for a better demonstration."

Veronica hissed, "You're sick."

"No," Xander said. "That would be your boyfriend's Dad, and all those other poor saps out there."

Alex winced.

Glancing at the nearest screen, Veronica now saw the previous view of the exterior, and a shattered section of the fence, where a blur of something huge moved out of sight, leaving behind several grisly pieces of what had been soldiers.

"Now," he said, "what to do with you?"

Alex shook himself off. "Well, trying to get us eaten didn't work out so well, and now we're in here with you, on an island overrun with these things plus a trio of prehistoric monstrosities, so can I make a suggestion?"

Xander shrugged. "No. I'm not working with you and we're not in this together."

Veronica rubbed her jaw, and then clenched her hands into fists. "We're in agreement there."

Alex shook his head. "So we're to be zombie bait again, is that it?"

Xander was about to reply when the main screen blinked off, fizzled, and then sparked back—with an image of DeKirk's looming face.

"Ah," he said, glancing around the scope of the periphery, "Xander. Figured you'd be in the control room, and you've brought friends! How quaint."

"'Sup, Mel?" Alex said, trying to downplay his nervousness and possibly to get Xander to drop his guard. With him distracted now with DeKirk, it was two against one, and they could take him. *Just wait for the right opportunity...*

"Mr. DeKirk," Xander bowed to the screen, but kept his eye on the captives. "I'm sorry to report that your security here on the island has been rather..."

"Not up to the task?" Alex supplied.

DeKirk shot him a sharp look and Xander shook the gun toward him. "As I was saying, sir, there may be need for...additional forces." Xander glanced to one of the other screens where the ridge of the *T. rex's* head broke through a canopy of trees outside the fence to roar at the clouds. "...including air support."

DeKirk never blinked. "Despite what I've seen from the feeds—and yes I have been glued to the happenings like this was the Moon Landing—none of this particularly worries me. That's why I chose to send you to an isolated private island, after all. It's contained. *You're contained.*"

Xander tensed. "Your foresight has indeed been uncanny, as always sir, but there's still the matter of control. Your product—this discovery of a lifetime—has some inherently chaotic flaws."

DeKirk glanced off-screen as if reviewing some footage. "Nothing insurmountable. At least not compared with the potential."

Veronica stepped into view. Arms at her side, heart pounding. This was it, the first time she could finally address her quarry. "And what, exactly, is that potential?"

DeKirk just smiled. "And who is this lovely vision?"

Xander was about to speak when DeKirk held up his hand. "Just a sec, running some facial recognition software. Should have our answer in a moment."

Oh shit, Veronica thought. Cover about to be blown, she looked down and held her hand over her face.

"Sorry, too late, Miss... Winters...Veronica." DeKirk smiled, and then directed a glare to Xander. "You let a CIA agent into your midst? I see you have a gun, Xander. What, do you want to give her a chance to take you out or call for help? You realize she's trained seven ways from Sunday in how to kill people a lot more dangerous than you? I'm sort of surprised she hasn't eliminated you already. Are you going to give a long monologue and then leave the room so she can escape and kill you later?"

Xander reddened, but then tapped his gun. "I think we're covered there."

"Don't take anything for granted," DeKirk snapped. "I never have. Which is why I've made it this far. You've slipped up again."

Xander grit his teeth. "I released her into a horde of zombies. What more do you want? She snuck aboard *your* damn boat before I even got there."

"Regardless," DeKirk said, "I've had a communications dampener on the island for years. For security purposes. Only I have direct access. I see everything, know everything."

Veronica lifted her chin and stared at the image of the man—the monster—she had come to know only too well. "Great. Well, even gods can fall. And this... whatever the hell you have here, it's way beyond your control. There's no hope to contain it, or use it for anything profitable. These are no zoological attractions to line up in some park for the world's entertainment. They're voracious, unstoppable predators who—oh by the way—will turn anything they don't kill outright into reptilian zombie things until there's an unstoppable army—"

DeKirk started nodding vigorously about halfway through her speech, and when she finally noticed, she stopped. Alex took a step behind her. "Oh Jesus, I think that's what he freakin' wants."

"An army?" Xander perked up. "Sir, if you'd wait a moment. I've been in here analyzing the biology of these things. The capabilities and characteristics of the virus."

"Time well spent, I'm sure." DeKirk feigned a yawn.

Xander continued unfazed. "We now know how fast the virus replicates, how there's no defense against it, especially after the host is already dead. I've analyzed how it effectively establishes control in the brain stem and not only reanimates the body's muscles and tissues, but also rearranges and splices some reptilian-saurian DNA strands into the host's to create a nastier, tough-skinned predator with superhuman senses, reflexes and...well, appetites."

"Everything you're saying only makes me more certain that I'm on the right path," DeKirk said.

Xander sighed, almost exasperated. "So, after I found myself essentially trapped in here against a growing horde outside, all of them wanting to devour me, and since I had no desire to be zombie food or to become one of them... I started working on a cure."

DeKirk raised his left eyebrow. Alex and Veronica stiffened. The floor now his, Xander began again.

"Well, not a cure, per se, but more of what I'd expect is the reason you brought me here." Xander licked his lips. "A failsafe."

"Yes, I'm aware of your specialty and I'm happy to see you didn't disappoint when placed in a scenario that might stimulate your talents."

"Okay...." Xander eyed him carefully. "I'm not sure if that means you're just happy the events transpired in such a way as they did, or if you actually had a hand in said events, but in either case, you're right. I rose to the occasion. Tested various possibilities, ran a few thousand computer simulations to determine how the virus would interact with certain synthesized enzymes. I believe I've found one that will break down the virus, eliminate it completely."

DeKirk pulled away, his expression darkening. "I already know all this. My techs shadowed your laptop, captured every keystroke and download."

Xander swallowed, and then shrugged. "Then you should also know that we don't have the required inputs here on this island."

"Yes, I do know that. Because your research is now *my* research. If you've found the cure, or the *failsafe*—we'll know soon enough. Congratulations will be in order. It's all I hoped for from you. Let me worry about the details from here on out."

"But there's more," Xander said, thinking fast, seeing where this road was ending. "There's more I didn't share, lots more up here!" He tapped his forehead, realizing that to DeKirk his brain might now represent little more than potential zombie nourishment.

"Give it up," Alex whispered behind his back, "you've lost your chance."

"No, wait," Xander pointed the gun at them again, and then leaned toward the screen. "I know how I can synthesize it from here, and your techs will be able to, also, I'm sure. With the right procedures and some trial and error, but you really need more than an antidote. You need a reliable method of *transfer*. What are you going to do, try to shoot hypos full of the stuff into them?" He laughed. "Just try breaking through their scales with a needle."

"True," Veronica said. "Ka-Bar blade barely does the trick."

"Fill some hollow-point rounds with it," Alex offered. Xander shot him a death glare.

DeKirk cleared his throat. "I was thinking gas grenades myself. Or drop it like pesticide from a crop duster plane."

Xander faced the screen again. "Too slow and unreliable once you factor in wind and mobile targets."

"So then, what other options," DeKirk continued, "might you have rattling around in your oh-so-brilliant brain? So far, I actually favor the hollow-point idea." He shot the dreadlocked environmentalist an appraising stare. Xander also looked at Alex, his face paling as he realized his importance to DeKirk was rapidly waning.

"Microchips." Xander stood back, rubbing a finger nervously against the gun. "That's all I'm going to say, but there's a transfer method we could use to outfit healthy individuals at the outset, before the introduction of the virus. Then, after they've turned, they do their thing, serve their purpose and before they go on to consume more than you want or turn the whole population into yellow eyed freaks, we click a button that triggers a micro-explosion in the brain stem, like an aneurism, and terminate their asses."

DeKirk smiled. "Now *that*, Dr. Dyson, is something I might be willing to wait around for. Great minds do think alike, however, and as it turns out, I've had my people working on just such prototypes. But of course, I realize your product will be so much more efficient and of demonstrably higher quality, am I right?"

Xander nodded with an enthusiasm that was pathetically close to desperation.

"So I'll make a deal with you."

"Okay. What is it?"

DeKirk leaned in closer. "Survive the next twenty-four hours, and when my rescue-clean up team arrives this time tomorrow, they'll pick you up and we can collaborate on your technology and build on it to continue our partnership."

"Twenty four *hours*," Xander mused, listening to the muffled sounds of cacophony outside the walls of the room. "That's... going to be difficult. Can't you fly any faster?"

"It's all about the scenery, my friend, and the journey. Now, I forgot to mention. If you're going to survive, you'll have to do it... out there."

"What do you mean?"

DeKirk looked away and his arm reached beyond the view, fingers tapping some buttons. "I'm opening up all the exterior doors and unlocking every door inside the facility."

"What? Sir—"

Alex clenched his fists, hoping to buy some time, and to speak before DeKirk could turn off the connection. "What the hell do you hope to accomplish with all this? My Dad's discovery— you've seen what it can do, the unexpected horrors it's released in just under twelve hours..."

DeKirk's eyes softened. "Yes, but it wasn't unexpected. In fact, I've had a little theory for quite some time now. I never did buy into the whole asteroid-killed-the-dinosaurs explanation. Scientists looked at all the evidence of violence among the fossils and concluded that food supplies were vastly diminished after some cosmic event, leading to more aggression and intra-species violence—much as what might happen if our own crops failed."

"Cannibalism," Xander said.

"Yes. So much so that the more obvious interpretation would be that these dinosaurs literally ate each other to extinction. Screw the asteroid, it was this... and now I know exactly what drove them to it. A parasite. One glorious, devilish little bug that can bring down the mightiest of species. Including our own."

He let out one more long sigh. "My whole life, in fact, has led to this moment." He leaned back, folding his arms and closing his eyes. "I've been chosen, you see. I've always been an outsider, standing above the world, watching it slide into chaos and misery, wishing there was something I could do. With all my talents, with my resources and perspective. Knowing, hoping, that in time I'd be given the tools to bear out such change, and this...this now is validation of my mission." He opened his eyes and leaned forward, his face filling the entire screen. "There's one thing you missed, Xander, in your rush to find a cure."

"And what is that?" Xander hefted the gun, tensing his fingers on the trigger as if he wished he could shoot DeKirk through the screen.

"You missed the following extrapolation: that this virus, if it could be modified, could offer certain...benefits."

"Modified how?"

"To keep all the good bits like strength and sensory improvement, speed and longevity—if not downright immortality. Imagine if you could block the parasite's ability to take over the brain stem, to overcome the host's consciousness. If someone...if *I* could be transformed, and yet still be..."

"In control..." Xander whispered it. "All the benefits of being a zombie—the near indestructibility—without the drawbacks—the mindlessness and the rotting flesh."

"*Yes.*" DeKirk leaned back. "I intend to become—as you said yourself Miss Winters...a God."

She shook her head and glared at him. "Yeah, well God or not, a bullet to your head will still put you down. Come out here for a little stay on your Zombie Island Retreat, we'll see how immortal you are." She was stalling, hoping to buy them a way out. "And oh, I got a message off on the ship. They're coming for you."

DeKirk laughed. "I'm sorry, but I know you didn't, and even had you managed it, help wouldn't come in time. Now, goodbye Xander. Goodbye Alex and Veronica. I expect to see you again, but not…quite in your same senses."

DeKirk's dark laughter filled the room until he killed the connection.

32.

Alex moved closer to Xander. "Your boss is a lunatic, you realize."

"I'm aware of that fact," Xander said. "Had my suspicions before, but really, what geniuses aren't a little insane?"

"Um... Einstein?"

"Shut up," Veronica hissed. "What are you doing?" The screens had returned to their surveillance mode—revealing swarms of zombies running headlong toward the facility, lured by the open doors. The hallways were filling with undead, moving with deliberate speed, as if sniffing them out, eager to explore new territory.

"We don't have much time," she said, "either shoot us or figure something out."

"I'd actually prefer getting shot," Alex said, watching the horde converge from various entrance points, seeing them running up stairs, drooling, snapping at each other, yet moving with a singular purpose, like a colony of ants.

Xander's screen was different—showing scrolling lines of code on one side, offset against facility schematics on the other. "It may still come to that but for now, I need you. We need each other."

"Afraid you'd say that," Veronica said. "I won't—"

"Whatever you're doing," Alex interrupted, "please do it fast, or like I said, shoot us, 'cuz the other option is we open that door and run for it."

"Never make it, kid. Not without... Here, got it!" He pointed at the screen, traced a line from one central-looking rounded room, down one section, a right then a left to a door. He hefted the gun. "Okay, munitions room one floor down, a right and a left."

"Munitions..."

"Yeah," Xander said, "and I know, I'm going to have to trust you won't blow a hole in my back."

"Wouldn't dream of it," Veronica said, and then added: "I'd shoot you in the leg and let the zombies eat you piece by piece."

"Lovely," Xander said, running to the door. He opened it and peeked outside. Alex could hear the trampling of feet coming from the hall to the left.

Xander pushed out into the hall and aimed toward the noise. "I'll slow them down. You run for the exit sign, then into the stairwell and down. It should be clear. I'll be right behind you."

Alex didn't need to be told twice. He ran, with Veronica at his side. Gunshots roared at their backs, and they flinched, fully expecting a double-cross.

Every step closer and still no bullets in their spines, Alex skidded to a stop at the door. More snarling and rapidly thumping feet came from this direction. "Oh shit, Xander?"

Veronica pushed past him and opened the exit door. "Come on!"

A lab-coat wearing zombie hurtled around the far corner, bounced off a wall and came tearing at Alex, waving its arms frantically and snapping its jaws—then its head exploded in a microburst of gunfire.

Xander ran past him into the stairwell, shouting back. "Thought the plan was clear, no stopping!"

Alex followed, hauled the door closed, and ran after Xander and Veronica. "Um, this part of the plan was Phase One, what's Phase Two?"

They rounded the bend, and then got to the lower level's door. Veronica backed away after placing her ear on the surface. "Your move," she said to Xander, nodding to the gun. "We may have guests on the other—"

Xander moved into position. He nodded for Veronica to get ready to pull the door open. From up one level they heard sounds of clawing and banging at the door. The zombies would figure it out in a moment and rush down upon them, attacking from both directions.

"Here we go," Xander said, checking his clip.

"Want me to take that?" Veronica asked.

"You'll get some hardware soon enough. Stay focused."

"Um..." Alex hung back, glancing up. He felt useless, dead weight.

That all changed with the next words out of Xander's mouth, before Veronica flung open the door and they rushed into the thick of battle.

"Be ready, kid, you're up soon. Phase Two? It's to fight our way back up the stairs to the roof. There's a helicopter, and I'm hoping you have enough skill to fly us the hell out of here."

#

Veronica had to admit, for a biochemist nerd, Xander was pretty dead-on with a gun, and that was a good thing when only a headshot would suffice, A real good thing. He took down two raging ex-soldiers to their immediate left as he exited the stairwell, then shot down three in quick succession on the other side. Veronica saw her chance—a .45 clipped to one of the zombie guard's belts—and snagged it just in time.

Xander, on her right, mowed down another four charging creatures, sweeping at head level and blasting their skulls open, while she covered them from the left, firing ten rounds at the five lurching figures as they marched around the corner like dumb AIs in a shooter video game.

In the ensuing silence, they heard rumbling steps and echoes of hungry wailing somewhere else on the level. The corridor was littered with zombie corpses and the walls were sprayed with gore and bullet holes, but for now, they were safe.

They approached the munitions door. It had a hand print scanner as well as a key code entry system.

Alex tried the door and breathed out in relief as it opened right up. "I guess we have DeKirk's overzealous sense of drama to thank for this."

"Just get in," Xander said, turning and giving the hallway a once-over as he checked his gun's magazine—one round left. "And gear up. This was just a prelude to the fight we're going to have getting to the roof."

Alex stood there in awe—not so much because of the shelves and racks full of ammo, weaponry and stacks and stacks of guns, grenades, crossbows and body armor and helmets—but because of Veronica's sudden burst of unbridled enthusiasm.

She slung a heavy automatic rifle over her left shoulder, and once she was done stuffing magazines into her pockets and a knapsack, she grabbed several handfuls of grenades and set them inside on top. She zipped up and slung that over the same shoulder before grabbing, cocking, and loading two stainless steel .45 handguns and slipping them into the back of her jeans. She considered the crossbow for a moment, hefting it, and then tossed it to Alex.

"Here you go, Daryl."

Alex fumbled with it and tried to fathom how to load it when Xander reached in, plucked it from his grasp and threw it to the floor. "Quit kidding around. This isn't *Walking Dead,* let's not alert them with loud noises' bullshit. They know where we are— whether its smell or superhuman hearing or fucking ESP. Whatever it is, we need firepower. We need it fast and loud. Gather that gun there, and... well hello, baby!"

He slung the M5 over his shoulder and made his way to a green crate with Asian lettering. "Oh, I really hope my translation is right, and no one took this out already..."

The crate opened, and he whistled. "There you are." He reached in with both hands, and straightened up, setting the back end of a cylindrical weapon over his right shoulder while he turned and aimed through the sight on the end.

"Bazooka?" Alex whispered.

"RPG," Veronica said. "Looks to be circa nineteen-eighty. What was this, some hidden military base for the Japanese?"

"Koreans," Xander corrected, "and...there they are. He pulled out a square sack and looked inside. "Four rockets, in prime condition." He grinned like a teenager just given the keys to a sports car. "Let's gear up. We've got a flight to catch...and some dinosaurs to kill if we get the chance."

Veronica stared at her enemy, this cold calculating killer, and Alex could tell she was weighing her options, trying to judge which threat to take out and when. Whether to just draw those .45s and shoot Xander full of holes right now, or to rely on his knowledge of the facility to get them out.

Logic apparently won out—either that, Alex thought, or she was just biding her time, waiting for a more fitting moment to exact her revenge. Whatever the case, Alex had to focus. He'd been defenseless up to this point, and lucky. No more. He licked his lips, surveying the room for whatever was left for him.

"Just take a damn AK," Xander said, "and one of those .45s, and let's move."

33.

The stairwell was a little more crowded than when they left it, and the gunfire echoed painfully in the narrow quarters. At least it blocked out the hideous sound the zombies made: the hissing, scratching and gnashing of teeth that went with the high-pitched cries of insatiable hunger and brutal bloodlust.

Veronica took the lower section and Xander started to work clearing the upper stairs, while Alex stood at the door, guarding their flank. His hands trembled as the AK-47's barrel swept back and forth, seeking targets in either direction, although Alex feared it would take him the whole clip before he would be able to hit something's head. Wishing he had time for practice, all he could think about now was getting to that roof, and then…whether or not he could actually pilot a freakin' helicopter.

It had to be close to flying a prop plane, right?

Deal with that when you get there, he thought, flinching with every burst of fire at his back, every guttural cry, every scream from Veronica—who probably couldn't even hear her own battle cry over the explosive echoing rounds.

The coast clear, he risked a glance over his shoulder and immediately spun around. Veronica was out of ammo, bending over to reach for another magazine. She had forgotten about the guns at her back—or else figured her best bet was still the rapid-fire automatic, but she wasn't going to make it.

Xander was busy mowing down a seemingly endless onslaught of ex-doctors, janitors and soldiers pouring down the stairs, clambering over the comrades, so he couldn't help. Alex swung the AK around and aimed. Took a deep breath and just as he focused on the first pair of yellow eyes belonging to a bald, freakishly heavy ex-scientist, he felt his finger tighten and pull—as enthusiastically as he could.

The recoil kicked back and he stumbled then righted himself, ready for another shot, even if he would just get off a burst at the thing's chest to knock it back. When he looked back, the overweight zombie was toppling backwards, a neat chunk of its skull blown away and gore spilling out.

"Nice shot," Veronica said, slamming home another magazine before she casually turned and blasted through another wave of undead. Alex stepped in, braced himself and fired off a half dozen more rounds, two of them connecting, before aiming up the stairs and taking out one more, riddling bullets up its chest before connecting with its chin, and then punching through its open mouth.

Xander shot one more with a .45 as it rounded the bend, gnashing at them. When it was down he gave Alex a nod. "Thanks for the assist, kid. Now let's move."

Alex chose his spots without much concern, stepping on the backs and chests of bloodied corpses, trying to get to the clearer stairs beyond. Veronica followed, but Alex hesitated, glancing at a few of the faces on these stairs, then below.

"What are you doing, kid, looking for loose change?"

Alex swallowed hard, still trying to peek around all the shattered skulls and look for eyes that held some familiarity. "Looking for my Dad."

Veronica paused. Xander sighed and shook his gun in a waving motion. "Haven't seen him in this bunch, so stop wasting time."

"Where did you last see him?"

"Outside, okay? He kind of…went berserk and busted free after wasting a few guards. I opened the lab door and let him out. He's probably…" Xander made a shooing motion over his shoulder. "Out in the world somewhere, hopefully roaming free, doing what zombies do."

Shaking his head, Alex started after them. "I'm not giving up on him. He can fight this, and it was just an extremity wound."

"From a freakin' dinosaur," Xander snapped, skipping to an empty stair, and then running around. "Let's pick up the pace, I hear them."

Alex did too—down the stairs below them. Doors banging against walls, more trampling feet. *Definitely brought by the gunfire,* he thought. *The hell with whatever other senses they've got.*

"Uh… one last question."

"Come on," Xander called from above, exasperated.

Alex stopped in mid-step, seeing a tear in his boot, and then looking at all that blood on the floor, among the corpses. *Hell, on my own clothes...* "When you studied this virus thing, did you happen to conclude anything about like...how it infects somebody?"

Xander's head peeked over the railing. "What?"

"Well, you looked in the microscope and saw the microbes in my Dad's blood, just swimming around, so those things—they've got to be everywhere, right? And if they touch our skin, or get in a cut, or our eyes, or we breathe them in..."

"Jesus. You a germophobe or something? That's not how it works. They're activated through enzymes in the host's saliva."

Alex frowned. "So...we have to be bitten?"

"Yes!" Veronica shouted, picking up the logic faster. "Just step on 'em, and get the hell up here."

Alex moved his foot, but stretched and found a clear spot, then jumped over the remaining heap of bodies to land on another empty space. *Taking no chances.*

He ran after them.

34.

Veronica burst out onto the roof, wincing against the intense sunlight bearing down from a crystal blue, cloudless sky. It took her eyes a few moments to adjust and get her bearings, and then Alex was all but smashing into her.

"They're coming! Right behind me!"

She turned, pulled the door shut and looked around, cursing. Grabbed Alex's rifle and slid the barrel through the handle slot, flush against the external wall, then backed away. Something slammed into the door from the other side, and a barrage of thumps and howls of frustration followed as the creatures threw themselves against the door and tried pulling it and pushing to no avail. The gun held.

"Okay, let's pray that keeps them out. Now..." She turned and Xander was already heading toward the landing pad—a giant painted X on a flat concrete section in the center of the roof. The helicopter itself was painted white with red stripes, and looked shiny but a little beat up, with scratches and dents along the outside edge and nicks in the windshield.

"All ready for you, kid," Xander called when he got to the door and peered inside. "Keys in, locked and loaded, or in this case..." he opened the door, "...unlocked. Get in and get it going, we'll stand guard." He motioned Veronica to the north edge of the roof as he slung the RPG's strap over his right shoulder, took out the M5 and reloaded it, heading toward the south edge.

Veronica watched Xander as she gripped the AK in her hands, raising it, then pointing it in his direction, wavering. Did she still need him? He had just turned his back on her. Was he that confident? Alex was getting in the cockpit. Looking like a lost, scared puppy, but if he could fly that thing...

She tensed, about to aim. It was the perfect chance—shoot Xander down now, end all the pain and anguish. He more than deserved it, whether or not this was personal. Clearly justified, she just had to...

Something caught her attention and caused her to flinch, shifting her aim. The southern edge of the rooftop... beyond the edge she could only see a beautiful view of the Pacific stretching out into the lighter blue horizon, and off to the right, rising from the jagged hills and brush carpet, a smoking volcano.

Again, the sound of scrambling, hissing and scraping.

She approached, tensing, her feet nearing the edge. Behind her the chopper's engine turned, sparked, died. She heard Alex cursing, muffled behind the glass as he tried again.

Her feet neared the edge, where the sounds were getting stronger, more intense and *closer.*

Finally there, she looked back first, to see Xander patrolling the opposite edge, gun tip down. She watched him turn to the chopper and yell something disparaging at Alex—something lost in the ferocious hissing of the thing beneath her.

Snapping her head around, she leapt back out of sight, but not before a glimpse of the impossible: one of the Cryos, its ferocious snout and flaring crown only a few yards away.

Its dead dragon-like eyes locked on her, and she felt sixty million years of hunger and absolute ferocity wash over her senses, along with the revolting scent of blood and death that issued from the depths of its throat.

#

It hadn't climbed the building's four levels, but instead—if she could believe her eyes—it had ascended a mound made up of writhing, reaching, climbing zombies. Several dozens of them, all piled onto each other like ants working collectively, creating a ramp the Cryo just ran right up and ascended.

Still can't get up, she thought. Didn't build it high enough… yet.

That's when another influx of zombies tore around the corner. Heads up, they seemed to unerringly locate her on the roof's edge, and they ran. Two of them accelerated as if getting a burst of nitrous. They bounded up the ramp and leapt ten feet into the air— onto the tail and back of the Cryo...

Where they climbed up the spine of the creature, tensed, crouching at its neck and shoulders, eyes on her—

And they sprung…

Veronica fired as she fell backwards, strafing the first zombie in mid air, the slugs knocking him back, but still he landed on the edge in front of her. All the rounds had missed its head, and it rose in a flash, growling.

Her finger still on the trigger, she raised her aim, and this time blew its skull open, just in time to roll out of the way of the other leaper.

Again the engine cut, caught and then revved up, competing with the sound of her gun—and Xander's now, joining the action. She wasn't sure if it was her shot or his, or both, but the leaper's cheek blew apart and a hole punched through its temple simultaneously, taking him down.

She scrambled to her feet just as another zombie leapt into the air, arms spread wide.

This time Xander shot him twice in the face, and the mindless attacker fell in a heap at Veronica's feet.

"How the hell are they climbing?" he shouted, joining her side.

"You don't want to look." Veronica pointed over the side, where now the Cryo was doing a little hopping dance, allowing more and more zombies to jump onto the pile so it could step on their bodies and raise itself up.

"Holy shit," Xander said, returning the M5 to its strap around his shoulder—and taking out the RPG. He checked the rocked magazine, clicked the release, and lined up a shot. "Stay still you son of a—"

"Wait!" Veronica yelled and tried to deflect the shot. "You'll blow open the—"

The rocket streaked out in a blast that went wide by a few feet, missing the Cryo's head but tunneling between its forearms, where another zombie had been climbing under its neck. The explosion knocked Veronica back into Xander, who dropped the RPG and scrambled to catch it before it rolled off the side.

"What the hell, bitch? I had it!"

Veronica got up fast, gun ready, pointing at his face. "You idiot! The explosion could have… Oh shit…" She looked down, and tore her eyes away from the sight of the Cryo writhing on the ground below, its chest cavity torn open, its rib cage blasted apart, internal organs sliding to the dirt, its lower jaw demolished and smoking, blackened tongue wriggling—but still trying to get up.

She looked at the hole in the side of the building, a hole that enlarged as she watched, collapsing a full quarter of the roof.

She backed away, as did Xander, backed almost to the western edge, until they were sure they were safe from further collapse. Still she couldn't look away, couldn't move or respond enough to raise the gun until it was almost too late.

The floor below them was now exposed. A floor full of hungry, crazed reptilian zombies who had—until now—been denied their prey.

They jumped for the roof.

#

Alex saw the explosion, saw the roof almost collapse completely, concrete tumbling away and supports failing, and he had a moment's terror where all he could think was: *get this bird off the ground or you're going to be buried in it...*

He grabbed the collective pitch, the stick-lever on his left, turned a few dials, flicked the release switches—, and prayed. Pulled back and felt the helicopter ease up, getting the landing skids off the roof, then it lurched backwards—and stalled like it got too much clutch.

It slammed back down onto the roof, then the engine caught and it again roared into life. He looked up and out the cockpit window and saw thankfully that the damage to the structure at least was over, and limited to the farther section of the collapsed roof. That was the good news. The bad news was that a countless rush of zombies were climbing, leaping and running across the remainder of the roof, chasing after Veronica and Xander who were now sprinting desperately for the chopper. They'd given up on all but a few backwards bursts of fire that did nothing to slow down the horde.

Shit, shit, get this working!

It was all up to him now.

He leaned over, unlatched the door, and kicked it open for them as Xander shouted, "Get it off the ground, kid!"

Alex pulled back on the stick, gentler this time. It was going to be tight. If he could raise it and keep the bird there about six feet up, they could leap and grab on to the landing skids like in the movies and—

They were almost there, leading the zombies by a shrinking distance.

Xander was faster and while the craft was still rising, he leapt into the passenger hold, then turned and let loose, emptying the M5's clip, spraying cover fire behind Veronica and over her head, knocking back the first row of ravenous creatures. Veronica skidded to a halt, ducking her head again as the chopper dipped, angled, and almost sheared off her head.

"Sorry!" Alex yelled. "Get in already!"

"Wait," she yelled. "Something..." She turned, aimed and fired in another strafing angle, blasting apart three more heads and ripping into legs and kneecaps, tripping up another row of attackers—attackers that suddenly slid to a halt as if listening to some distant orders. They turned their heads and looked backwards toward the gaping rooftop hole, and they started to move to the sides.

"What the hell are they doing?" Veronica shouted.

"Who cares?" Xander yelled back. "Come on, super agent, or I'm ordering the kid to leave you up here."

She backed up, right to the edge of the chopper, the wind from the rotors and the engine roaring in her ear, so she couldn't—and didn't—hear the other roar. The undamaged Cryo that had leapt over its wounded and writhing sister climbed the ramp, and in a huge bound, jumped to the bombed-out third level, then extended and locked its jaws around a jagged section of the rooftop and hauled itself up.

It shook itself, raised its head and, seeing the chopper, sniffed the air. As its crest changed color to a burning crimson, it bellowed out a challenge.

With the battalion of slavering zombies in its wake, following it like it was a medieval battle ram, it charged toward the chopper.

#

Veronica dove in as Alex fumbled with the controls. He shifted and pressed the wrong foot pedal at first, turning the nose toward the rampaging dinosaur. Then he tried to compensate by pulling back on the cycle pitch lever between his knees, but the nose was already tilting up. The tail rotor sparked against the rooftop surface and Alex cursed and grabbed the collective on his left side. He pulled that back to urge the craft upward.

It wobbled, tilted, and Xander and Veronica went tumbling to the side.

"*Kid!*"

"Trying," he shouted back.

"Try harder!" Veronica shouted, sitting upright through the next turn. She aimed at the Cryo—only twenty feet away now and gaining. She fired one burst, but then the helicopter rotated in a 180-degree spin and Alex cranked the lever in front of him, the chopper soaring ahead and over the roof.

He looked back—and wished he hadn't.

The Cryo, with three zombies riding maniacally on its back, never slowed down. Caught in bloodlust, it took two huge strides and then threw itself off the roof after its prey.

No, no, no! Alex was lost in the act of trying to control this unwieldy bird with a combination of both hands and feet, forgetting which limb did what. He gripped the collective lever, twisted and sped up just as he felt the jarring impact along the tail. A series of screams and gunshots and scraping sounds like giant nails on a metal chalkboard, and then the chopper was spinning and spinning.

Falling.

#

As they plummeted, the Cryo hung on with an unyielding grip like a mad pit bull at first, but then crunched through the metal, dropped from the tail, then caught on the landing skid.

"Son of a bitch!" Alex shouted, heaving back on the lever, trying to keep them from falling, even as the forward trajectory kept them moving ahead, still spinning. Victoria fired a volley of bullets out the open doors at the flailing beast, but then had to brace herself before slamming hard into a seat and flying into Xander against the inside wall.

Trying to work the pedals and counter the Cryo's weight, Alex screamed. "Not working! Can't shake it and we're going down!"

Not entirely true, he thought suddenly, seeing the landscape spinning around, and the research facility closing in. They had spun around, and now the acceleration took them back toward the building.

Gritting his teeth, Alex leaned back and to the side, tugging hard on the cyclic pitch. The chopper turned sharply just in time, its nose missing the wall, but the tail banked fast—and slammed the dinosaur right into the brick.

Take that! He thought in short-lived exuberance. The weight dropped as the screeching Cryo finally let go, stunned, and fell to the ground. Alex was about to yell back that they were free, but then he saw the gauges spinning, the warning lights flashing, and felt a pit in his stomach.

"We're going down."

#

"I thought you could fly!" Xander yelled, shoving Veronica aside and grabbing onto the nearest chair to brace himself. She scrambled to do the same.

"Single engine props!" Alex shouted back, kicking at the pedals and madly wrestling with the levers as the craft banked left, then right. It spun again in a wild 360 as it dropped, rose, and then dropped again. "Big freakin' difference!"

"Great, but a landing is a landing," Xander yelled. "Just get us down, preferably away from the—"

Maneuvering and precision were the last things in Alex's thoughts at the moment. All he could do was fight the rotors, bent tail, and eke out enough control to keep the skids level as they dropped. "Hang on, going to hit…!"

Alex winced and the others gripped the seats, expecting a massive crash… which never happened. Opening his eyes, Alex looked out on the courtyard, peppered with corpses and bullet-ridden vehicles and trees. He took a deep breath. They were on flat ground.

Near perfect landing. He smiled and started to turn to check on his passengers when his heart stopped.

The Cryo that he had knocked loose had fallen some fifty-feet, crushed a Jeep and rolled off, but now was up, shaking its head, straightening its spine and turning to face them.

It charged.

Not again! Alex looked down, wishing this was some military grade Apache with side mounted machine guns or missile launchers, but they had nothing. A sitting duck, wounded and flightless at this point. Worse than nothing, really.

"Guys?" He tried to yell over the roaring engine.

Their door was still open, but there was no way they could get a clean shot, even if they could react in time. Paralyzed, Alex couldn't move, couldn't cry out, couldn't do anything but sit and accept his fate as the beast screeched maniacally and bounded toward him, head on, head—

Alex blinked and saw it—and made a silent prayer that the angle was just right, that the height was lined up.

Unlike so many other times, with his father, his mother's cancer, his own life's wildly chaotic events...this prayer was granted.

The Cryo never knew what hit it. Charging upon the defenseless bird, it opened its jaws wide for a killing blow to tear open the metal skin and devour the occupants, when it ran directly into the whirling path of the main rotor blade.

It sheared off half the creature's jaw, and kept thunking into its carapace, slicing through its temple, ripping off the crown, then gouging through the right eye—and jamming nearly through the skull. There was a wretched squealing sound—whether from the rotors or the dying beast, Alex wasn't sure, but then the rotor assembly sparked and popped. The chopper itself tilted toward the beast until the blades snapped off and the craft rocked back with such force it tilted over and dropped hard on its side.

After shaking off the minor bruises, Alex climbed into the back, grabbed Veronica's arm and helped her up. Xander, rubbing his head, collected himself from a heap behind the cockpit.

They climbed up and out and jumped onto the ground. Alex stood, still staring at the twitching dinosaur with a helicopter blade lodged in its skull.

"Creative kill, kid." Xander slapped Alex on the back and shoved a backpack into his arms, bulging with grenades and spare magazines. "Carry this shit for us. Now..."

"We have to move," Veronica said in a deathly voice. She hefted the AK and pointed to the building, to the roof to be exact.

Where a crowd of zombies perched, wavering, watching, and then, like lemmings, one leapt, and the others followed.

#

A wave of bodies jumped from four flights up. They struck the ground—and each other. Some tipped or bounced off one another and fell headfirst—bursting their skulls on the ground, but the others landed upright enough that their craniums were spared.

"Please tell me," Alex said over the sound of the sputtering engine behind him, "that they're not getting up from that. Their legs are broken, and…"

"Shit." Veronica aimed at the first wave of reptilian zombies, rising and stumbling on legs with bones protruding from the split flesh. Some crawling, some hopping. None stopping.

"Xander?" Alex asked nervously. "Sorry about the flight disaster, but I hope you have a Plan B?"

Cocking the M5 and slamming another magazine home, Xander grumbled. "Yeah, I have a Plan B, but it sucks, and it involves getting to a Jeep, like that one there, across the courtyard."

He pointed over the heads of the onrushing zombies, across the way, where something else just lumbered into view from around the building's west corner.

Missing half its insides, its ribcage blackened and its neck torn out so that a flopping black gullet flapped in the wind, the other Cryo staggered toward them.

It screeched, and rushed them.

35.

"Screw this," Xander said, unleashing a spray of bullets at the wave of zombies charging from the right. Five went down in an accurate blast that ripped through skulls, eyes and cheekbones. "We're not going to make it."

Alex, gripping the bag, had an inspiration. It didn't happen often, but something clicked, and he remembered Tony, remembered his sacrifice—and his specialty. Digging into the bag, he turned and ran around the chopper. "Follow me!" He yelled back. "Get behind the chopper."

Veronica didn't need to be told, she was backing away anyway, firing at the onrushing dinosaur. Even though gimpy and nearly slipping on a flood of yellowish-red blood oozing from its wounds, it was gaining fast, marching ahead of the zombies—the ones that weren't getting picked off by Xander's shots.

Bullets scattered across the Cryo's body as Veronica led Xander back around the helicopter. She adjusted her aim, trying to hit the head, but the beast kept shaking and roaring, its bounding movements making it a hard target, even if the bullets could penetrate the thick skull.

Xander followed, emptying his clip at the horde that continued to grow as the rest of them leapt from the roof, then got back up, chasing and hungry.

"What are we doing? The Jeep is the other way."

"Got to clear the roadblocks first," Alex said. "Trust me, this'll work. I think…"

"Great."

"Or," said Veronica, emptying her clip, "Xander, you could load another rocket in that RPG and try to hit the thing's head this time!"

"Only one shell left," Xander said, "and not enough time to load it. Give me the time, and…"

"Don't need it." Alex led them back at an angle now, so that the rattling and busted chopper was in the path of the onrushing dinosaur as well as the rampaging crowd of zombies.

He smelled gas from the ruptured tank, hoped it was enough. He reached into the bag, yelled, "Run!" and pulled out a grenade. He yanked the pin and dropped it back in the bag with the other three grenades—then tossed it at the rear of the helicopter.

"Shit, kid!"

Now that they understood what he intended—they ran after him, turning and sprinting for the nearest cover—the only cover—a stack of crates and barrels near the back wall.

They didn't get there in time before the explosion.

Alex glanced back as a wave of kinetic energy roared through him. Shrapnel exploded in all directions and a piece of the tail rotor spun like a boomerang just over his head.

He had a glimpse of the Cryo's neck and head lording over the helicopter. It was in mid-jump, attempting to leap on the chopper's body and then over it in pursuit, but then the grenades exploded, igniting the fuel tank. All Hell roared out in fury. The chopper's insides gutted the dinosaur, shredding it tooth to claw, scattering bones and flesh high into the air in all directions. Metal pieces flung out in an enormous radius, fragmenting and blasting through the crowd of crazed zombies, annihilating their flesh and bones, the force pulverizing their bodies as the heat incinerated their flesh.

Veronica peeked up through her arms and Xander lifted his face from the dirt. Alex, on his knees, rose with his ears ringing painfully. He was bleeding from a half dozen cuts, so far all minor.

They surveyed the smoking ruin in front of them and watched as more pieces of the helicopter fell to the ground, interspersed with falling bits of dinosaur cartilage.

Xander pulled out the .45 and aimed as he walked ahead, firing a few rounds into dazed zombies' skulls. One was on fire, waving its arms in the wreckage, unable to get its bearings. Another dragged itself into their path on shattered legs.

Two more shots and the courtyard was quiet.

He and Veronica looked back to Alex.

"Good going," Veronica said, "even if you did blow up our ride off this rock."

Alex shrugged. "Wasn't fixable anyway. Hopefully, your buddy there has a good Plan B."

"Let's get to the Jeep," Xander said, "hotwire it, and start hauling ass out of here before the rest of this bunch smells us and comes after us. I'll explain on the way."

Veronica loaded another magazine as she followed behind Xander, aiming at his back.

Alex figured he'd better say something, or they were going to be back to two members in this team, the two without a plan. "And hey, let's not forget about—"

Behind him, the trees crunched, the wall shook and cracked, and a sound like a wrecking ball cut through the silence, just as the ringing in his ears had quieted.

"—*that.*" Alex whispered, backing away.

"Shit," Xander shouted. "Run!"

The wall split open and with a deafening roar, the *T. rex* burst through.

36.

Alex reached the Jeep first, but Xander got in and shoved him aside. He shook the RPG off his shoulder and thrust it in the back seat with Veronica, who leapt in, about to aim back with the AK.

"That won't do a thing against it!" Xander yelled.

"Maybe we should've run back inside," Alex offered, sitting helplessly—without even a weapon, just watching as Xander fumbled around for the key and luckily found it under the visor. "Sweet, I hate hotwiring."

Trying not to look as the ground trembled with each stomp of the seven-ton dinosaur roaring toward them, Alex fidgeted as the engine started—and stalled.

Veronica stood up, aimed anyway with the AK, and for all the good it would do—opened fire. Sparks flew off the *T. rex's* teeth.

The engine turned again, and this time caught. Xander thrust it in reverse and hauled back, and then out in a whiplash-inducing J-turn that propelled them just ahead of the dinosaur's snapping jaws. It swung its head down and roared at them.

Veronica screamed, leaned back against the inertia and emptied the clip. Bullets tore through the dinosaur's chest cavity, ripped up the tough hide and blasted out pieces of its thorax before again deflecting off teeth or being swallowed up in the gaping maw—where Alex saw the gruesome signs of recently devoured prey: tattered soldier's uniforms, an arm, and a partially chewed abdomen.

The Jeep kicked up clouds of dirt and obscured the view as it spun out and ripped free. Out of the compound and racing down the dirt trail, Xander banked hard and then accelerated and tore ahead, gaining distance between them and the pursuing beast.

The *T. rex* bounded after them, its dead eyes flashing in the low-level sun, shimmering red, feral and entirely remorseless. Its shoulder broke through the masonry on the side of the entrance and it kept going without so much as breaking stride.

"Faster," Veronica said, reloading, "and I'm out of ammo after this!"

"That's why I gave you the RPG!" Xander yelled back as he twisted the wheel, dodged an outcropping of boulders, and twisted shrubs lining an embankment. The volcano rose in their view through the windshield.

Veronica set the AK down and picked up the RPG, grabbed the case and reached inside for the last shell. The Jeep hit a hole and jarred her grasp and the rocket ammo almost slipped from her hand. She gripped it tighter, shooting a glare at Xander. "Loading it," she yelled, fitting it carefully into the slot.

The *T. rex* tore around the corner, almost slipped, then lowered its neck. It bared its monstrous teeth and picked up steam.

"So what the hell's our plan?" Alex asked, fastening his seatbelt.

Xander pointed way down into the valley, east of the volcano, where the road banked and Alex could just make out a small domed-shaped building at the end of a long, straight road.

"Is that—?"

"An airstrip! Yes, kid, you have good eyes. DeKirk kept quiet about it, but I checked when I first arrived. There's a plane there, resupplied only two days ago. Should be fueled and ready to go. It's a Cessna, something I hope you can actually keep aloft this time."

"Shut up, I know planes, not damn helicopters."

"Both of you shut up," Veronica yelled, "and drive straight so I can get a shot off."

Xander banked and accelerated again on the twisty road as it turned into a steep decline. "Your target's about forty feet high and twenty long. You can't miss, just aim and fire!"

"Trying for the damn head," Veronica shouted back, "and I haven't exactly had a lot of practice with this weapon back on the range at Langley!"

The ridge temporarily blocked her sight of their pursuer as they roared down the hill, but then it was there, airborne, leaping after them with surprising speed.

"We can just outrun it," Alex said. "It can't do over thirty, maybe forty if I remember right."

"Textbook theories don't count here," Xander said.

"I don't think," Veronica added, "that this creature read any of those books. It seems to be gaining!"

She aimed again, trying to keep her body steady through all the bumps and jolts.

"Oh *shit*," she heard Xander say as she felt a drag on the transmission and a slowing of the Jeep.

"You're not going to believe this!"

Alex looked back, his face deathly white. "Veronica... Fire— we're out of gas!"

#

She didn't even think, couldn't respond. She heard them arguing that maybe the gunfire had ruptured the gas tank and that's why they were now dead in the water, miles between them and the airstrip, miles between any cover except for some woods on their right, leading up the way to the volcano.

All she could do was line up the best shot she could, before the *T. rex* could get any closer, and fire.

The recoil slammed her back hard against the metal frame. She had the immediate fear that she had let the launch push her aim too high. Then a concussive roar blasted back at her, and a shotgun-like burst of blood, bone and gristle exploded past her and all over the Jeep. She dropped the RPG and covered herself with her arms, but with the ringing in her ears and the wave of nausea she at first assumed to be from the gore, she didn't realize the Jeep had gone partially airborne—its rear wheels lifted off the earth and the entire back half of the chassis spinning to the side. The proximity of the explosion tossed the decelerating vehicle sideways and around, and as it came down it crunched hard on the driver's side, tilted and—

"*Oh nonono!*" Xander yelled.

—The Jeep rocked hard on its side, stalled, then tipped onto its roll bars. Xander grunted as he fell hard on his left shoulder, but quickly recovered and scrambled out. Alex fumbled with his seatbelt, and then finally got it loose and wriggled free, bleeding from a few more cuts.

Dazed, Veronica lay on the ground, her neck at an awkward angle, the Jeep's cargo bed above her. She fought a rush of unconsciousness, but a nagging voice in the back of her head—one that sounded like Alex's voice—urged her to 'get the hell up!'

She blinked and actually let out a chuckle. *Why?* What was the point? It wasn't like they had anywhere to go. It wasn't like they weren't being hunted by an army of zombies racing after them down the road from the facility, hungry for their flesh, and it wasn't like the *T. rex* she just shot was dead, right?

Blinking again, she turned her head and dared to look.

"...get out, get out!" came the diminishing voices outside.

She laughed again, looking out the gap, right into the eyes of the prehistoric monstrosity, the beast that pulled back, revealing that she had indeed, missed its head.

It trilled at her, loud and piercing, yet full of frustration, and she saw why a moment later, when her gaze moved down and she saw it was lying on its left side, struggling to get up. Its right side was a different story, a sight to behold: from the initial chest cavity there was now an enormous smoking hole.

It roared, and its neck lunged forward, snapping at the Jeep and missing by a foot.

"Get out!" Alex hollered, this time closer, and followed by a barrage of gunfire. Bullets tore up the road, and then ripped into the beast's snout, between its eyes to scatter off the ridges on its skull.

The *T. rex* shrieked at them, shook its head and rocked side to side until it flipped—and started to rise.

Veronica finally cleared her head and got moving. She scrambled out, snagging her AK-47 at the last second, then—with a glance back at the struggling *T. rex*, ran after Xander and Alex, already bounding for the meager concealment of the woods.

She risked a backwards glance, just as the *T. rex* righted itself. It called out again as it sniffed the air and its head turned from the Jeep to the rain forest. Behind the beast, the road suddenly filled with movement.

Before the trees obscured her view, she saw the rush of blood-soaked bodies, the reptilian skin and diseased eyes that locked onto her with such hunger that her blood went cold.

As soon as Veronica had caught up to the others, leaping over brush and fallen trees as well as the odd volcanic rock, Alex yelled ahead to Xander: "What the hell is Plan C?"

37.

"Run!"

Xander bounded off through the forest away from the zombie horde and the closing *T. rex.* Alex and Veronica took off after him. The going was tricky, with hiding tree roots ready to trip them up and random volcanic rocks poking up out of the soil. Head-high ferns whipped their faces as they ran.

The terrifying cacophony of the approaching zombie horde, that wheezing, fighting mass of former humanity crashing through the trees with no regard for its own safety, spurred them on. That, and the Tyrannosaur, which they could hear screeching somewhere behind them. They saw no animals as they made their way through the forest—no birds, no insects, nothing, as if every living thing knew that this was no longer a safe place to be. There were no longer living things here, except for them, and if they wanted to keep it that way they needed to keep running.

Alex patted his pockets as he ran, hoping to feel the outline of a spare AK magazine he had somehow overlooked, but he came up empty. All three of them were out of ammo. The only working weapon among them was Veronica's Ka-bar, and a lot of good that would do against a seething wall of undead with a few rampaging dinosaurs thrown in the mix. They were alive, and when you were alive there was one thing above all others you wanted to do, and that was to stay alive.

"Shit! Shit-shit-shit-shit!" Up ahead, Xander stomped the ground in time with his profanity. He had run right into a natural alcove of sorts, comprised of a rocky hill and tangles of fallen trees and vegetation that had succumbed to a landslide in the recent rains. The peak of the smoldering volcano was visible over the lip of the amphitheatre-shaped formation Xander had led them to. Alex and Veronica came to within conversational earshot of him and stopped, looking right and left at the curve of the obstacle now hemming them in.

"We might be able to get up that way." Alex pointed to a fallen log leaning up against the muddy hillside. It only reached about halfway up, but at that point a jumble of loose rocks looked like it might provide enough footing to make it to the lip of the cul-de-sac.

Xander eyed the log dubiously.

"It's either that or we start running around this dead-end," Veronica said, looking back toward the sound of the coming horde.

"Screw it." Xander ran to the log and jumped up on it. He steadied himself and then began to walk up, arms outstretched for balance like a tightrope walker. He got about two-thirds of the way up and signaled for Alex and Veronica to start up after him. "It's good, we can make it, c'mon."

First Alex, then Veronica began to ascend the log ladder. By the time Alex was almost halfway up the log, Xander was very near the upper end of it, but then the high end of the log began to sink into the muddy hillside. Xander started to fall with it. At first the movement was imperceptible.

"Once we get to those rocks right up here it'll be smooth sailing." But no sooner had Xander completed his sentence than the log began to sink under their weight into the muddy hillside. Once it got going it happened fast.

"Jump!" Alex warned, aware that Xander was about to be dragged inside tons of wet mud and could easily be trapped there and suffocate before they could get him out. If Veronica even let him get him out. Xander pushed off the log, extracting his lower half from the mud pile and tumbling down the hill to the forest floor below, passing Alex and Veronica with a disturbing glare and a breathy "fuck" on his way down.

"Let's go." Alex turned around on the log and was shocked to see the crowd of zombies approaching the open cul-de-sac. "Go, go, go! They're almost on us!"

Veronica skip-hopped down the log and reached the ground by the time Xander had gotten to his feet. Alex was there a few seconds later, interrupting their I-wish-I-could-kill-you-right-fucking-now stare-down.

"Quick, which way?"

Veronica looked back toward the zombies and the beach beyond. "Back to the ship? Hide out and barricade ourselves in there until DeKirk arrives?"

"Then what?" Alex asked. "Take on his army of the living as well as the army of the dead?"

Xander shook his head. "Before even considering that, we'd need a working vehicle to make it back to the ship. Plus it's a wreck anyway, probably on the seafloor right about now."

"What about the airstrip?"

"Also too far. We'd be overrun before we got there—either those infected things or a dinosaur." Xander pointed up toward the volcano. "According to the facility map back in the control room, there's an old World War Two bunker at the base of the volcano built by the Korean to house munitions. Not one of DeKirk's facilities, so it'll lack modern amenities, but if we can get inside we can hopefully lock everything out and wait out the twenty four hours."

"Could've mentioned a bunker earlier," Alex grumbled.

No one had a better plan, so they set off running out of the cul-de-sac and to the left. The dinosaur's shrieking was louder now, coming from almost directly behind them, but at the moment that wasn't their chief concern. As the unlikely trio reached the wall of the cul-de-sac they saw the first of the zombies. He wore a shredded crewman's uniform, stumbling rapidly toward them with arms flapping. A long line of undead trailed after him, a thick, shambling horde, cracking branches and toppling plants in their wake.

Xander cleared the wall of the amphitheatre completely and squinted past it. "Volcano! C'mon." he took off at a sprint. Alex and Veronica still stared back at the monsters heading their way, mesmerized by the deadly spectacle. Veronica tugged at Alex's hand.

"We need to go."

"Hold on!" Alex stared at one of the zombies in the front line. Its clothes were not a uniform, either military or ship's crew, but rather normal civilian clothes.

Then, with mounting horror, he recognized the face.

His father's face.

#

Even with the sickly pallor, the blood and gaping wounds, even with the sunken cheekbones and vacant, thousand-yard-stare from reptilian eyes, he could see beyond a shadow of a doubt that it was his father, Marcus Ramirez.

"Dad? *Dad*!" He shouted and the zombies ambled faster towards them. Alex started to run to the thing that used to be his father but Veronica grabbed him by the shoulder and held him back.

"Alex, no! He's not your father anymore."

"But—" His mind simply could not reconcile this hideous creature with the man he had known all of his life, the man who had in fact given him life.

"He's dead, Alex! He's dead! We will be too if we don't get inside that bunker. Come *on*!"

She tugged him by the arm and together they ran after Xander toward the volcano.

38.

They heard Xander before they saw him, his voice sounding like it was echoing inside a tunnel. "I'm in here. Hurry up, I can see them coming!"

The air took on a hint of sulfur and a brownish hue as they neared the cone-shaped mountain. Veronica wrinkled her nose. "It's like L.A. smog."

Alex looked up at the smoky fumes belching from the volcano. "Yeah, it's *vog*. Like a combo of smog and fog, but from a volcano. I've seen it on my surf trips to Hawaii."

Veronica gave him a look that wasn't all exasperation. "I hope you get to go on more trips after this one, surfer boy. I really do. Let's get inside."

They stood at the base of the rocky cone, unbroken except for the obviously man-made feature that stood before them. A sizable rectangular opening had been cut into the side of the smoking mountain. Rusty iron bracing framed the doorway, the door itself having been retracted or swung inward, they supposed by Xander, who called to them from out of sight inside.

"It'll take some time to shut this big-ass door after you get in. Hurry the hell up!"

Alex took a glance back at the oncoming zombie mob (*my father is one of them!*) and then raced for the volcano entrance, Veronica bounding close on his heels. His calf muscles burned on the way up the short but steep incline, and then he crested the ramp and entered the volcano's interior. Peering inside, he saw that it was a large, flat space, perhaps a square mile, roughly circular in shape. The ramp eased back down to a smooth dirt floor dotted with vegetation, and a few footpaths meandered in different directions. Xander stood at the entrance, fretting over the huge metal door.

"I don't see how we're going to get this thing shut." Xander inspected the door where it retreated into the rock wall. Metal tracks above and below indicated that it slid back and forth.

"Didn't you open the damn thing?" Alex asked.

"No, it was already open."

"What's that down there?" Alex pointed down to the volcano floor where an entrance of some sort was set directly into the ground.

Xander perked up at the sight of it. "That could be the munitions depot! Let's head for that, maybe we can barricade ourselves in there. If we're real lucky the zombies won't even notice this entrance."

"Think again." Veronica stared out into the jungle. "They're coming straight for us."

Gazing out at the coming horde, Alex could see the flicking of tongues and the rapid up-and-down head movements, en masse as though at a rock concert listening to a beat only they could hear.

"Let's move!" Xander charged down the ramp to the floor of the volcano, followed by Alex and Veronica. Thorny scrub brush dotted the reddish ground, but they avoided most of it by following the path. Xander reached the small door first and bent down to examine it.

"Looks like one of those old fashioned cellar doors," he said, commenting on the twin doors slanting down at an angle into the earth. They had retained none of their original paint, but the color of the rust caked onto them blended well with the surroundings.

"The first ones just entered the volcano! They're pouring in fast." Veronica monitored the main entrance, the Ka-Bar clutched in her right hand, while Xander and Alex each flung one of the cellar doors wide. Alex turned his head to the side as a blast of cool, moldy air wafted out.

"C'mon kid, smells like air freshener compared to those things out to get us. Down we go."

Xander produced a small flashlight from a pocket and shone the beam down a rickety wooden staircase. "You two get down there first."

Veronica stepped inside, the knife passing dangerously close to Xander's throat. He ignored her, encouraging Alex to hurry by waving an arm at him. When all three were crouched on the stairway, Xander and Alex reached out and started to pull the doors closed. Alex took a last peek at the zombie pack now shambling en masse into the volcano. They moved through the brush directly toward the cellar doors, ignoring the paths. Then, as he and Xander were about to slam the doors down, they saw something that stopped them cold.

The main volcano entrance door slid shut all on its own, slicing a couple of zombies in two as it slammed into its frame, sealing the volcano's interior with a resounding metallic clang. The head of another zombie, leaning awkwardly backward as if in a limbo pose, was crushed and separated from its body, dropping its now truly lifeless corpse onto the floor. One of the half-zombies managed to clutch the shirt-tail of a former doctor and was dragged across the dirt, his open entrails smearing the reddish earth as he bounced along, snarling and snapping his jaws as he went.

"How did that happen?" Alex gaped at the closed volcano door, now smeared with gore.

Xander shook his head, and then muttered, "DeKirk."

"Nice of him to wait for the zombies to get in here with us before he shut it."

"Somehow I doubt *that* was an accident," Veronica said, eyeballing the ravenous monstrosities as they made their way toward the ground door.

"Forget about DeKirk," Xander said, gawking at the rag-tag horde of undead invading the volcano. He slammed the doors closed and flicked the rusty deadbolt. "That's not going to hold them long. We've got to find another way out of here."

39.

"They'll be on us in a couple of minutes!" Alex shouted over the clang of the doors banging shut in front of him. Xander's artificial beam was now their only light. He directed it down the stairs, where a few long-gone steps gaped like missing teeth in a smile, but overall the stairs looked passable.

The doors behind them jarred with multiple impacts and the clanging of flesh on metal as the first zombies bombarded the entrance to their shelter.

Xander shone his beam back down the stairs. "Better go one at a time down these, not sure they'll support all of our weight. Veronica, you go first, you're the lightest. I'll hold the light."

"You're the light of my fucking life, Xander." She descended rapidly, not resting her full weight on any of the steps for more than a split second, and then she was on flat ground, looking off to her right.

"Looks a like a tunnel goes off this way for quite a ways. Can't see any detail."

Xander held the light for Alex to descend the stairs and then he made the trip himself. With all three of them on the bottom, Xander aimed his beam down the tunnel, comprised entirely of natural volcanic stone, with no bracing or mining supports of any kind. The obvious threat of a cave-in, of being entombed in this place for eternity went unspoken.

They moved down the passage, the sound of zombies banging on the doors receding as they went. At the end of the long tunnel a door was open on the right while the passageway curved out of sight to the left. Xander shone his beam into a room and took tentative steps inside. He flipped a light switch on the wall with an audible *clack* that echoed throughout the room. They were all surprised to see a bare bulb hanging from the ceiling flicker, then catch, bathing the room in dim but steady illumination.

They cast their gaze around the space, taking in the sheer sense of history about it. Clearly, it was an old room, filled with dusty metal shelves lined with crates and cases. Large pieces of military and industrial equipment lay about the floor, some covered in now shredded tarps.

"Munitions room!" Xander exhorted, moving deeper into the space.

"Let's see if there's anything we can use." Veronica set her weapons down on a wooden table and began slowly walking about, examining items. Xander did the same, picking up a case of shells, plucking one out to look at it and dropping it when he saw it was the wrong size for his gun. He found an old rifle and picked it up, tried the action and found it jammed.

Alex, meanwhile, headed to a far corner of the room that had been partitioned off with what looked like plywood crates. At first, he thought it formed an uninterrupted walled-off area, but then he found a small gap where one side didn't quite reach the actual room wall, which was itself carved directly from the volcanic stone. He felt something liquid splash on his scalp and looked up to see water dripping from the ceiling, having percolated through the soil above.

He passed through the narrow opening into the walled off section of room, and caught his breath.

"We've hit the jackpot."

Bombs.

Lots of them. Old-looking ones, with big bulbous metal bodies and little stabilizing fins, stacked not just ceiling-high, but in actuality even higher than that. A circular opening had been bored into the floor and Alex could see that the bombs were stacked well down into that, farther than he could see, deep into the volcano's innards. Even more troubling, an assemblage of wiring and little metal boxes was integrated among the bombs. Alex was no explosives expert, but even to him it looked suspiciously like a trigger mechanism.

"What the hell is DeKirk planning with all this shit?"

"What do you—?" Xander was there in a flash, looking over his shoulder, eyes scanning, taking everything in. "Holy..." He whistled, and then looked up and around the chamber. "I wonder if he's planning a little failsafe of his own..."

"Guys!" From behind them, Veronica's voice was fraught with worry. "I hear them coming down the tunnel!"

Xander threw a case of 50-cal machine gun bullets down on the floor in aggravation. "This old ammo isn't going to fit our guns. Gimme some 9mm rounds. Shit!" He looked around the room in desperation, eyes alighting on a metal gas can against the wall. He went to it and hefted its weight, feeling liquid slosh inside. Unscrewed the cap and sniffed, recoiling at the sharp tang that assailed his nostrils. Satisfied it was some kind of fuel, he picked up the can and carried it to the doorway, where Veronica's eyes grew wider by the second.

The sound of the zombie horde grew louder, their feet scraping the floor as they transited through the tunnel toward the munitions room. Xander eyed Veronica. "Got a light?" She shook her head. He looked over to Alex, who was still out of sight behind the walled-off area.

"Hey, kid, what're you doing over there? Find anything else we can use? Because it's decision time. Make a stand here or run for it to the unknown at the other end of the tunnel. Could be a dead end for all I know. Literally."

"I'll go check." Veronica dashed from the room out into the tunnel.

"I'm still thinking about this." Alex said, staring at the bombs.

"Kid, that's not helping now—"

"No, really. I think we can use this..."

Xander unscrewed the gas can cap and dumped the liquid out into the tunnel, opposite the direction in which Veronica had gone. Shining his light down the passage, he spotlighted a sea of red eyes moving his way, glowing orbs sunken into heads that gasped, moaned and screamed senseless utterances that reverberated around the tunnel, making it sound like a carnival funhouse on Halloween. He ducked back inside the room and ran over to Alex.

"Lemme see again."

Alex withdrew from the bomb space and pointed inside. Xander slipped through and Alex heard him take the lord's name in vain several times as he took in the inventory in more detail. "So DeKirk was probably thinking, set these off... maybe start a volcanic eruption in the process...the volcano has been getting hotter lately. An explosion could really disturb the geothermal stability of this thing..." Xander let a smile form. "If we can blow this place up—and escape—we'll take out a lot of those freaks in one fell swoop."

Alex backed up. "I like it, but if something's wrong with the trigger system, we could die right here."

"Kid, there's no time to sugarcoat it for you. We're probably either dying quick, like this..." He stared up at the mountain of antique incendiary devices, then down into the bored hole full of more bombs, before cocking his head out toward the hall, where the jarring cacophony sounded like it was about to reach them. "Or die relatively slow, out there, and become one of those things." He focused some more. "This mechanism here has got to be the timer."

Suddenly, Veronica burst into the room. "What the fuck are you guys doing? If it wasn't for your gasoline slip'n' slide out there those things would already be in here!"

Xander's voice came from behind the partition.

"Veronica, is there a way out from that end?"

"Yes. There's—"

He cut her off. "All I need to know. You ready to run?"

The first of the zombies made its way into the munitions room.

"Hell yes."

"Yeah." Veronica's and Alex's responses overlapped.

"Go! Go! Go! Five minutes to boom!"

Xander exited the bomb area, now wearing a heavily loaded canvas backpack, and saw the zombie, still wearing a white lab coat with a stethoscope around its neck. Veronica held her trusty Ka-Bar at the ready, still hoping she could slip past the threat to the tunnel outside the room. Alex followed her.

Xander picked up one of the smaller warheads, maybe eighteen inches long, with a skinny end and a fatter, spherical one. He gripped the thing by the thin end like a club and made his way to the exit. The zombie followed, almost cat-like in its movements while in a burst of speed, but then slowing once again to an uncoordinated, rambling walk as it neared Xander for a bite. Xander swung the warhead and caved in the side of the zombie's skull, forcing its grayish tongue far out of its mouth in the process.

182

He let go of his impromptu weapon and sprang for the door just as three more zombies reached the munitions doorway.

He heard Alex shout, "Look out!" then saw the spark of a Zippo lighter in Alex's hand. As if in slow motion, he watched his arm wind up for the pitch and release the weighted flame. It flew over Xander's head and landed with a *click* that was drowned out by the *whoosh* of erupting flames as the gas went up. In a tunnel of flame the advancing zombies shrieked, thrashed, and caterwauled while the three still among the living sprinted down the unlit portion of the subterranean passage. Almost as an afterthought, Xander stopped, shrugged off his newfound World War Two backpack and tossed a handful of 50-cal rounds into the fire.

By the time he shouldered his pack and was running down the tunnel again, he heard the snapping pops of the shells being forced from their projectiles, knowing that the brass casings were flying around inside the fire. When he reached the end of the tunnel where Alex and Veronica had already made the left turn—the only available option—he turned back for a look down the hall.

A zombie completely engulfed in flames from head to toe continued to walk toward him, arms outstretched, screaming, screaming, wailing as though it were in unfathomable agony. Yet still, it kept coming, driven through its fiery anguish by the insurmountable urge to consume raw human flesh. Others like it burst forth from the flames.

Xander felt palpable relief when one of them toppled and thudded to the ground, its brain having been boiled inside its skull, its cranial lining drooling from its charred mouth. They could be killed by fire. Then it was trampled over by a procession of burning zombies, a few dropping as their brains cooked, but many still forging ahead, alight, shrieking hopelessly out of their shapeless, melted faces.

Xander turned the corner and ran into another room—a cavernous area serving as another storage zone, full of crates and boxes. There ahead of them...Veronica was behind the wheel of a lone Jeep, turning the key, letting loose a little holler of joy as the engine cranked to life. Alex was hefting a rocket launcher and lugging it over to the Jeep, followed by one more. He stuck them in the back of the vehicle like they were a couple of snowboards for a weekend trip. He found a luggage-sized case of extra rockets for the launchers leaning up against a wall and tossed that in the Jeep, too.

"Not long before it all blows, if it's going to blow." Xander checked his watch.

Suddenly, a charred zombie staggered into the room from the tunnel, still smoldering.

"Little help here!" Xander called. He faced off against the zombie, preparing to fight it hand-to-hand. Veronica left the Jeep idling and stepped out while Alex went to a roll-up door and reached down to pull it open.

The zombie lurched but Xander evaded it. Veronica circled around the dead one's backside, blade at the ready.

Two more smoldering zombies entered, one leaning over to chew on the other's burnt shoulder meat despite multiple swats to the face as they walked. Xander continued to circle until he was between the Jeep and the zombie he squared off with. There was a rushing sound of metal on metal as Alex threw the roll-up door open. Veronica slashed at the first zombie with her Ka-Bar, missing its neck and slicing it under an armpit. The creature pounded a blistered hand that was missing all of the fingers onto her back, knocking her to the floor.

Xander looked over at her, beneath the zombie with two more undead a few steps away, and then out the roll-up door to the outside. The view surprised him. It wasn't merely the inside of the volcano, but actually led outside to the rest of the island. The way out.

Alex, now carrying a tire iron he'd picked up somewhere in here, ran over to the melee. He cracked the zombie falling over Veronica in the skull, dropping it on top of her. She yelled for him to get it off her. While he did, Xander slid into the driver seat of the Jeep and quietly put it into reverse. He rolled the vehicle out of the garage and put it in park, got out and walked to the entrance.

Alex and Veronica had dispatched the first zombie but now battled two more, and Xander could see a whole gang of them—some still on fire—about to pour into the room from the tunnel. He reached up and grabbed the handle on the roll-up door just as Alex looked up from the fracas.

"Help us!"

Xander smiled back at them—a devilish grin. "Actually, I've got a better idea!"

He proceeded to pull the door down, slamming it hard. Then he took a chain he'd seen in the Jeep and used it to wedge into one of the tracks just above where the wheels were on the track, fastening it tight, effectively blocking the door from rising. Trapping Alex and Veronica inside the bunker. There was no way in Hell they'd be able to fight their way back through that burned-out tunnel.

Smiling at his ingenuity, Xander hopped back into the Jeep, honked the horn, and sped off.

40.

Alex's watch beeped and he looked up from kicking a zombie in the head to glance at it.

"Time's up! Brace yourself, it's gonna blow!"

Veronica tried lifting the roll-up door but it was jammed.

"Goddamned, Xander!" She hurled herself against the metal barrier in frustration, bouncing off of it and back into the zombie melee, where she jammed the tip of her Ka-Bar into a bloodshot eye. Then, seeing Alex ducking for cover, she crouched and covered the sides of her head with her elbows, bracing for the impact...

Which never came.

"I thought you said time's up?" She looked up at Alex, who had dispatched another zombie by shattering its skull with the tire iron. He backpedaled away from two more as he continued to consult his watch.

"I guess that old stuff doesn't actually work. We lucked out!"

Veronica glared at him from the bloody floor. "Lucked out? Oh yeah, locked in here with these monsters that want to have us for dinner. Oh, and a *T. rex* roaming around out there if we do manage to get out. We lucked out, all right."

Alex sighed, looking around. "There's got to be a way out of here. Plus, you never know, those old bombs could go off at any moment."

"We're not getting out through that tunnel. Too many of those things."

Alex had piled a bunch of oxygen tanks, munitions, spare tires and other random objects in the doorway, slowing the progress of zombies into the room, but they still crawled and climbed in one at a time. Three moving ones occupied the room presently, one with half its face burned away, the other half a normal zombie pallor, as if it had fallen on one side onto the burning floor and been held there for some time.

"Need some help here," Alex said, casting about for a weapon of opportunity, his tire iron having bounced out of his hand when it glanced off a zombie skull. Veronica got up, brandishing her knife.

"You look for a way out, I'll hold them off."

She walked up to the closest zombie and feinted left, then stabbed right, plowing the blade up through the neck of the undead monstrosity all the way into its brain cavity. She withdrew the slimy, black metal and eyed her next victim as the first dropped to the floor, dead for good.

Alex tried the roll-up again, almost dislocating his shoulder with the effort. He kicked the door repeatedly, checking to see how it would give. Maybe he could ram something heavy into it, but no. It was stout. More trademark DeKirk quality—or a holdover from Korean wartime engineering.

He glanced over at Veronica to make sure she was handling herself okay. A flood of zombies were bottlenecked at the barricaded entrance, fighting and biting each other while occasionally one made it through. Veronica was battling them one and sometimes two at a time, becoming brutally efficient with the Ka-Bar, learning how to distance herself from the threats, only going in close when a high-value target, such as an upturned chin, presented itself.

Alex spotted a tarp-covered object in the corner and ran to it. Something he could use? He ripped the cover off and stared at a green-painted forklift. It looked like it might be operational—and gas powered, most likely used recently by the looks of it. His eyes traced a path from it to the door, making a connection. He'd never operated one before but how hard could it be? He heard Veronica grunt with the effort of stabbing another zombie, looked over, saw her drop the thing, and back off. She looked back at him, made eye contact that said, *please do something,* and turned back into combat.

Alex pulled himself into the forklift with a handhold and studied the controls. Key in the ignition, thank God. Turned it, and the engine rumbled to life. *Yes!* He lurched forward, tentatively rolling ahead. Realizing he needed speed for this to work, he floored the gas pedal and was surprised at how much acceleration the vehicle had to give.

He pressed the button to raise the forks off the floor so that they would hit the door higher up, and then steeled himself for the impact. The lift rammed the door at an angle, causing the machine to turn violently to the left when one fork poked through the metal before the other one. Alex was jolted from his seat and almost thrown from the vehicle but grabbed the seatbelt strap (that he hadn't bothered to put on). He dangled from the side of the forklift as it punched through the door, taking Alex through a jagged rip in the metal sheet that tore at his left arm and leg, flaying his skin.

He could see sky! Sky that was filled with volcanic smoke, and a fine black ash that now rained down upon them, but still. How good it looked after being underground and inside for so long. How sweet it was, to breath the open air, even filled with volcanic ejecta as it was. He dropped off the lift and was turning to run back inside for Veronica when he saw them.

Zombies.

A dense gathering, fanned out into a more or less horizontal line that advanced on the garage, faster than usual. Some of them, Alex noted, looked as if they were of South Pacific islander descent. *How many damn employees were on this island?* There was no time to speculate, for the pack approached, gaining speed when they saw new prey.

"Veronica! More outside, let's go!"

He heard the ring of metal on metal followed by a guttural yell—he wasn't sure if it was Veronica or a zombie—and then the agent came crashing through the gouged-out door, eyes widening in abject horror as the phrase *out of the frying pan into the fire* draped over her consciousness like a shroud of doom.

She was bloody.

Sheets of crimson washed down her right arm and leg.

"Veronica! Were you—?" He couldn't bring himself to say it. *Were you bitten?*

She read the anguish on his face. "Negative. It's from the door on the way out. Could have left me a bigger opening. I have to say, your vehicular skills do not impress me thus far. I hope you can fly a plane better than you can use a forklift or a helicopter. "

"Get me to a plane, I'll fly it," Alex said confidently. Inwardly, he flashed on his arrival to Antarctica in the chartered plane from Chile—the sketchy landing and how Tony had questioned his abilities, too. He shrugged the thoughts off. "What about this?"

Alex looked back at the nearing throng. Behind them, two zombies pushed through the ripped door without any care whatsoever for sharp edges, one of them cutting itself so badly in the process that a sizable slice of flesh unfurled from its side, flapping obscenely as it bounced along toward the pair of humans.

Veronica whirled around, head on a swivel, knife at the ready.

Alex tried to see through the oncoming wall of zombies, to see past them to what lie ahead. He registered some trees on the right and no sign of Xander, that bastard...But there, on the left! Something leaning against a boulder. Something black and chrome...

A motorcycle!

He pointed it out to Veronica, but to get to it, they'd have to force their way through the horde.

She took one more glance back at the garage, where another burnt zombie was grating itself though the ruptured door, and then set off at a jog toward the bike. "I'll fight 'em as long as I can, you get through to the bike and get it started. Trusting you not to leave me behind like Xander."

She reached the first of the zombies and exploded into a fury of slashes and jabs, parries and thrusts, nearly decapitating the lost soul. She quickly realized that she'd put too much energy into that single encounter, however, and then found herself having to deal with three of the creatures simultaneously. She inflicted quick but deep face and neck wounds to each of them before whirling around into an open pocket for some running room like an NFL player looking for a first down.

Alex was farther ahead, weaponless but nimble, avoiding fights, taking advantage of the fact that more of them were drawn to Veronica's bloodletting than to his rapid dodging. The motorcycle was probably only fifty feet away, but it seemed like a mile.

He continued to hear Veronica's effort-laden gasps as she fought off the horrid abominations. He knew that as good as she was, she could only keep this up for so long. All it would take was one slip-up, one little momentary lapse of reason, and she would dissolve into nothing in the undead mob. With this many, there would be so little of her left that she wouldn't even return as a zombie.

In an odd sort of detachment, Alex wondered what the point of it was, the zombified existence. Was it life, was the reanimated corpse just a host for transporting the virus and replicating it, but to what end, if all it did was spread and eat... and eat? Everything in sight including, ultimately, others like itself. He didn't know, but he sure as Hell didn't want to find out, and the sight of the bike ahead galvanized him to action.

He made a beeline for the next open patch of ground, where he then had to jog right, then back left, in order to forge ahead again. He had just allowed himself the first faint touch of optimism when he looked into one of the zombie's eyes...and stopped dead in his tracks. This particular zombie carried a gun, dangling carelessly from one finger, while the sleeve of its sweater hung loose from the wrist of the other arm. That was not what made it remarkable to Alex.

"Dad?"

His father's face was unmistakable, even zombified, but in spite of the fact that his brain tried to tell him, *no, you're wrong— that's not him!*—there was no way it could with the tattered turtleneck, khaki pants, and especially the alligator boots it still wore. Marcus Ramirez' last outfit. Chosen in some department store on a day when simply going to pick them out was a chore, something to get over and done with so that he could get on with his life. Now, he had no life, at least not one that was recognizable to Alex or any normal human. He had an existence, but certainly not a life. The maggots and flies residing in his rotten cheeks had more of a life than he did, Alex reflected.

And yet...

"*..lex!*"

It had formed a word.

The seething, writhing mass of zombies, Veronica's tortured cries born of a single furious blade, the smoking volcano, all of it receded to the back of his subconscious as he stood in place and focused on the figure before him who used to be his father.

"*Aaaaaaal...*"

It seemed like a terrible effort for the creature to formulate words.

"Dad!" He unconsciously reached out to his father—to what he thought of as his father but surely was no longer. He watched, unable to move as a mounting internal struggle waged itself inside the zombie's virus-addled mind as it tried to call upon the last remaining vestiges of its former self. A blanket of ash fell upon its upturned face as it slowly raised the hand with the gun.

"Prowwwwd..."

The gun went off, shooting another zombie right in the forehead, dropping it like a sack of bricks.

"fffYouuuuuuu."

"Dad...!"

Then Alex's zombie father pointed the gun at itself, at its right temple, but the aim was unsteady, and it succeeded only in blowing a hole in the shoulder of its shooting arm, making its aim even worse.

"Stop!"

"Allllllllex!" It shot again, this time putting a round into the base of its neck. It slumped to the ground, reaching out a hand toward its still-living son.

Another shot, to the scalp, this time.

"Runnnn..." and a final one, entering its mouth up into its brain. Its eyes opened wider with the realization that, even for whatever Hell of a dimension it found itself in now, this was it.

Show's over, folks.

As he toppled to the dirt, Alex's father reached up in a spastic motion and dropped the firearm. Alex took it, whispered something to his father that for years he would not be able to recall that would haunt his dreams in different ways, and then used the gun to put some lead into the head of another zombie that stood in his way.

The motorbike waited, just ahead.

Alex blasted one more zombie out of the way and then saw Veronica waving him on to the motorcycle as she broke into a run through an open pocket. He turned and sprinted to the bike. An old Honda. Key in the ignition, the whole cycle wet and covered with sludgy ash. He mounted the seat in a daze and prayed while he turned the key. The motor turned over once and died. He looked back and saw Veronica on the losing end of an altercation with two zombies, one of them very tall and thin with a long reach.

He steadied the pistol's barrel on the handlebars and took aim. Held his breath, squeezed the trigger...

Dropped Mr. Thin Man.

Veronica looked over, smiled, side-stepped past the last remaining zombie in her way and broke into a full-out run.

Alex tried the key again. It turned over twice this time, and then died.

"Shit!"

"Go, Alex, I'll hop on!"

"Trying!"

Then he looked to his right, wondering why she sounded even more panicked, and he saw four zombies, tearing through the brush toward them.

He turned the key one more time. Heard the motor rev...rev...and catch!

He threw the machine into gear as he felt Veronica leap onto the seat and throw her arms around his waist. "Move!" He gunned it, just tearing into the terrain and onto a path and racing at a right angle away from the zombies, who all stumbled ahead, waving their arms and squealing in loss.

"I hope you can actually drive one of these," Veronica yelled, tightening her grip.

"What direction?" Alex didn't dare take his eyes off the terrain, fearing one wrong bump or tilt would send them flying to the ground—where they'd be dinosaur bait in no time.

She pointed ahead in the distance, to a flat plain beneath a forested slope. "That way to the airstrip."

41.

Alex jockeyed the old motorcycle along a dirt road through a rain of sooty ash, Veronica's arms around his waist, no zombies or dinosaurs in sight for the first time in hours. Even so, he didn't feel good about anything after having seen what had happened to his father. He was numb and looking forward to only one thing: getting to the airstrip and finding a way out of this hellhole.

"Hold on." He warned Veronica as he went airborne off a rock, the wheels landing two bike lengths away on loose packed soil. He swerved hard to the left, and then recovered, gunning it once again in the direction of the airstrip.

Then they heard—and felt—the explosion.

The ground shook beneath their wheels with the force of it. Alex braked, slowing them enough so that when they fell off they avoided injury. They lay sprawled out on the forest floor while a series of muffled booms sounded back at the volcano.

The ground shook as another series of explosions went off, like a Fourth of July fireworks finale—more impressive and longer-lasting than the volley preceding it. Veronica dusted the leaves off of her and stood, surveying their surroundings while Alex righted the bike.

"The entire bunker must be destroyed," Veronica said, mounting the cycle once more.

Alex looked back at the volcano, the apex of its cone now brimming with fire. "I think that might just be the beginning."

"Storing the munitions there...the bomb..." Veronica shuddered as a pall of ash sifted down, intensifying. "Was that the failsafe? Instigating an eruption?"

"I don't want to wait around to find out. Let's—"

They both heard it at once: the sound of a large beast trampling the ground and crashing through the brush somewhere nearby. They couldn't see anything, but set off again on the bike. A path forked ahead and Veronica pointed left. Alex went that way and soon after they crested a steep rise, from the top of which they could see the airstrip not far below on flat ground.

Something else, moving, and it caught Alex's eye.

A Jeep, tearing down the path, kicking up dirt clouds in its wake.

"There's Xander!"

"He's going for the plane, too. We've got to catch him."

"Why? He can't fly."

"He's probably thinking of hiding out in the hangar and waiting for DeKirk, and...even if he can't fly, he might blow up the plane just to spite us."

"If he knows we survived."

"Well, there's not really anywhere to hide between here and there. He's going to know."

Alex shrugged. "Nothing to do about it but catch his ass."

"And take him out now, at last." Veronica gritted her teeth, tightened her grip around Alex and nodded. "Go!"

#

The idea of being trapped on this rock where such a ghastly fate had befallen his father was beyond unthinkable to Alex. He throttled the bike up and riveted his gaze to Xander's Jeep, which was rolling along faster than was safe, the RPGs jostling around in the back. The bike had horsepower to spare, though, and so Alex yelled for Veronica to hold on and jammed the throttle all the way back. They raced down the rugged trail, which at times felt like an expert ski slope, all moguls and sharp declines. Alex and Veronica hunched low on the two-wheeler, careening faster and faster, approaching a larger set of boulders and gaining on Xander, who Alex saw was glancing back, with sudden alarm.

Why's he so acting so shocked? Alex thought, a moment before it dawned on him that there might be another reason for his fear.

Was it the volcano, or just the fact that they had survived, or was it—?

The bike's front wheel thumped hard on the leveling ground, they skidded but stayed on balance, but when they emerged from beyond the outcropping of boulders and fallen rocks, they were met with another fright.

Alex knew what had Xander had seen.

The *T. rex* lurched out from the side of the boulder where it had been crouching, almost blending in with the rubble and the mountainside. It straightened its neck, stretching its entire body to its full length. Stories high, it was crawling with zombies, the undead humanoids latched onto its tail, its flank, even sitting atop its back, cowboy style.

It roared and swiped at them—but just missed the back tire with its giant jaws.

Furious and frenzied, it gave chase.

\#

The sky had darkened, with rolling black clouds of ash belching up from the volcano. The ground rumbled and the winds turned cold and full of swirling black flakes.

Alex veered to the left shoulder of the road, feeling his hands vibrate as they rolled over jagged volcanic rocks. He was about to stop, forced to either crash or run into the *T. rex's* tail, when the beast leaned forward and raised its tail in a swishing motion that lifted it just higher than the bike.

"Duck!"

Alex gunned it and they shot forward beneath the dinosaur's massive appendage. A zombie dropped off the *T. rex*—whether by design or by accident, Alex didn't know—and landed a split second behind them, the fingers of one of its hands shredding off in the spokes of the rear wheel. Alex looked back over his right shoulder and saw the dinosaur roar in frustration, then turn on a burst of steam and race after them.

"Go!" Veronica urged, but he needed no encouragement. He fell into a trance state with the bike, seeing only the road's obstacles immediately in front of him, feeling the rhythms of the machine as he coaxed the needed movements from it. He focused on Xander's Jeep, trying to match its movements and keep gaining on it. Behind them the Tyrannosaur tore down the road on its powerful hind legs. Alex leaned into a curve and when he straightened out, Xander's Jeep was not far in front of him.

Xander glanced back, saw them following, and with shock at the proximity of the dinosaur and the cycle, so close, he swerved and accelerated all at once—and at the absolute worst time.

His left front wheel slammed into a rocky patch and the Jeep cart-wheeled to the right, completely out of control. It wedged into a patch of mud and tipped up, nearly flipping before coming to rest again on three wheels, the fourth having snapped off at the axle. Xander was tossed from the Jeep and lay sprawled in the road. He sat up, clutching his arm—where a jagged white bone stuck out of a bloody fissure near his elbow. He looked dazed but furious, regaining his senses.

Alex skidded the bike to a stop sideways to avoid hitting the Jeep, losing traction and coming to a stop. No other option, he tried to right the bike but Veronica's weight tugged him off balance. Turning his head to see where the *T. rex was,* sure it was right there about to devour them, he felt it rush past the bike in a blur, then saw its red eyes full of mindless rage, its gargantuan head towering above them, the zombie riders fearlessly hanging on.

There was no doubt as to its intentions. It went after the wounded prey.

Alex felt a rush of thrill and felt for a moment what he imagined Veronica was feeling at the same time.

Get him, he thought, silently rooting for the monster as it bore straight for Xander.

#

Grimacing in pain, clutching his arm, Xander realized he hadn't many options left. A sitting duck, bleeding out at that, a perfect meal for the rampaging dinosaur and its riders. Hungry, the *T. rex* was whipped into a violent frenzy of white-hot fury that went beyond mere animalistic self-preservation. Awakened after eons to an unfamiliar place in a disease-ridden body, not even possessing a functioning heart and plagued by a retinue of parasitic zombies, this creature was compelled by the forces of its own evolution to do the one thing in this world that it knew how to do: attack and feed.

Xander saw it coming for him and pushed up with his good arm to his feet. Timing it perfectly, he ran forward as the creature rushed in a burst of speed toward him. Throwing off its timing, Xander ducked and rolled under its swooping jaws, between its legs and past its flailing tail.

Without looking back, not sure of how much time he had just bought, hearing only the roar of frustration and fury from the beast, he ran to the Jeep, knowing that fleeing any other direction would result in his death as surely as if he had remained motionless in the road. At the Jeep, in a movement that he knew would bring him great pain, he slid one of the heavy rocket launchers from the back of the vehicle and balanced it atop his right shoulder, the side of his good arm. With the monster bearing down on him, he turned around and took aim with the weapon.

He lined up the bouncing *T. rex* head in the rocket's sight and prepared to fire. Consumed now by dread so real it overshadowed the pain of his broken arm completely, Xander tried to block out his mind from telling him that his life was about to come to an end in the festering mouth of a prehistoric animal.

Making his last stand, Xander flipped a lever on the launcher. The *T. rex* paused, perhaps having learned the lesson and steadying its approach, and lowered its head. One of the zombies slid down the *T. rex's* snout like a kid on a slide, careening past Xander and taking a swipe at him in mid-air. Reflexively, Xander dodged the zombie and squeezed the trigger, aiming right at the dinosaur's head in his line of sight.

Got you, he thought with giddy exuberance—that suddenly turned to outright horror…

Nothing happened.

He lowered the barrel of the RPG, wincing with renewed pain from his ruined arm.

Shit.

His mouth opened and he stared at the bullet-ridden, drooling draconic visage in front of him, the demonic eyes and jagged teeth in a rotting mouth expelling a breath so foul he started to gag.

It was over, and just as he heard the revving of a motorcycle, and saw a blur in the corner of his eye, as Veronica and Alex tore away to safety, he knew it: there would be no escape. No second chance, no tomorrow.

All his genius, his plans, his brilliance, undone on this blasted island, undone by something, at last that he couldn't foresee.

The *T. rex* moved lightning-fast, thrusting its jaws forward and its gaping maw closed around Xander's entire body, its head twisting to the side so that its prey's feet stuck out one side and the arms and head out the other. Blood rained from the sides of dinosaur's mouth as it raised its head to full height, its jaws crushing Xander's ribs and gouging into his organs. The zombie that had slid off the beast stood in place and raised its face up, accepting the bloodbath that rained down from the dinosaur's grinding jaws. It opened its mouth as wide as it could, catching Xander's fresh-squeezed blood, like the pulp of a shredded orange, gargling it when it overflowed down its face.

Still clutching the rocket launcher but now in his death throes, Xander reflexively pulled the trigger one more time, and this time the RPG fired.

#

Alex slowed the bike.

He and Veronica both looked back in time to see the rocket that seemed to exit directly out of the *T. rex's* mouth, sending a missile slamming into the Jeep where it exploded into a fiery ball of wreckage. The zombie standing nearby was engulfed in fire, the flames burning Xander's blood off its rot-riddled skin before consuming its flesh and incinerating its bones.

The Tyrannosaur reared back in surprise, feeling the heat of the explosion. It reacted by tossing its prey and catching it deeper within its jaws, then clamping down on Xander. The pressure cut—or more like pressed—the biochemist in half. His head and upper torso remained in the creature's jaws, trapped like portions run through a meat grinder. His lower body—shredded flesh and bone—tumbled out into the burning Jeep, where moments later the remaining RPGs exploded. Shrapnel blew out in random directions, one jagged piece of the Jeep slashing through the *T. rex's* leg, which didn't seem to affect it as it wolfed its meal down its straining gullet. Another flaming piece of debris caught a zombie on top of the *T. rex's* back, pulverizing its cranium like a watermelon disintegrating under a sledgehammer.

Back on the road, Alex tightened his grip on the motorcycle's handlebars as the airstrip beckoned. He took off, even as he felt Veronica's grip loosen slightly, and felt her breathe a long sigh and say something like, "Rest now, Edgars..."

Without asking what all that meant, Alex checked the mirror—and then gunned the bike even more.

The *T. rex* certainly wasn't sated.

It turned, howled, licked its teeth clean, and then loped after the bike.

42.

The air grew darker, thicker, and more sulfurous as the motorcycle rolled onto the airstrip. The airplane was at the other end, and Alex strained to see what kind it was as he coaxed every last bit of speed from the bike. He needed it, because the *T. rex* ran surprisingly fast for such a large animal, its hind legs making short, quick, bird-like steps as its head remained level.

Although the outsized lizard was fast, it was not as fast as the Honda, and by the time Alex and Veronica were halfway down the runway to the plane, Alex was pleased to see that the *T. rex* had fallen behind. Perhaps it was like a cheetah and could only sprint for a short time, or maybe its cadre of zombie parasites was weighing it down or causing too much damage. Whatever the case, Alex rejoiced over the fact that he would have a little time to fire up the plane without the dinosaur breathing down his neck—or attacking it and destroying their one chance at escaping this island.

Just then, something more dramatic took their attention away.

"Alex, look!" Veronica pointed behind them, but not at the dinosaur, which still pedaled its legs down the runway after them.

The volcano's top frothed with orange. They heard a deep rumbling, and without warning, an explosive geyser of red-orange magma blew from the volcano's center.

"There we go," Veronica said. "Eruption!"

"The failsafe," Alex added with some satisfaction as he drove the bike faster toward the plane. It was fine with him if this whole goddamn place went up in flames forever. He felt like he had nothing anymore. Everything he had thought he stood for in the past was wrong, he now realized. Dead wrong. He flashed on his friend Tony, the first to die in this mess. On his father. On all those people who came here simply to work... But he, of all people, at least had a chance to escape with his life, and with Veronica. Almost as if she could read his thoughts, he felt her hands squeeze him, and not because she was about to fall off the bike. An unspoken signal, to which he responded by leaning back into her, relishing in the touch as if to say, *under other circumstances—*

once we're free of this—maybe there's something for us, something, someone we can each cling to.

Then the airplane loomed before them, a Cessna Citation. *Yes,* he thought. *I can fly this...if it works. If it's fueled...if, if if...*He tried to shut off the worrying part of his brain so he could focus. The *T. rex* was still coming for them, and the volcano was erupting, and even with the lead they'd gained they needed maybe three or four minutes to get that plane moving.

Probably not enough time, the nagging voice told him. He glanced right and left off the runway. The terrain on either side was wholly unsuitable for takeoff. That meant that should the *T. rex* charge at them during the takeoff attempt—and based on its behavior so far, *why the hell wouldn't it?*—he would have very little room to maneuver around it. Simply leaving the runway was not going to be an option. Rugged, uneven terrain on one side and a field of jagged volcanic rocks on the other. *That dinosaur might just plow right into us before we go airborne; it'd be like running head on into a 18-wheeler.*

This small airplane was it, he reminded himself as he skidded to a stop next to the Citation. There were no other aircraft, no ships, boats, nothing. If they were going to escape this island, this was it, or wait it out for DeKirk and find a way to overpower his goons and... But he couldn't even think of any way that could come out in their favor.

God help them if he couldn't get this airplane started. Even without the *T. rex,* the idea of trying to survive here indefinitely with that horde of zombies...

"Alex!" Veronica's voice snapped him out of it just as they neared the plane. They ditched the bike, letting it fall to the ground as they ran across the hot dirt toward the pilot side of the plane. Alex threw open the door to the cockpit and Veronica jumped in and slid across to the co-pilot chair before Alex leapt in. She kept her voice calm so as not to distract him from his task of starting the plane.

"Not to state the obvious, but get this thing in the air!"

Alex didn't look up from the control panel as his eyes did a quick scan of the instruments. Veronica watched him, concerned that he wouldn't be able to start it. "You know how to fly one of these, right?"

"Slightly different model than the one I learned on, but yeah, I got this." He took a deep breath, studying the controls before starting up. "Okay, this is your captain speaking. Fasten your seatbelts. We hope you enjoyed your stay on Fucked Up Island. Next stop, Anywhere But Here." His hands flew over the controls, pushing buttons and throwing switches.

She released a smile at last, one that quickly faded as she hastily clicked the lap belt into place, while glancing over their shoulder at the dinosaur barreling headlong down the runway.

The engine rumbled to life, vibrating the seats beneath them as the propeller started to turn. Alex patted the dashboard. "That's it, baby. We can do this!"

He gripped the steering column and eyeballed the runway. He would need to taxi the aircraft to the left in order to have the proper approach. Farther down in the takeoff zone, the *T. rex* ran slightly left of center. One of the zombies fell out of a laceration in the carnivore's neck, only to be trampled underfoot by the storming beast, but Alex didn't allow himself to reflect on it for even a split second. As soon as the aircraft began to move, his brain locked on to the set of pre-flight activities he'd been trained on. He sought them out now, focused on them like a kid with a security blanket, to the exclusion of everything happening around him, including the *T. rex*, including the volcano spewing molten fire, threatening to flood the island.

He spun the plane into position and throttled up, starting the aircraft rolling down the runway. Veronica gripped one of the hand holds, or "oh shit handles" as he recalled one of his instructors joking long ago. Then he heard her voice, and what she said cut through everything.

"Alex! Shit, lava's spilling onto the airstrip!"

He lifted his eyes from the controls for that, and halfway down the strip, past the *T. rex*, which had thankfully slowed to eat another zombie it had shaken loose during its run, and he saw the dull glow of orange laced with black, oozing onto the runway from the left side, the rocky side. It coincided with right about where his wheels-up point should be, but he was all too aware that should even one of his wheels come into contact with the molten sludge for even a split second at near-takeoff speeds, the plane would spin out of control and wreck on the ground.

The whine of the engine increased in pitch and volume, causing the *T. rex* to pick up speed. A membranous sac of entrails dangled from its clenched teeth and flopped up and down as it bounded toward them. Alex eased the plane to the left side of the runway as it picked up speed. Closer to the rushing lava, but a little further from the *T. rex*. The aircraft began to rattle and he knew take-off velocity was approaching.

A bright splash of lava distracted his eyes as the magma flow was forced over the shallow lip of the airstrip by the vast volume pushing behind it. The Tyrannosaur broke into a trot, aiming straight for the Cessna. It canted to the right and its right leg splashed into a pocket of yellowish lava, splattering a shower of molten rock across its already shredded hide. Even above the roar of the plane's engine, Alex heard the scream of the creature as it reared in place and leaned backwards, zombies careening from its back. One of them fell into the advancing lava sheet by the side of the runway, dissolving its body while its head, propped up on the lip of the airstrip, was spared, the jaws working of their own accord as the brain waited to burn, watching the *T. rex* go bounding off again.

It came right for them, charging head-on like challenging a rival in a game of chicken.

"Fly Alex, fly!" Veronica white-knuckled the oh-shit handle. "Now!" She shrieked as the airplane went aloft but then came back down, bouncing down the runway on the very edge of take-off velocity, the wings wavering each time it went airborne again. A zombie wearing a tattered soldier's uniform, automatic rifle still dangling unused over its raw, red shoulder, stumbled across the runway, directly in the path of the plane.

The Cessna took another hop and Alex flicked his hand out for the switch to retract the landing gear. He punched it without taking his eyes off the runway, hands immediately back to controlling the wheel. They felt a thud as the bottom of the left tire rolled over the zombie's head, breaking its neck so that the former human hung there for a moment with its head dangling at a sickening angle, before crumpling to the lava-streaked runway.

For one terrifying second, Alex felt the aircraft dip, as though it was going to bounce off the runway yet again—right into the *T. rex*. He pulled back on the stick and the nose of the little Cessna pointed skyward...

...and stayed that way. The scarred, bloody head of the *Tyrannosaurus rex* filled the windscreen as Alex yanked the stick all the way back. Veronica threw her arm across her face. The dinosaur snout barely passed below the plane and Alex looked out the pilot-side window in time to see the beast toss its head back and forth, roaring in rage. Its tail swiped the ground like a meaty windshield wiper, flinging gobs of lava this way and that, searing the faces and bodies of the zombies, which now regrouped on the ground to attack it.

It roared again, and again, even as it failed to move anymore, as waves of lava rolled over its feet, consuming its legs and still rising. It bellowed and shrieked, less from pain than from utter denial of its prey. It roared until it finally lost all balance and toppled forward—face-first into the searing liquid, where it thrashed and chomped and bit without purchase into the implacably searing foe. Finally, its flesh and bone melted away, its eyes exploded, and its brain burst into flames and it rolled sideways, the rest of its bulk consumed by an even stronger adversary.

#

Ahead, the volcano continued to erupt, with geysers of magma spewing from deep within the Earth to wash down the steep cone and over the island, drowning it in fire, challenging it to begin life anew.

A little voice in Alex's head told him to beware of stalling, and he leveled the plane out, passing above and to the right of the volcano to avoid the tricky updrafts he knew would be waiting above the open cone. Little meteors of shooting magma traced by the windscreen as the Cessna bolted across the sky.

Then they were past the active volcano, looking at the strip of beach up ahead and the great blue ocean beyond. Veronica let her arm drop from her face and looked out the passenger window behind them, then over at Alex, whose slate gray eyes she could now see held a wisdom born of experience that hadn't been there when she had first met him.

"Was that close? That was close, wasn't it?"

He reached over and took her hand.

"Nice flying. I think you'll make a better pilot than a forklift driver."

"Thanks. I think you'll make a better secret agent than you will a doctor." She poked him playfully in the ribs, laughing more out of the sheer joy of being alive than the joke.

"So where to, Mr. Pilot?"

"Like I said, it's a non-stop flight to Anywhere But Here. Fuel tank's full."

Veronica leaned over and kissed him softly on the cheek, then brought her lips close to his ear. "When can you engage the auto-pilot?"

43.

South Pacific airspace

The sleek Learjet 35 hurtled south, its crew of four transporting only one passenger. That client also happened to be the owner of the aircraft, Melvin DeKirk, who reclined in a leather couch in the plush cabin, partitioned off for privacy. He wore a pressed dark suit and a power red tie, sharp Italian loafers on his feet, crossed in front of him. A table made from a slab of old growth redwood supported a silver bucket filled with ice, a rare bottle of French champagne and a satellite-connected laptop computer. DeKirk looked up from the current issue of *Fortune,* where his grinning face was on the cover, to see an icon blinking on the laptop screen.

His lips tugged downward at the corners as he recognized the program—an automated application that was set to notify him of any problems on his island facility. He dropped the magazine and dragged the laptop closer to him, opening the software. Multiple warnings and critical messages awaited him: *Working threshold temperature exceeded here, minimum air pressure not met there, multiple fire alarms triggered, perimeter security breach alarms...* The place was falling apart. Then, with a start, he clicked on a blinking red bomb icon. The screen refreshed and a new window displayed a message: SELF_DESTRUCT _STATUS=ACTIVATED.

Wow! So that old crap worked after all these years! DeKirk stroked his chin in thought. *They really knew how to design shit back in those days.*

DeKirk pressed the call button for his flight attendant. In less than thirty seconds, an attractive brunette slid the partition aside and stepped into the cabin, all smiles, asking politely what she could do to make his flight more enjoyable.

He eyed the champagne with distaste. "I won't be needing this after all. Get me something stronger, say a whiskey on the rocks?"

She told him she'd be right back.

"One more thing."

She looked back at him expectantly.

"Tell the pilot I wish to change our destination. We won't be going to the island."

"Very well, sir. What shall I give the captain as our new destination?"

DeKirk shrugged. "Honolulu for now. We'll figure it out from there."

"Excellent, sir. I'll let him know immediately. Aloha!" She smiled at him again before leaving in a whirl of legs and perfume.

DeKirk's laptop made some more noise. He shut down the Adranos facility program, but even after that he could still hear something. Incoming Skype call. He checked the caller ID and then accepted the call. The harried face of his Security Chief for the Antarctica site filled the screen—a very hairy face with a gray beard and long white hair drooping over his forehead. *What is it with these cold weather roughneck types and beards?* DeKirk wondered.

"Strasser, fill me in."

"Mr. DeKirk, sir, good news!"

"Perfect timing, Strasser. Just what I'm in need of hearing." DeKirk waited, glancing to the cabin, hoping for the return of the attendant and his drink. *Well, what is it you idiot?* He drummed his fingers on the two thousand year old wood.

Recognizing that silence was his prompt, Strasser went ahead. "Sir, we have more specimens. Here, take a look..." He tapped some buttons and then the video changed to a split view, with Strasser taking up half the screen and the other half showing a live feed of the drill site.

DeKirk was looking deep into the excavation pit. It looked like a war zone down there, with the Russian crew and plenty of his own crew, all zombies, tooling around aimlessly, attacking one another, the drill apparatus mostly in disarray.

"Bear with me, sir, going lower..."

DeKirk watched as the camera descended rapidly—mounted on a cable system that was being controlled remotely by Strasser—deep into the pit from which the *T. rex* had been raised. DeKirk leaned in closer to his screen. The ice was almost crystal clear down here, and he found he could see individual forms in the layers of frozen fresh water. Some were just beneath the surface, like more of the Cryos he could see, and—was that another *T. rex?*

DeKirk beamed, his hand groping for the call button again. This was fantastic! More specimens, and they looked to be in even better condition than the first batch. DeKirk licked his lips at the thought of it, ignoring whatever the hell his guard dog was blathering on about now... and then the flight attendant was back.

She started to set the whiskey on the table but he held up a hand. "Turns out I'd like that champagne after all." Her face registered confusion for a second, but she got over it quickly. "Absolutely. Right away, sir." She bounded off with the untouched whiskey.

DeKirk sat entranced by his computer. On screen, a zombified pterodactyl broke free of a thin sheet of ice, shook its wings, stretched and took flight, spiraling up toward the top of the pit. DeKirk beamed at this, his mind burning with possibilities, thinking about the research Xander had completed, and was now DeKirk's property, thinking about failsafes and virus modification, about immortality and power, and about a future of his own making.

Below the first winged reptile, others emerged, blinking yellow, primordial eyes.

DeKirk watched, enthralled as they took flight and followed the leader to the surface.

END

Jurassic Dead 2: The Dead World
Coming Spring 2015

After the discovery of a dormant zombie virus in preserved dinosaur specimens, billionaire visionary and megalomaniac Melvin DeKirk proceeds with his plan to unleash a zombie-dinosaur army upon the world, starting with Washington DC. The US military struggles to prevent the contagion's spread and defend against the onslaught of prehistoric monstrosities, including pterodactyls and aquatic behemoths, as all-out war breaks out between the living and the dead.

Made in the USA
Middletown, DE
15 December 2014